LIEUTENANT
HENRY GALLANT

D1710357

H. PETER ALESSO

Novels by H. Peter Alesso
www.hpeteralesso.com

THE HENRY GALLANT SAGA

Midshipman Henry Gallant in Space © 2013

Lieutenant Henry Gallant © 2014

LIEUTENANT HENRY GALLANT

This is a work of fiction. All characters
and events portrayed in this book are
fictional, and any resemblance to real
people or incidents is purely coincidental.

VSL Publications
Pleasanton, CA 94566
www.videosoftwarelab.com

Edition 1.01

ISBN-13: 978-1500726805
ISBN-10: 150072680X
Library of Congress Control Number: 2014914368
CreateSpace Independent Publishing Platform
North Charleston, South Carolina

A warrior fights with honor.

Pride is his just reward.

1

RUN

Gallant ran—gasping for breath, heart pounding; the echo of his footsteps reverberated behind him.

He hoped to reach the bridge, but hope is a fragile thing.

Peering over his shoulder into the dark, he tripped on a protruding jagged beam, one of the ship's many battle scars. As he crashed to the deck, the final glow of emergency lights sputtered out leaving only the pitch black of power failure— his failure.

He lay still and listened to the ship's cries of pain; the incessant wheezing of atmosphere bleeding from the many tiny hull fissures, the repetitious groaning of metal from straining structures, and the crackling of electrical wires sparking against panels.

Thoughts flashed past him.

How long will the oxygen last?

He was reluctant to guess.

Where are they?

The clamor of dogged footsteps drew closer even as he rasped for another breath.

Trembling from exhaustion, he clawed at the bulkhead to pull himself up. His hemorrhaging leg made even standing brutally painful.

Nevertheless, he ran.

The bulkhead panels and compartment hatches were indistinguishable in the dimness. Vague phantoms lurked nearby even while his eyes adjusted to whatever glowing plasma blast embers flickered from the hull.

As he twisted around a corner, he crashed his shoulder into a bulkhead. The impact knocked him back and spun him around. Reaching out with a bloody hand, he grasped the hatch handle leading into the Operation's compartment. Going through the hatch, he pulled it shut behind him.

He started to run, then awkwardly fought his own momentum and stopped.

Stupid! Stupid!

Going back to the hatch, he hit the security locking mechanism.

It wouldn't stop a plasma blast, but it might slow them down, he thought. *At least this compartment is airtight.*

Finally able to take a deep breath, he tried to clear his head of bombarding sensations. He should've been in battle armor, but he'd stayed too long in engineering trying to maintain power while the hull had been breached and the ship boarded.

Now his uniform was scorched, revealing the plasma burns of seared flesh from his left shoulder down across his back to his right thigh. He had no idea where the rest of the crew was; many were probably dead. His comm pin was mute and the ship's AI wasn't responding. He had only a handgun, but, so far, he didn't think they were tracking him specifically, merely penetrating into the ship to gain control.

Gallant tried to run once more, but his legs were unwilling. Leaning against the bulkhead, like a dead weight, he slid slowly down to the deck.

Unable to go farther, he sat dripping blood and trembling as the potent grip of shock grabbed hold. The harrowing pain of his burnt flesh, swept over him.

Hope and fear alike abandoned him, leaving only an undeniable truth; without immediate medical treatment, he wouldn't survive.

I'm done.

Closing his eyes, he fought against the pain and the black vertigo of despair. He took a deep breath and called upon the last of his inner resolve and resilience . . .

No! I won't give up.

Exhaling and opening his eyes, he caught sight of a nearly invisible luminescent glow of a Red Cross symbol, offering him a glimmer of hope. He stretched his arm toward the cabinet.

"Argh."

He heard a cry of agony and only belatedly realized it had escaped his own lips as he strained to pull twisted metal away from the door to a medical cabinet. Reaching inside, he grabbed a damaged medi-pack.

Painstakingly he used the meager emergency provisions to stop the bleeding and to infuse blood plasma. His limited mobility prevented him from reaching awkward areas, but he managed to insert an analgesic hypodermic into his raw blistered flesh. Next, he crudely bandaged his suffering body.

He relaxed momentarily as the medication coursed through his veins working to stifle the worst effects of shock and blood loss. His parched throat demanded . . .

Water.

He looked at more cabinets, but was unable to make out their markings in the dark. Stretching his fingers, he opened the nearest one, groping for something familiar inside.

No.

He opened the next.

No.

And another.

Yes. Finally, he snatched a half-buried survival kit. Greedily he drank and even managed to take a few bites of an energy bar.

A surge of adrenaline helped him shift his position to sit more comfortably as his mind came into sharper focus.

As he examined his surroundings in the faint light, he spotted an interface station. He was about to reach up and patch into the ship's AI to get an update on the ship's defensive posture when he was disturbed by the dismal clangor of footsteps.

He held his breath.

Are they coming this way?

2

FTL

FOUR DAYS EARLIER . . .

The cold midnight black of space was indifferent to the warp distortion of the United Planets' *Intrepid* on its maiden voyage to Tau Ceti. Exotic dark matter fueled the ship's warp drive to create a space-time distortion bubble around the ship. Even while exceeding the speed of light, everything within the bubble appeared normal, including the perception of time.

One of Earth's nearest cosmic neighbors, Tau Ceti is a yellow dwarf star at about 11.5 light-years distance. The star's brilliant radiance beckoned the *Intrepid* deeper into its gravity-well, while the ship's forward view port allowed the bridge crew to witness its inner fusion turmoil, converting over six hundred million tons of hydrogen to helium each second.

Officer of the Deck, Lieutenant Henry Gallant, stood at the center of the *Intrepid's* bridge. Tall and athletically built, he seemed perfectly at ease as the focus of attention. His symmetrical facial features and square jaw made him appear forthright and earnest. His steely gray eyes might have deemed him overly intense, but in a curious way; a single careless curl of brown hair drifting across his forehead hinted at a youthful exuberance which combined with his good-natured smile left a reassuring impression.

In stark contrast to the vast emptiness outside the ship, inside the *Intrepid*, the dozen members of the bridge crew were crowded into a circular hi-tech equipment-packed bridge with three inner concentric circles. The innermost circle was around the command chair with its virtual support screens. It was normally occupied by the commanding officer, but the OOD was currently sitting there. The next circle was the command and control, and weapons stations, while the outermost ring consisted of sensor, navigation, and communication consoles.

One hundred and eighty degrees of the bridge's circumference was occupied by a front wall displaying a high resolution view screen showing the star system ahead of them.

From their demeanor and casual posture, the team gave the air of routine—nothing remarkable going on here. Yet there remained eagerness in the faces of the men nearest Gallant, causing him to savor the moment before issuing the next series of orders. The crew was so well coached on the ship's evolutions they could predict his exact words.

That was Gallant's perception as he stood at attention, careful to display a neutral facial expression while anticipating the coming maneuver.

He turned his attention to the youngest member of the team—the twenty-year-old helmsman—only one year younger than Gallant.

"We've reached the system threshold, sir," reported the helmsman, prodding the OOD to end the FTL flight. Within the star system they would be limited to sublight drive to avoid passing through a consequential field of matter; a planet, a large asteroid, or even worse, the star itself, which would bring their voyage to a swift and fatal conclusion.

"Very well, prepare to exit warp," said Gallant. On the ship-wide communication system, he announced, "All stations, standby to collapse warp bubble. Standby to collapse warp bubble."

Turning to Chief Howard, he said, "Chief of the Watch, sound three blasts of the drive alarm."

Chief Howard complied and the racket the alarm made ensured the whole crew knew what event was about to transpire.

"Helm, collapse warp bubble," ordered Gallant, ostensibly monitoring the virtual screens surrounding him, but in actuality, his attention was keenly focused on the actions of the helmsman, cautiously checking every movement to ensure exact performance—waiting, watching.

"Aye, aye, sir," responded Second Class Petty Officer William Craig. Short and wiry, with a ruddy complexion, he was young for a second class PO, but his outstanding performance and Chief Howard's recommendation had spurred his advancement. Using a methodical touch on the controls, he listened to the AI's prompting and made subtle adjustments. He watched as the three dimensional image projected on a virtual screen showed the warp bubble as it writhed and gyrated in response to his manipulations.

The *Intrepid* dropped smoothly out of warp. The subtle changes to the surrounding space-time fabric were inconspicuous to the crew; nevertheless Gallant detected a subtle difference to the ship's rhythmic vibrations beneath his feet.

The intricate operation complete, Craig reported, "Warp bubble collapsed, sir."

The bridge crew's placid response to the event, prompted Gallant to strike a similar blasé pose.

"Ahead standard," he said.

"Aye, aye, sir," said Craig, registering the signal on the AI display, which alerted engineering to start the sublight antimatter fusion reactors. As the reactors went critical, the ship ejected minute particles that produced only a tiny amount of acceleration, nevertheless the thrust compounded over time and the ship was soon propelled by the fusion engines.

"Nicely done, Helm," commented Gallant a few seconds later when the ship was operating on fusion drive.

"Thank you, sir," said the petty officer, unable to suppress a prideful nuance in his voice. He was one of the most popular young men on the ship. His bubbly personality and gregarious nature made him welcome, wherever he went. Even now, while on duty, he exhibited a contagious joyful excitement.

Gallant was pleased with the maneuver, but as the ship's Engineering Officer, he would withhold final judgment until he conducted a thorough series of tests to review data and garner more details on the performance of both propulsion systems. After probing the Faster-Than-Light (FTL) frontier, busy evaluation days were ahead.

He waited expectantly for the keen observations and appraisal of his captain, but Dan Cooper made no historic comment.

Instead, Cooper sat relaxed, leaning against the bulkhead, quietly chatting with the ship's senior chief.

"What do you think, Chief Howard?" he asked.

"Oh, she's shiny and new, I'll give you that, sir, but I'll take old *Repulse* any day of the week. They don't make ships like her anymore."

The captain chuckled. "I was asking about the FTL performance."

"Well, I'll wait until my engineering gang finishes tweaking and fiddling before making my official report, but my first impression is, she's"—the chief paused and looked over the bridge with a sweeping glance then finished begrudgingly— "okay."

"That's good enough for me, Chief," concluded the captain, giving him a good-natured slap on the back.

Outwardly the captain seemed unconcerned and it crossed Gallant's mind that behind this man's calm exterior, and dignified composure, was an underlying alertness conjoined with an abiding trust in his crew, such that, he felt prepared for any emergency. A methodical man, Cooper expected precision and discipline to be a natural consequence of his crew's training. Despite being brawny and self-assured, Captain Cooper was surprisingly unassuming. Clean-shaven with well-groomed wavy black hair, square shoulders, and a ruggedly handsome face, the captain was approachable. His good-natured, loud, infectious laugh was frequently heard throughout the bridge whenever someone ventured a quick joke.

Gallant took a moment to survey the state-of-the-art bridge with its veteran crew, from among the best the fleet had to offer, especially picked for this mission. From their relaxed, casual appearance, they might have seemed slack, yet their eyes showed the keen resolve of a skilled meticulous team. They had each endured considerable privation and many challenges to reach their position.

It was natural enough to consider his career and what opportunities might await. He let his fingers touch his lieutenant bars as reassurance. They reminded him of his own struggles in the service. Fighting alien threats had been secondary to the concerns most senior officers expressed about his fitness since he had entered the Space Academy.

His reflections were interrupted when the astrogator reported, "Sir, we're twenty light-minutes from Tau Ceti. There are five planets visible. The nearest to Tau Ceti is designated Tau-Alpha and has an orbital radius of thirty-nine million kilometers. Spectral analysis shows it's a composite of a carbonaceous, silicate, and metal-rich rock covering a barren volcanic mantle."

The planet's radio-telescope image offered Gallant interesting views.

"No moons," commented the senior chief, distracted from his conversation with the captain. Chief Benjamin Howard was a highly decorated veteran. His uniform's well-creased trousers and mirror-glossed shoes reflected his pride of service while his significant physical musculature belied his thinning gray hair.

"The second planet, designated Tau-Beta, has a 121 million kilometer orbit. It's a warm-water planet, Earth-type in size and character, sir," continued the astrogator.

"With one large moon," contributed Chief Howard.

"Very well," acknowledged Gallant, his curiosity roused.

"The next two planets are gas giants with no moons. There is a small asteroid field followed by the last planet with a 311 million kilometer orbit. It's a gas giant composed of hydrogen and helium with numerous volcanic methane moons, sir."

At last, Captain Cooper stirred and moved to the astrogator's station to examine the findings.

The semicircular bridge's efficient layout with the captain's chair in the center allowed for numerous AI and virtual screen resources. The entire bridge was buzzing with watch personnel conducting analyses, but everyone moved aside when the captain moved.

A variety of different active and passive sensor arrays supplied real-time data to supplement known astrophysics stats, which together plotted the planets' orbits and looked for any contacts to compute their course and speed. The sensing equipment included seven different types of active radars and four passive telescopes as part of operations. Every contact tracked had a specific emission signature they could identify. The spectrum of the *Intrepid's* emissions, electromagnetic, Fermion, and dark matter, on the other hand, was strictly controlled to prevent others from detecting and tracking them.

Gallant leaned toward the captain and quietly suggested, "I recommend we investigate the Earth-type planet, sir."

The captain nodded and said, "Agreed. Officer of the Deck set course for Tau-Beta."

"Aye, aye, sir," acknowledged Gallant and soon the fusion engines reached their top speed of 0.002c. He calculated their flight path and reported, "We'll reach Tau-Beta in about one hundred hours, sir."

"Very well. I think I'd like to deploy a probe to investigate the moons of the last gas giant."

"Aye, aye, sir."

Gallant touched a few tabs on the virtual control screen sliding open the massive drone hanger hatch in the midsection of the ship. He called up the AI settings for plot control and touched the destination spot on the screen while adjusting the final coordinates. He looked at the captain. At his nod, Gallant pressed the Launch tab. Deep Space Probe 16 left the *Intrepid* and the eighteen-meter-long-projectile journeyed toward the largest moon around the fifth planet.

"Probe away, sir. It'll be a week before it begins transmitting."

The captain didn't respond, but Gallant could guess what he was thinking . . .

Tau-Beta—an Earth-type planet?

3

RUN

Clang! Clang. Clang . . .

The footsteps were fading away, allowing Gallant to exhale in relief.

Ever since he had started running, he had been operating on raw nerves and guesswork. Now with the medication taking effect, his natural mental and physical toughness began to return.

The enemy was an aggressive predator, but Gallant didn't intend to be a passive prey. What he needed was a way to fight instead of run. He didn't know how knowledgeable his opponents were about his ship, but he would need to adapt to stay alive and possibly help retake the ship.

With the AI and comm down, how can I contact the captain?

The captain would rally the crew around the bridge, so Gallant started walking on his still unsteady legs. Ideas flew through his mind while he tried to ignore the raw emotions tugging at him.

I can still fight. I know every bolt and duct in this ship. I'll find a way to buy time for the others.

After a few minutes, he reached a point where several corridors and decks converged into a funnel-like passageway approaching the bridge.

This spot is defensible, he thought. *I might be able to hold them here, at least for a while.*

He found a weapons locker and pulled out a plasma rifle and several grenades. Abruptly he stopped to reassess his opponents. They were well-trained warriors in battle armor with plasma blasters, as well as AI assisted sensor equipment. Even in the pitch-black of the ship's interior, they could track him using thermal imaging. If he fought using conventional weapons and tactics, he could expect to pick-off two or three in a firefight before they killed and bypassed him. He decided to fight asymmetrically.

He evaluated his assets: hand-to-hand combat skills, superior knowledge of the ship, and fighting in an oxygen environment against methane-breathers in environmental suits.

If I could mask my thermal image, I could become a stealth fighter, he considered. *I could pick them off one at a time before they knew they were in danger.*

He hesitated only a few seconds before adapting the risky strategy.

Taking a deep breath, he pulled a hose from the bulkhead and covered himself with cold lube oil to disguise his thermal signature. Then he picked up a crowbar and a titanium blade knife.

He hid behind the twisted door of an equipment panel and waited. He was ready.

Someone's coming.

He timed his attack and threw a metal bolt across the room to let it strike against the metal bulkhead. The *twang* drew the attention of a pair of aliens entering the compartment. He stood up, moved quickly behind them, and with cat-like reflexes struck.

Whack! Whack!

The crowbar was sufficient to break the tubing to their methane-feed breathing apparatus. As they struggled to get their breath, he inserted his deadly knife into what he hoped was a vulnerable seal around their armor plating and completely cut open the breathing apparatuses, one after the other. Both aliens were dead in a minute. Not a shot was fired; no noise was made.

Looking down at their lifeless bodies, Gallant felt a moment's hesitation. He'd killed before; it was never easy—never solely about right or wrong—just necessary.

For a second, he imagined the aliens standing over his dead body. *Would they hesitate?*

The escaping methane gas caused him to gag and interrupted his introspection. Dragging the bodies to a storage locker, he placed them inside and shut the cover. With this act, he banished any misgivings.

The hunted is now the hunter.

He waited once more.

After several more minutes, two more aliens were similarly dispatched.

With his confidence growing, he decided to become more aggressive. Expecting all live crewmates to be with the captain on the bridge, he set a series of trip wires attached to grenades at key access points in the Operations compartment. Then he left the section and entered the engineering spaces. He found half a dozen aliens gathered nearby and quickly tossed several grenades into their midst which exploded destructively. However, the blast concussion knocked him down.

Quickly recovering, he got up and continued his breakneck ride through the deadliest battle he had ever fought. He fired his plasma rifle at the wounded aliens and tossed another grenade. The noise was thunderous and the flash of light gave him a chance to see down the corridor and get his bearings. His sense of smell detected the acid fumes rising from the explosives followed by smoke. Looking away, he sprawled across the deck and crawled back to the operations compartment. Losing himself in the smoke and confusion, he retreated to his hiding spot at the passageway junction and listened to the turmoil he had caused.

Adding to the chaos, several trip wires went off. Blast followed blast across the nightmarish metal landscape. He was satisfied he had disrupted the boarding party's advance. Possibly he had given the captain enough time to organize the bridge's defense.

Again he waited.

After a few moments of agreeable respite, he was beginning to enjoy a glimmer of optimism when . . .

Why has everything gotten so quiet!

4

RIVAL

EARLIER IN THE DAY . . .

Gallant stood in the entrance to the wardroom where half dozen officers congregated around the dinner table. From the variety of their comportment—good-natured bantering, rapt debate, disgruntled complaining—they could have been young businessmen casually relaxing after a hard day's work, yet the subtle tension of their body language suggested they were concealing a shared disquiet. Noting the absence of the captain, Gallant tried to further assess the tenor of the room, but his fellow officers' temperaments were distorted by the executive officer's presence. Such was his insight—garnered over the course of their interstellar journey, wherein he contrasted the inspiration of their amenable captain against the repression of their perfectionist XO, Anton Neumann.

H. PETER ALESSO

Lieutenant Commander Anton Neumann let his perfectly even white teeth sink into a succulent piece of filet mignon. He chewed the morsel thoroughly before fixing his strangely penetrating blue eyes on Henry Gallant. For a brief moment their gaze met and exchanged a measure of their intense dislike.

"You're late," Neumann said mildly with a questioning nuance.

"My apologies," Gallant replied formally. "Number two reactor's criticality safety rods required recalibration." He selected the seat at the foot of the table—the farthest from Neumann.

"Is there a problem, Mr. Gallant?" asked Neumann. He paused, waiting for a reply, and then added, "I trust you completed the realignment protocol."

"No, sir, no problem, and yes, I completed the protocol realignment according to standard procedure," said Gallant. While Neumann was strict about protocol and performance, he couldn't be called a martinet; still Gallant resented being questioned by the XO in front of his peers.

"Very good," concluded Neumann.

The son of a rich and powerful asteroid-mining magnate, Neumann had enjoyed a life of privilege, growing up poised and self-assured. "*Winners always win*," was his favorite saying, and, having inherited his father's ruthless competitiveness, he seemed to epitomize it. Tall with a powerful physique, jet black hair, and cold blue eyes, he was strikingly handsome. When he chose to, he could display a dazzling smile. He looked every inch the "winner" he professed to be. He had even represented the Space Academy in the 2166

Solar System Olympics where he had won two gold medals in track and field events, which were prominently displayed in his quarters. A product of advanced genetic engineering, he was, in every way, the prototypical example of Earth's evolutionary aspirations.

In contrast, Gallant was born without genetic engineering, and, as an orphan, he had to struggle above his family's poor circumstances to reach his current rank and position. Ironically, the lack of opportunity which had deprived him of the advantages of genetic engineering had resulted in his emerging with unique mental abilities—the result of a natural selection mutation. His goal of being the engineer on the first FTL spacecraft was the culmination of all his endeavors. Now that he had achieved the desired position, serving under Neumann cast a pall on it.

The two men had first met several years earlier, both as midshipmen aboard the battle cruiser *Repulse*. Both were fighter pilots with exceptional records, and, after a while, they had developed a healthy respect for each other. However, their rivalry intensified when they each began wooing the same young woman, Kelsey Mitchel.

Gallant served two years at the Space Academy on Mars, before traveling to Jupiter for a two-year deployment on the battle cruiser *Repulse*. Attractive brunette Kelsey Mitchel was assigned as the navigator on his fighter. They served together through many hazardous missions, and, as their relationship thrived, Gallant took it for granted she would eventually choose to marry him. That she made a different choice surprised and disheartened him—she agreed to marry Neumann when he returned to Earth after this voyage.

Given what Neumann had to offer, Gallant never blamed her. Rather he harbored an abiding spite toward Neumann, who Gallant suspected merely pursued Kelsey as a prized conquest.

Now the die was cast, and despite Gallant's best efforts to forgive and forget, serving with Neumann rubbed salt into the wound.

"Kelsey," muttered Gallant as he played with a small object in his hand. Out of the corner of his eye, he caught the sharp look Neumann gave him and realized he had been overheard, but he didn't care.

The small coin-like piece he rubbed in his hand wasn't a coin at all, but a music box capable of holding every piece of music every recorded. In actuality it retained exactly one recording—the only recording that mattered—Kelsey's.

He let his mind drift back to a place far away several years earlier. He recalled people and events passing through his life with a swish and then they were gone; their importance—to what might have been—remained in his memory of what was.

One night at The Lobster Tavern on Jupiter Station—*Kelsey was dressed in slacks and a sweatshirt with the letters UPSA. She was sitting in the center of the room, tapping her fingers impatiently on the top of her table. Her brown hair was pulled back from her face into a ponytail and fell across her shoulder. When she wasn't tapping, she was making faces of displeasure, as if something important of hers had gone astray. With all of that, her classical facial features still made her the most striking woman in the room.*

Unceasingly, men she knew, as well as locals she didn't, would come over and try to join her.

"Hi," she would say. "It's great to see you, but I'm waiting for someone." Then she would tilt her head to one side and flash a big smile, which somehow said she was disappointed and she hoped he would understand. This placated most, but one hopeful suitor remained hovering over her until she spotted Gallant. She stood up, waving her arms excitedly. As he approached, her last admirer capitulated and withdrew as Gallant sat down.

After a while the crowd convinced Kelsey to use her lovely voice to sing. She chose a sweet melody of passion and farewell. It mesmerized all who listened. The melancholy tones touched Gallant so much, he made a recording and kept it ever since.

Unfortunately, after her song was finished and she joined him again at their table, Gallant sat passively, looking on as . . .

Neumann crossed the room and asked Kelsey for a dance. She stood up, and he took her hand and led her onto the dance floor.

"It's been quite an evening," she said, placing her hand on Neumann's shoulder, her bright eyes shining with delight.

"A wonderful evening—thanks to you," he said as he drew her closer.

Kelsey nestled comfortably into his arms. Her sweet breathe brushed past his cheek; her soft hand gently caressed the nape of his neck.

Kelsey and Neumann made such an attractive couple they invited stares from the evening's crowd, but they seemed indifferent to their momentary celebrity as the joyful participants of the evening's festivities swirled around them in rhythm to the music.

Gallant's mind refused to shrink from the churning desires of the memory—Kelsey would remain an unsatisfied yearning of his past.

Gallant looked down the length of the wardroom table. *Damn him.*

The boisterous and good-natured atmosphere of his fellow officers did nothing to improve his spirits. During their journey together from Sol, Gallant had come to know his colleagues, their likes and dislikes, as well as their eccentricities.

The ship's weapons officer, Lieutenant Stahl, was short and squat, but with broad shoulders and giant muscular biceps. He was a consummate professional. He never wanted to discuss anything but tactics or equipment, especially the latest upgrades.

Stahl nodded to Gallant and punched in his authorization code on the galley panel. The auto-server popped up and displayed a tray of synthetic entrees and side dishes.

"We're getting close to the Earth-type planet," he contributed, sparking a discussion on the planet's attributes.

"What do you think, XO? Will we have real steak and potatoes instead of synthetics, sometime soon?" asked Lieutenant Rogers, the ship's supply officer. Sitting there eating synthetic foodstuffs, only whetted their palates for the goodies they expected to find on the planet.

"Don't get your taste buds all excited—we don't know what will be edible," piped up the ship's medical officer, Lieutenant Marcus Mendel. Despite the fact he was responsible for the crew's physical conditioning, he was overweight and the least likely officer to be found working out in the gym. The ship's "class clown," he frequently victimized his shipmates with his witticisms. "I could save endless hours of toxicity testing if you would volunteer to be our guinea pig, Rogers."

"No thanks," said Rogers.

"In any case, we'll have an opportunity to explore a planet comparable to Earth. It should be a treasure trove of new knowledge," said Stahl.

Mendel smiled and held up crossed fingers.

The youngest members of the wardroom, Lieutenant Junior Grade Richard Palmer and Ensign John Smith, stood up and showed thumbs-up. Palmer and Smith were spending every available hour of the day working to qualify for their duty assignments, Officer of the Deck and Engineering Officer of the Watch, respectively. Their study and duty cycles kept them fully occupied, so any chance for a diversion was a welcomed opportunity.

Neumann made a wry smile. "Does anyone have further data on Tau-Beta?"

Gallant said, "I stopped in the CIC earlier and left the captain there reviewing the latest info. The images are showing many varied life-forms. We've rescheduled engine maintenance tests to avoid any delays."

"I thought you still had engineering update issues to resolve, Henry?" asked Lieutenant John Paulson, one of the officers who shared a tiny stateroom with Gallant.

"Yes, Gallant, I'll be conducting an informal inspection of the engineering spaces on the mid-watch. I'll review your recalibration results then. I'll expect them to be up to standards," said Neumann.

"Yes, sir. Please excuse me," Gallant said, rising from the table, annoyed by Neumann's criticism in front of the wardroom officers. "I've got the next OOD watch and it's time to start my walkthrough."

His chest tightened and he gave Neumann a withering look as he left the wardroom.

Egotistical bastard.

He stopped abruptly in the corridor and reflected on his behavior and emotions. While he didn't want to be jealous or bitter, he had to admit those passions had found fertile ground in his heart, and he was hard-pressed to exorcise them.

No matter how much he denied it, he would never find peace until he found a way to move on from Kelsey.

———

Twenty minutes later, Gallant had completed his walk-through and arrived on the bridge in time to witness the *Intrepid's* approach to the Earth-type planet, only four days since they had entered the Tau Ceti's system. He was glad it was impossible to die of curiosity because he certainly would have tested the proposition.

"What do you think is going to be down there, sir?" Chief Howard asked Gallant.

"I don't know, but I can't wait to find out."

"I've got a theory."

"Spill it."

"We're going to find tropical islands with dancing girls—paradise, simply paradise."

"Well, you would know. You've visited enough ports. I hope the natives are friendly."

"Aren't they always?"

"Mr. Gallant, we've reached the two hundred thousand kilometer limit," reported Helmsman Craig.

"Very well," responded Gallant. He pressed his comm pin and said, "Captain?"

"Coming," responded the captain.

In a minute, Captain Cooper came bounding onto the bridge from his ready-cabin off of the bridge area. The captain used his ready-cabin during eventful periods to be able to respond instantly to emergencies. His normal quarters were an additional deck and compartment away, but they included elaborate furnishings and provided a small reception area which he found useful when he was receiving visitors while in port.

Gallant considered the *Intrepid* to be a sleek and beautifully designed ship. Its 180,000-tons were shaped like a huge missile with a length of 710 meters and an extended beam of 133 meters. It housed the engineering compartment's dual engines. *Intrepid's* limited armament included short range plasma and laser cannons. Her crew of twelve officers and 214 men were highly trained and fully prepared to face any challenge.

"Captain on the bridge," announced the Chief of the Watch.

The captain waited expectantly on the OOD.

"Captain, request permission to enter geosynchronous orbit," asked Gallant as he admired the sights in the main viewport, which extended the entire height of the bulkhead.

"Permission granted," said Captain Cooper.

"Ahead, slow. Helmsman, place the ship in stationary orbit over the planet's equator at the specified coordinates. All stations evaluate data from land masses directly below."

Gallant's attention was momentarily captured by the sight of the curvature of the planet flashing across the viewport along with the detailed telescopic images at the nearby science station of the planet's surface.

This was the United Planets' (UP) first journey to another star system and they had an endless list of information to collect about the planets. The operations personnel were already collecting so much data the analysts were hard pressed in evaluating their windfall.

Gallant reported aloud, "Tau-Beta has all the characteristics of an Earth-type planet complete with oceans covering ninety-three per cent of the planet's surface in comparison to Earth's seventy per cent. There are no large continents, however, only numerous island groups. The largest island group is in the temperate zone and geographically resembles Earth's Hawaiian Islands only much larger, volcano included. And one more thing—I'm delighted to report—*life*," said Gallant, his voice characterized by a higher than normal pitch. "Sensors show flocks of birdlike creatures, herds of mammals, and other abundant creatures of all kinds."

"Are there any signs of intelligent life?" queried the captain in a general, informal way inviting all personnel to contribute.

Lieutenant Commander Reed, the *Intrepid*'s Operations Officer, sat with his face buried in a virtual display. He was barrel-chested with a craggy face. His station was cluttered and his ruffled hair and scraggy beard, along with his wrinkled uniform, reflected his demanding schedule.

"Sir, I think I can make out fabricated structures clustered along the shore of the main island of the largest island group," said Reed.

Gallant bumped into Captain Cooper as they bounded forward to catch a peek.

Gallant stared in bewilderment. *Is there a civilization?*

5

RUN

Crouched behind a metal cabinet, Gallant remained waiting near the converging passages in the Operation's compartment for the Titan warrior's next move. The unnerving quiet was finally broken by a series of earsplitting explosions.

Kaboooom! Kaboooom!

The shocking roar briefly rendered Gallant deaf. He instinctively raised his hands to his ears. As he fought to shake off the concussion, an acidic stench of smoke and ash invaded his nostrils, forcing him to cover his mouth to suppress a spasmodic cough. The blinding flashes of plasma weapons shrieked into the compartment and left a smoldering display of fireworks.

What happened?

His methodical mind searched to unravel the possibilities.

His overwhelmed senses forced him to keep his head down as the aliens attacked the Operations compartment in force. The exploding grenades and plasma flashes splashed against the bulkheads seemingly aimless from all directions. Sound was the first of his senses to return, leaving a buzzing in his ears. He realized the attackers had no idea where he was hiding, but were merely laying down suppressing fire to flush him out as they moved forward. Breathlessly, he shrank into the depths of his hidey-hole, but the game was up.

His hit-and-run maneuvers had paid dividends, but ominously, the tactic was no longer viable. Feeling he had achieved all he could under the circumstances, he decided to execute his escape plan.

Touching the bulkhead behind him with his left hand, he extended his right hand toward his rifle. When his outstretched fingers grasped the weapon, he pulled it close. Then he crawled to a nearby duct vent and squeezed his body inside, vanishing from his enemy's advance.

Calmer now, he peeked out of the vent to observe a large group of aliens swarming into the compartment. They passed his previous hideout and continued through the funneled passageway toward the bridge. After a few minutes, the sound of a raging battle made it clear the captain was mounting a robust defense. Gallant heard blaster shots and screams.

Focus!

He crawled through the ductworks until he reached an exit point aft of the bridge, directly behind the aliens. As he squirmed out of the duct, he clutched his plasma rifle and pulled out several grenades from his pockets. Then he moved forward into the battle.

As he climbed up a ladder, behind the aliens who were engaged in the firefight on the bridge, he caught a glimpse of Captain Cooper jumping from spot to spot while engaging the aliens.

Gallant methodically targeted the aliens with his rifle, hitting those who could not be clearly seen by their companions. As a result, they didn't know they were being fired upon from their rear. A few moments later, he again caught sight of his captain in the thick of the fighting, rallying his crew.

Gallant pulled the trigger on his plasma rifle and held it down, letting a continuous stream of hellish fire flow at his enemies, but soon the flashing red light indicated the weapon was completely discharged. Letting it fall from his hands, he pulled a grenade from his pocket and hurled it forward.

He then fired his hand blaster, but his luck finally ran out as he attracted heavy return fire.

A blast burned through the hatch he was hiding behind.

"Ugh—" he cried from the scorching heat of the near miss.

Got to keep firing . . .

6

AMBUSH

SEVERAL HOURS EARLIER . . .

"It looks like a civilization. There's an entire community on the main island," said Gallant, animated by the scene. "The structures appear to be mainly small habitats in clusters along the shoreline with a large central plaza. Along the southern perimeter there are a few industrial buildings, possibly factories, and then on the western side, segregated somewhat, are farms and animal enclosures."

Captain Cooper examined the telescopic display as he zoomed in on the areas highlighted by Gallant. Nodding, he asked, "Are there any other inhabited areas?"

"No sir. This is the only visible settlement on the main island chain. The rest of the planet's land masses appear bare of habitation, nevertheless they are teeming with plant and animal life."

"I see large herds of various mammals roaming freely across the main island. Are there any signs of domestication?" asked the captain as he watched the rapidly changing color images come skidding across the screen.

"There are a few hundred animals in corral pens on the outskirts of the settlement. The rest appear to be running wild," said Gallant, sweeping his arm in a wide arc to illustrate the free range the animals enjoyed.

"Agriculture?"

"There's a desert to the west and a volcanic region on the northern section of the main island, but lush vegetation covers the temperate portion of the islands. Irrigated farming activity is abundant near the western part of the settlement, sir. The crops under cultivation might support a population of several hundred to several thousand individuals."

"Can you estimate their level of technology?"

"There is a road system crisscrossing the settlement with several fossil fuel ground vehicles in transit. Surprisingly, there are glass and steel industrial buildings showing a sophisticated construction we would normally find on Earth. By all appearances, this looks more like an advanced, yet isolated, colony rather than a naturally developing indigenous population, sir."

"What kind of population?"

Deadpan, the ship's surgeon, Lieutenant Mendel, said, "Human."

"Right . . . humans," responded Gallant dryly. "Eleven light-years from Earth? How is it possible they got here, ahead of us . . . the first FTL ship?"

"You caught me, Henry. I told an outrageous lie for no reason," said Mendel raising his hands over his head in mock surrender.

"Funny, Doc," said Gallant. "You shouldn't be such a smartass when the captain's on the bridge. I might have to put you on report."

"Oh, no! I guess my punishment will be getting reassigned to engineering," said Mendel.

Gallant sighed, shaking his head. "And you used to be such a respectable medical doctor."

"I'm only along for the ride now."

Unable to keep a straight face, Captain Cooper put his hand over his mouth to suppress a snort.

"Yeah, Yeah. Enough. How about evaluating the inhabitant's physiology?" asked Gallant.

"I completed the physiological scans two minutes ago. Like I said, they're human. I wasn't kidding. They're human!"

Suddenly, no one was smiling, it wasn't funny anymore.

"A colony? A human colony?" asked the captain, perplexed. "From where? Surely not from another planet in this system?"

No one could think of a response to the *Intrepid's* commanding officer.

Cooper looked directly at Gallant and said, "I don't like this, Gallant. Not one bit!"

For several seconds, it remained disarmingly quiet on the bridge.

"There's something strange," started Gallant, when he was interrupted by the exclamation of the senior sensor technician.

"Radar contact! A high speed ship is emerging from behind the moon. Designate, Tango-one."

The comfortable atmosphere on the bridge spontaneously changed as every station galvanized to face a potential interloper.

The Chief of the Watch reported, "Tango-one emissions' signature is identified as a Titan vessel, destroyer class."

While the announcement surprised everyone on the bridge, they showed their professional poise by rapidly adjusting to the arrival of the enemy threat.

"Sound General Quarters. Full power to the shields," ordered Captain Cooper.

Gong! Gong! Gong!

Battle stations brought a flurry of activity on the *Intrepid*. A moment of bustle and movement erupted as men proceeded to their duty stations. Mendel left the bridge to prepare the medical center for casualties while other personnel quickly got into their battle station assignments. Multiple reports from various stations fed into the CIC, attesting to their readiness.

"Captain, there are no other contacts," said the sensor technician. "We'll be within Tango-one's missile envelope in seven minutes, sir."

His illusion of an amiable mission shattered, Gallant thought, *The destroyer must have been hiding in the moon's radar shadow while we were making our way across the star system. How could a war we left light-years away have followed us to Tau Ceti? Damn!*

The Titan destroyer charged directly at the *Intrepid*. The Titans were not known to have FTL drive, but their fusion engines were capable of 0.0022c. Their destroyers were armed with anti-ship missiles, lasers, and plasma cannon systems, and this one was attacking at full throttle.

On the other hand, the *Intrepid* carried minimal weapon systems. It had only a few pulsed lasers and plasma cannons for short range defense. Without anti-ship missiles and carrying no anti-missile missiles, she was completely outmatched. By attacking them while they were entering planetary orbit, *Intrepid* was caught operating at minimum sublight speed on its fusion engines. In addition, they couldn't use their FTL drive while within the star system. This ambush caught them at their most vulnerable.

Several years earlier, UP had fought a series of space battles against the Titans after discovering they had colonized the outer planets of the Solar System. The Titans had traveled in generation ships from Gliese-581, and the methane-breathing Titans were Gliese-forming the volcanic moons of Saturn and Uranus. Gallant had fought in the *Battle of Jupiter* where, he had played a pivotal role in the great victory that drove the Titans back to the outer edges of the Solar System.

We beat them before—we can do it again.

Gallant shared the faith and confidence the bridge team had in their captain. Far from Earth and about to face battle, the crew, surrounded by the virtual screens and scanned reports, worked feverishly to prepare for action against a familiar foe.

"Helm, break orbit, steady as you go, full speed ahead," said Captain Cooper.

"Aye, aye, sir," said Craig, focusing on setting the course and ringing up the speed.

A moment later Cooper ordered in a calm, but commanding voice, "Engineering, I want everything those engines are capable of and I want it now!"

"Will do, Captain," said Lieutenant John Paulson.

Then a few moments later the bridge speaker blared, "Answering, all ahead emergency, sir. Both reactors are RED-lined!"

John's always been fearless. I hope he isn't being reckless.

Gallant visualized the excitement on his roommate's face. Paulson would ride those engines to the edge of a core meltdown.

The fusion reactors, working beyond their safety limits, increased the momentum of the *Intrepid* and accelerated her out of orbit. Still, the crew could only watch as the Titan destroyer continued to close the distance preventing their escape.

Like the rest of the crew, Gallant wore a tight-fitting pressure suit for survival from large G-forces during routine operations. In addition, he was strapped securely into his acceleration couch because as the *Intrepid* left orbit and accelerated at an abnormal rate, the crew was pressed forcefully into their chairs.

Gallant watched in fascination as the forward view screen showed the Titans launching two medium anti-ship missiles. They separated from the destroyer and began their journey to attack the *Intrepid*. They grew visibly as he looked on. They were known to carry multiple one hundred megaton thermonuclear warheads.

"Incoming missiles designated, Tango two and three," reported the radar operator.

A continuous stream of reports was coming in from every direction, but Cooper remained calm and organized. "Concentrate port laser and plasma weapon systems on Tango two and starboard batteries on Tango three."

"Sir, the missiles are closing and moving so fast we're having difficulty adjusting our target acquisition systems."

"Adjust your aim on-the-fly," was the captain's order, born from desperation.

The *Intrepid* had a titanium-molybdenum alloyed steel hull with powerful force shields. Together they helped minimize any effects of a nuclear blast. By using speed to distance the ship from an explosion, most of the blast effects could be avoided. Since any ships which moved at 0.001c would be in the vicinity of an explosion for only a tiny fraction of a second most of the blast would be dissipated into empty space. A missile would only do fatal damage if it hit directly on the ship's hull plates. Direct hits could penetrate the ships' shields and tear openings in the ships' hulls. However, near misses could damage the ship by weakening shields and armor over time.

The *Intrepid's* laser and plasma weapons struck the incoming missiles, but the missiles resisted immediate destruction. It took repeated hits on the warheads before they detonated. The multiple warhead vehicles exploded across a wide area of space around the *Intrepid*. A fitful red glow appeared on the port bulkhead side of the bridge. The end result was a thermonuclear fury which damaged the ship and wounded numerous crew members. The injured were taken to the medical center for surgical help.

"Damage control reports coming in from all sections of the ship, sir," reported Gallant.

The destroyer remained on the *Intrepid*'s starboard side and the range continued to close while the destroyer reloaded its missile launchers.

The Titans changed course to three-three-zero to close more quickly. As soon as the reloading was accomplished, the Titans launched another pair of missiles.

The captain gave a rapid fire series of orders. "CIC, give me a plot on Tango one. AI, show me the new missile projections. AI, show me the most effective laser fire options. Weapon's officer, synchronize laser fire and recharge all plasma weapon systems. Helm, come to course 090, azimuth up 10 degrees, increase speed to 0.002c, at time 1626."

The experienced crew responded without hesitation.

Again the *Intrepid* concentrated fire on the incoming missiles. One exploded short of its target, but the second explosion was a near miss, causing the *Intrepid* serious damage.

Reevaluating his position, Cooper ordered, "All stations, commence continuous laser and plasma fire." Then he added, "Helm—hard to port—come to course 180, azimuth up 10 degrees, speed 0.002c, at time 1647."

This gutsy call turned the ship directly toward the enemy and closed the range even faster. They were following their own laser fire toward the enemy ship. By this decision, he hoped to give his ship time to reach maximum speed while the enemy executed a difficult reversal of course and reloaded their missile launchers. The missile flight time was now mere seconds, which didn't allow the alien ship time to deploy more missiles. Instead of firing a salvo, the alien ship spent several confused minutes changing course.

As the *Intrepid* swept past the Titan destroyer, it once more opened the distance.

Rapidly, the Titans recovered and fired another pair of missiles.

The few moments lost before *Intrepid* was ready to respond proved fatal. The shock waves of the missile warheads' exploding rocked the ship. The violent repercussions of this salvo were devastating to the UP prototype spaceship.

The nuclear bursts damaged *Intrepid's* reactors and the ship's speed dropped drastically. In engineering, men struggled to keep the nuclear reactors functioning, the weapon systems up, and the environmental controls working. In the engineering control room, communications were lost and it rapidly became a death trap as fires from adjoining compartments roasted the inhabitants alive before fire suppression systems were able to counteract the flames.

Men struggled throughout the ship as damage mounted. The aft crew's quarters were completely demolished and the port laser batteries were bent like pretzels. The starboard repair shop was flooded when the main water recycling tank ruptured. Ironically, the spill quelled the fire in the area. Other compartments weren't so lucky. One of the plasma stations exploded from a direct laser hit and began to burn like a Roman candle. The heroic efforts by its gun crew failed to extinguish the blaze and most of the men perished in the attempt.

So the battle went; one horror after another. The small craft flight deck was hit by plasma fire and set ablaze. Craft after craft was disabled.

Little doubt remained amongst the survivors; the *Intrepid* was teetering on the edge of disaster. The only question was would internal explosions produce their demise, or would the Titans strike the final blow?

The men had one consolation during those horrific few minutes; the veteran crew stayed at their combat stations and continued to fire their remaining weapons' batteries, despite the cost in lives. They kept pouring laser and plasma fire at the Titan ship, inflicting whatever damage they could, until, they too, were silenced by return fire.

On the bridge, Captain Cooper, deprived of communications, visual images, and AI systems, had only a vague picture of the chaotic state of his ship. He issued orders in an attempt to readdress the damage, but the loss of communications, coupled with the destruction of men and material throughout the ship, reduced his efforts to near futility.

"Captain, fire in the engine room. We have several hull ruptures aft of the Operations compartment. Damage control teams are being dispatched. Hull integrity is dropping," said Gallant. He looked at the computer readouts and saw compartment lighting flicker on and off, and then the panel continued to function erratically.

In seconds, the *Intrepid* had become a derelict. At any time the enemy could take advantage of its vulnerability to either destroy or board and capture the ship, but the battle was not yet decided, as far as its captain and crew were concerned. No one was raising a white flag.

"Prepare to repel boards," ordered Cooper over the ship's speaker system, his voice still calm and reassuring. "All stations, don battle armor."

Cooper turned to Gallant and grabbed his arm. "Get to engineering."

Momentarily, Cooper's professional mask fell, replaced by his familiar warm smile; squeezing Gallant's arm he said, "Keep the lights on, Henry."

"Will do, Dan," replied Gallant, wondering how he was going to keep his promise.

Gallant left the bridge and ran through the Operations compartment. Briskly stepping through the hatch into the engineering spaces, he sealed the hatch behind him. The engineering compartments were normally packed with running equipment and humming machinery. Now it held mostly silent, mangled debris. Few pieces of equipment were working; a few were still being serviced by diligent crewmen who were trying to keep them going.

Gallant saw his Leading Petty Officer (LPO) frantically pulling on a broken frame beam along with several crewmen.

"Chief Howard, what's your status?"

Huffing from exertion, the chief said, "Both reactors are down. The control rods were inserted so they are at least safe, as long as we keep the fuel containment and keep cooling them. Of course with the reactors down, the weapon systems are offline. We're using residual heat to provide minimal power for essential equipment including life support. In addition, there are numerous small hull breaches in the aft portion of the ship and at least half of the engineering personnel are either injured or dead. I've counted five dead—so far."

A fresh barrage of plasma and laser weapons from the Titans struck the *Intrepid,* further damaging its titanium hull and shaking the men were they stood.

"At least they've stopped firing missiles," mumbled the chief.

"I'm going to the engineering control room and try to maintain minimal power. You keep the men working on the generators. Oh—and pass out weapons. We may need them before too long."

Gallant watched Chief Howard nod his head slowly and then he turned to go to the control room. The engineering spaces seemed like a strange new land with broken beams and busted piping. Numerous damaged sections of the bulkhead caused a dull glow from heat and radiation.

When he entered in the engineering control room, the first thing Gallant saw was the burnt and mangled body of his friend and roommate John Paulson. He forced himself to turn away.

He looked around the room at the rest of the electronic cabinets torn from the side of the bulkhead. Reviewing the engineering equipment status, he was able to tap into the ship's AI and get a virtual display of the ship. From the viewport, he could also see the planet below them.

"Make your report," he ordered the AI and listened to the endless list of damaged and out-of-commission equipment from the stream of data collected from all spaces. Evaluating his options, he issued a confluence of orders to the engineering gang in an attempt to patch things together to restore power. For a short few minutes, he thought they would succeed, but once again the lights went out and only emergency illumination remained.

The Titans soon came to understand the havoc they had wrought on the UP vessel and changed their tactics. No longer satisfied to puncture her hull and burn the insides, they decided to capture the behemoth hulk as a prize and seize the FTL technology. The destroyer dispatched several small craft, which approached the *Intrepid* and then latched on to the hull. They used explosives charges to breach the hull and were able to make a hole large enough for the Titan troops to gain access into the interior of the *Intrepid*.

The *Intrepid* was outgunned, crippled, and now the power was failing. The ship continued to drift slowly in space, and as a result of the battle damage, they were easily boarded.

Gallant quickly directed the engineering personnel to prepare for combat instead of repairing equipment. The corridors were lined with panels and cabinets storing all manner of things from emergency food and water to firefighting apparatus. He opened a weapons locker and distributed weapons.

The aliens were not aware of the *Intrepid's* layout, nor did they have a cohesive plan for taking their ship, but they were entering through the blown bulkhead access in fairly large numbers. They were well-organized and well-armed. Against them, the ship's small crew fought and resisted, but so much battle damage had been done to the ship's operations and communications systems that the men weren't able to mount a coherent defense.

While the combat raged, the shock of repeated plasma blasts struck the *Intrepid*. The concussion from one blast stunned Gallant. His senses told him something was seriously wrong; the sounds were the wrong noises for the engineering space. Loud cries of anguish and the jostling of crewmen combating fires reached his ears, but the rumbling of machines and the humming of equipment were absent. He looked into the chaotic darkness with uncomprehending eyes.

The firearms' noise sounded like continuous thunder. Sharp lights shone and invaded his consciousness. Yet a vague uneasiness swept through him as he struggled to grasp what was going on. Soon the uneasiness turned into apprehension as the battle drew nearer. The acrid fumes of the plasma beams stung his nose. Oxygen not being consumed by fire was being sucked out into space from small hull ruptures. Sick bubbly yellow and green smoke waffled throughout the compartments. Wounded men sat upright, being attended to by their comrades using local medi-paks.

Lieutenant Stahl left his weapons control station near engineering and came running past. He staggered and fell in front of Gallant, mortally wounded. Gallant could only spare a few troubled seconds to morn his friend before he was forced to address more crises.

The crew kept up a steady fire, and under his direction they wounded a Titan and drove them back momentarily.

Gallant finally shook off the effects of his concussion and thought of the captain. He considered the possibility of going forward to support him. He wanted to confer with Chief Howard.

Where is Howard?

He took a deep breath.

This is the first test of a UP ship far from Earth and we're losing.

The *Intrepid* engineering spaces were being quickly overrun, notwithstanding the crew's brave, but desperate defense.

He heard shouts and yells. Men were still struggling to get into battle armor and gather their weapons.

Once more he managed to gather a small group together and he coordinated their fire at the leading elements of Titan force. Tragically, all the crewmen were quickly hit by return fire.

A plasma blast splattered off the bulkhead next to Gallant, seriously burning him from his left shoulder down his back all the way to his right leg. He dropped to the deck in great pain from the burnt flesh. He lay there bleeding for several minutes.

Badly wounded, unable to repel the boarders, or fight effectively within the damaged compartment full of wounded, he realized there wasn't anything more he could do in engineering.

I've got to get to the bridge. That's where the captain will make a stand—got to get moving.

Run!

7

NO MORE RUNNING

The bridge was now the focus of battle.

Captain Cooper defended the forward section of the bridge with several men behind a makeshift barricade. They maintained a steady suppressing fire.

Titan warriors emerged from the Operations compartment and spread out into the darkened space, returning fire.

Gallant crawled out from the vent he had been hiding in and surreptitiously worked his way behind the Titans. As he emerged from his dark hideout, he fired his handgun and had to blink from the bright flash of his muzzle blast. He hit his target and one of the Titans fell. He moved along the deck stepping over the corpses of the fallen enemy and comrades alike. Screams and shouts echoed from crew members engaged in the fight.

From his position, behind the Titans on the periphery of the bridge, he was able to pick off several of the more exposed aliens. They couldn't shift their position to get a good shot at him without exposing themselves to the bridge crew's crossfire. His fire continued to be surprisingly effective. After an agonizing few minutes, he was able to drive away the nearest Titans. He found himself down on the deck once more firing in a prone position.

Gallant could see Captain Cooper and Neumann in pressure suits at the epicenter of the battle defending the bridge with a ragged group of men, only a few of whom were in their battle armor. The ferocious bloody battle was being waged as a wildly irregular series of personal combats, proceeding one after another. The struggle favored first one side then another. The action was close as the heavy fire continued.

The outcome seemed to be teetering precipitously.

Gallant continued to move forward closer to the fieriest fighting. The flash of a plasma discharge gave him just enough warning to throw himself flat down under the nearby shelter of a cabinet before a following plasma discharge came his way. Twice he felt the heat of near miss plasma blasts—once over his arm—another grazed his leg. Then the wave of the action washed past him and he found several men moaning nearby on the deck.

He tripped on the mutilated body of William Craig, his vacant eyes staring up at Gallant—his once youthful face was disfigured by burnt flesh and splattered with blood.

Bill . . ., flashed into Gallant's mind, but he quickly turned his thoughts away.

The struggling group of wounded men sought shelter behind whatever large metal objects afforded. As the fighting madness ebbed away, Gallant found shelter behind a large cabinet. He realized the nearby crewmen would die soon without medical assistance.

He leveled his pistol once more and fought his way into the thick of the chaos. He crept along the deck firing his gun as he moved, and then he jumped into a narrow hatchway. Nearby firing continued.

Grabbing, thrusting, punching, Gallant found himself in hand to hand combat with a Titan warrior. The tangled struggle ended with a thrust when Gallant grasped his knife and plunged into his adversary.

On the starboard side of the compartment, the fighting likewise continued at close quarters.

Fatalistically, his pistol redlined, out of ammo, forcing him to duck down as the captain charged forward directly at the remaining Titans. Time stopped for Gallant—he watched as a laser blast hit the captain squarely in the chest, a potentially fatal wound—splattering blood on the deck around him.

Several men laid down heavy covering fire while Neumann hurtled forward and dragged the injured commanding officer back behind the barricade.

Thank goodness, thought Gallant.

Gallant grabbed a nearby discarded rifle and rose once more into the action. He started shouting, "Intrepids! Intrepids! Here! Here!"

A few men rallied toward him and together they charged forward one more time, but the group was insufficient to drive the Titans out.

Gallant gave a sharp cry and fell to the deck when he was once again seared by a near miss plasma blast. Agonizing pain shot across his shoulder blade as the new plasma burn compounded his previous injuries causing him to reach the limit of his tolerance.

Weak from pain, he concentrated on thinking clearly. Weapons were once more being pointed in his direction. He moved farther behind the bulkhead before an irregular volley of energy streamed toward him. Once again, he found himself lying flat on the deck. His arms had no strength to lift him up. Still the bloody battle continued to be waged with undisciplined surges back and forth between the dwindling numbers of combatants on each side.

At last, the remaining members of the bridge crew popped up from behind the barricade, and made an audacious assault into the center of the bridge. There the struggle ended when Neumann killed the last of the Titans.

The Titan boarding party was eliminated. The internal contest was over.

Despite having reclaimed the ship, they had no time to rest. Somehow they had to defend the ship against further assaults.

What can we do about the destroyer?

8

HUMMINGBIRD

The Titan destroyer maintained its relative station off the *Intrepid's* starboard quarter, patiently awaiting news of their boarding party's progress.

A bleeding dysfunctional hulk, the *Intrepid* and its decimated crew remained sitting ducks.

Gallant sat amongst the dead and wounded on the burnt-out bridge gathering his thoughts. Despite his painful wounds, he had to persevere—there would be time to see the doctor later—hopefully.

"Gallant, status report?" demanded LCDR Neumann, as he climbed into the captain's chair in the center of the chaos.

"Yes, sir," said Gallant distractedly, as he watched the bleeding body of Dan Cooper being carried off the bridge by med-techs. Refocusing his attention on Neumann,

Gallant said, "We've retaken the ship and I've dispatched several men to patrol for any Titan warriors still able to fight, but the destroyer will send a new boarding party as soon as they realize we've prevailed. Or they'll start taking pot shots at us, depending on how badly they want to capture our FTL drive. Somehow we've got to disable their ship—and we've only a short window to act."

"Yes, time to act is short." Neumann shifted back and forth in his seat.

Gallant's brow wrinkled in thought as he continued, "We don't have an anti-ship weapon, but perhaps we can make one."

"I'm listening."

"We could put several nuclear warheads aboard the Titan assault craft they used to board us. Then using a Hummingbird's tractor beam, we could pull it into position and then launch it toward the destroyer. When it gets close enough, a remote detonation would cause one hell of an explosion."

Neumann nodded slowly. "It's possible, if there're any birds still operable."

"There's one."

"It'll take an exceptional pilot," said the XO, looking at Gallant with unblinking eyes.

"I'm ready," said Gallant, biting back the pain every movement cost him.

"I know you're wounded, but I have to stay to command the ship. Even wounded, you're the best man available."

"I understand."

"Carry on," said Neumann. "And Gallant," he added, "bring the Hummingbird back. I'm going to need it."

"Aye, aye, sir." Gallant looked at Neumann askew.

Was Neumann sending him on what looked like a one-way mission to finally be rid of him? Or was there something else at play? Gallant couldn't sort out the nuances at this moment.

Leaving the bridge, Gallant made his way to engineering, leaning against the bulkhead wherever he could. He found Chief Howard and quickly explained the plan.

Chief Howard said, "The assault craft is attached to the starboard side, aft the beam of the engineering spaces. I'll get men to move several nuclear devices there and meet you there, sir."

Gallant was glad the chief was so efficient and understood what had to be done. He had to carefully plot a course to target using the AI navigation system to reach the optimal launch point.

When preparations were complete, Chief Howard shook Gallant's hand. "Godspeed, Henry."

———

"I'm ready," reported Gallant, climbing into the Hummingbird and launching from the *Intrepid*'s main hanger bay.

Powering his tractor beam, he began towing the Titan shuttle, now loaded with nuclear devices. As the shuttle began to move, the Hummingbird registered the drag of the heavier craft.

Gallant loved flying the single seat U-707 Hummingbird with its powerful single anti-matter fusion engine. It was an all-planets, single man utility craft designed by Mars Douglas Corporation to transport individuals and critical supplies between ships and planets. Fast and durable, but unarmed.

She was a magnificent craft, cable of covering interplanetary distances swiftly with an elegance and responsiveness making the flight a delight. He considered it a thing of exquisite beauty.

He appreciated its compact size of fifty-six feet long, twenty feet high, with a wing span of thirty feet. Fully loaded it weighed twenty-eight tons. Its potent engine consisted of one anti-proton nuclear fusion engine capable of 0.01c for short periods and 0.004c for sustained travel.

In this case, its strong tracker towing ability would be essential. It had a titanium honeycomb fuselage with a shoulder cantilever wing. The fuselage, fins, and thrusters were made of similar material and all covered by a carbon composite skin. It could detect and track spacecraft and small high-speed meteorites at great distances with unprecedented accuracy.

Gallant would have sufficient room to stand and maneuver within the cockpit, albeit with discomfort. The remainder of the craft was occupied by engines, equipment, and supplies.

He patiently worked the tiny craft as it strained to tow the larger shuttle. He watched the Hummingbird's temperature start to climb from drawing ever greater measures of power and adjusted his speed until it declined back to acceptable limits. He tried to keep a constant acceleration to make the navigation problem as simple as possible.

He used a neural sensor interface to control the craft. The neural interface opened the surrounding space to his mind's examination. He controlled the tiny ship and began towing the Titan shuttle full of nuclear explosives toward its mother ship. Because the Hummingbird was so small and the shuttle was tethered so closely, he counted on it being difficult for the Titans to distinguish exactly what objects were approaching.

Eventually, the Titans made an effort to maneuver, indicating a sense of confusion as to why their craft was returning. Uncertain if their own crew was aboard, they trained their laser cannon at the Hummingbird and fired a warning shot.

Gallant remained calm as he approached the calculated launch position given him by the AI. Finally, by letting the Hummingbird drop its tractor beam, he launched the nuclear-explosive-laden shuttle toward the destroyer.

High-tailing it back to the safety of the *Intrepid* took all his coordination and concentration. Soon shots were coming his way and a near miss threatened to damage his Hummingbird.

However, the Titans were too late—the shuttle was well on its way.

Gallant worked feverishly trying to dodge laser beams while getting far enough away before the shuttle exploded.

Caught by surprise, the Titan destroyer was unable to maneuver sufficiently far away and was severely damaged when the shuttle exploded.

Once the shock waves passed him, Gallant was relieved to find he was still alive. He watched as the enemy retreated, limping away toward the outer reaches of the star system.

Relieved at driving off the Titans destroyer, the *Intrepid* was still too badly damaged for extensive flight and therefore was unable to pursue its enemy. In any case, they lacked the firepower to finish the Titans off. Instead, the *Intrepid* limped into orbit over the only inhabitable planet in the system, Tau-Beta.

When Gallant returned to the *Intrepid*, Neumann wore a scowl. "You let them get away."

Gallant matched Neumann's scowl and looked around the *Intrepid*, thinking, *How are we going recover from all this?*

9

SURVIVORS

Despite being severely wounded, Gallant was one of the fortunate *Intrepid* survivors. Seven of twelve officers and seventy of 214 crewmembers were dead. Many more were wounded and required treatment in the ship's severely damaged medical center.

Under heavy analgesics, Gallant lay still on an operating table awaiting surgery while the ship's doctor, Lieutenant Mendel, was desperately operating on Captain Cooper on the adjourning table.

Gallant observed Mendel performing surgical repairs to the damaged organs of the shattered body. Oxygen conduits, blood tubes, and electrical wires were connected to a multitude of locations on the captain's body—mouth, nose, veins, etc.,—allowing chemicals and nano-bots to be pumped throughout his blood and endocrine systems in an attempt to revitalize him and restore hope for his survival. The nano-bots traveled throughout his body conducting preprogrammed internal microsurgery and cell repairs. Electrical sensors were wired to his temple to control his brain functions, others to his heart and lungs. His complete body functions were transferred to the control of the ship's medical AI. An AI avatar stood by Mendel and coached him through the complex surgery.

The rest of the medical center was overflowing with the desperately injured. The few remaining med-techs available were frantically conducting triage and caring for the worst wounded. They injected stem cell rejuvenation fluids and conducted AI-supervised surgical repairs. Their efforts and the triage process were capable of healing much of the damaged flesh, including organs, such as the liver and kidneys.

Eventually, a med-tech came to Gallant. "You won't feel any pain. You can remain conscious and watch so long as you keep perfectly still, okay? You have first, second, and third degree burns over thirty per cent of your body, and you've lost a significant amount of blood, but your vital organs are intact and you will make a complete recovery using the rejuvenation bath after surgery. You should be up and around in four days and within a week, you should no longer suffer from chronic pain."

Gallant nodded and the med-tech, with the help of the AI, began operating on his wounds. He didn't feel significant pain, but could feel the pressure of the physical actions against his body and he was fascinated as the med-tech peeled away his damaged skin. Then collagen and the new skin, grown from his stem cells, were grafted onto his body. Finally, the surface was bandaged.

The med-tech smiled encouragingly. "It looks good. Though, if you had had genetic engineering enhancements, your stem cells would have produced a cleaner match."

Chief Howard came into medic bay while Gallant was receiving medical attention and wished him well, but mostly everyone was too busy looking after their own emergencies to pay more attention to him.

Soon after surgery, Gallant ended up in the regeneration chamber for twenty-four hours of rejuvenation. Nearby chambers were soon filled with his shipmates in various states of recovery.

When Gallant was released from the regeneration chamber, the first thing he asked was how the captain was doing.

The solemn med-tech mumbled, "He didn't make it."

Gallant's face fell. He said nothing. He had no words to express his personal grief.

Then he felt a moment of concern for how the *Intrepid* would fare under Neumann's leadership.

———

After he was released from sick bay, Gallant went to his tiny two-by-three-by-four meter quarters which he had shared with Paulson and Stahl.

They wouldn't be returning.

He stared down at his shoes and the burnt deck beneath them; he sat on what was left of his bunk in the shattered remains of his three-man stateroom. The cabin was sparsely furnished, revealing a traditional stark military room. A desk rested in one well-lit corner. The cubicle also included a tiny storage locker for each man to store his clothes and personal belongings. Three storage lockers had been under the bottom bunk bed and contained what personal property had escaped destruction. The rest of their personal effects were mostly distributed trash, strewn on the deck. The crumpled bunk beds were a heap of unrecognizable twisted metal. Along one wall was the closet containing uniforms. He managed to find one remaining disheveled but useable uniform he could wear.

He combed through the wreckage, but what remained of their personal items was unrecognizable. He bumped into a lump of melted material. He puzzled over it for a second and then closed his mind; he would rather not know what it had once been. The only area to escape incineration was the single utility sink in the corner of the room.

He picked up a few surviving remembrances—wreckage of shattered lives—an image stick with enough memory to hold millions of selected pictures, a personal jewelry pin which belonged to Stahl, and Paulson's UPSA class ring.

"Their family will want these," he muttered, and he continued to gather what he could, aware family members would eventually ask about them.

He would have to find other accommodations, but first he needed to get cleaned up and feel refreshed. He decided to take a quick shower under icy water for the prescribed thirty-second allotment. Pleased the water flowed when he stood under the faucet; he recoiled as the cold permeated his flesh. A twenty-second antiseptic cleaner and a ten-second rinse followed. He felt better after his shower.

He stood before the mirror while he shaved. His reflection showed a familiar face—one with a steely fortitude.

———

Burial in space was always an intense emotional experience, even when it didn't include the death of the ship's captain. Traditional space burials followed rituals from ancient burials at sea—which had been a practice for centuries, with the body of the dead sewn in a shroud. For in-space disposition, each body was suited in a pressure suit, covered with the UP ensign, and placed in a capsule.

The ship's general intercom heralded, "All hands prepare to honor the dead."

Neumann presided as acting captain over the solemn ceremony. All able-bodied crewmen assembled mid-ship at the hanger deck and saluted while the anthem played. Only the officer of the watch and the bare minimum watch standers remained at their stations.

Rows of flag-covered bodies lined the entire length of the corridor. Every hat was off; every head was bowed; they listened to the words of their new commanding officer as he spoke the funeral service. Then individuals came forward and spoke their peace, offered religious passages, or military readings, all seeking closure.

Gallant stood at attention with his shipmates. His eyes lingered over the flag-draped body of William Craig.

Chief Howard stood next to him and said quietly, "He was a fine young man." Then turning away, he added, "Sometimes the loss is more than I can bear."

Gallant nodded.

Yes.

The bodies were draped with the UP flag and their cap and insignia were displayed. The seventy-seven bodies were arranged to be individually carried to the discharge port and placed in a capsule for launch.

Upon completion of taps, the honor guard saluted. The chief master-at-arms presented the UP ensign to the commanding officer.

"We commit their bodies to the vacuum of space, to journey forever more. May they find a peace in death they didn't have in life," said Neumann.

One by one, the bodies were ejected into space.

Gallant brought his hand to his eye to salute each fallen shipmate. He couldn't find any better way to show his admiration. However, when the captain was released, somehow it felt too final, too conclusive to drop the salute. He waited for a long minute until he steeled himself, then as sharply as he brought up his hand, he snapped it down.

The ceremony finally over, men from all over the ship, got on with the job of saving the *Intrepid.*

———

"Mr. Gallant, it's good to see you returning to duty," said Chief Howard standing behind the port reactor compartment shield wall. "I've been supervising the ship's recovery and repairs while waiting for you to return from stasis."

"Thanks, Chief. I've been straining at the bit to get back to engineering. Doc Mendel was hard to convince, but I'm ready to return to work. He had me jumping through hoops and I mean it literally. He has me on a part-time schedule for the time being," said Gallant.

Howard nodded his approval.

For several minutes Howard walked beside Gallant sporting a frown, as they went through the engineering spaces looking over the compartment's damage.

They looked around, but couldn't find any of the familiar military spit and polish present a few days earlier. Everywhere around them was destruction and debris.

The *Intrepid* was still alive with bustling activities, however. Atmosphere venting from metal ducts provided fresh air while a multitude of machines produced a steady drone, as the air conditioners fought the heat buildup. Men were working and discussing their problems. Progress was slow, but steady.

"I guess I should get started by reviewing our operational status," said Gallant with a questioning inflection.

Howard shook his head, "Operational? Not much. We're working around the clock to restore what we can, but ... honestly... the ship is a mess. The men—those fit for duty—are exhausted. The XO has been driving everyone hard. I ..., I mean Captain Neumann," said Howard referring to his new commanding officer as captain for the first time.

Howard explained the entire propulsion plant was defunct. The crew was reporting numerous defects and major failures throughout the engineering spaces.

Gallant began to evaluate the sublight and FTL engines.

The Higgs containment field, required to maintain dark matter at negative temperatures and pressures, had ruptured, releasing their entire supply of dark matter.

The sublight fusion engine consisted of simple antimatter fusion reactors using an ordinary plasma containment field to drive the ship during normal planetary travel. The antimatter engines normally shot antiprotons into the nucleus of deuterium atoms, which caused a release of energy under the fusion process. However, even a small number of antiproton reactions could start a chain reaction which would otherwise have required a much larger mass of deuterium and tritium to sustain. With antimatter catalyzed reactions, only one gram of heavy hydrogen was required along with a microscopic amount of antiprotons. However, the antiprotons had to be kept isolated in plasma bottles surrounded by powerful superconducting magnetic coils.

The antimatter plasma containment field had also ruptured, thereby requiring more antimatter as well.

Howard said, "The fusion reactors are badly damaged; one critically so. The faster-than-light drive was also seriously damaged. A new inventory of exotic dark matter has to be acquired, or else we're not going any place."

After their brief physical inspection, Gallant went into the engineering control room located in the middle of the upper level of the engineering compartment. He pulled on his man-machine neuron interface headgear. This allowed him direct access to the ship's Artificial Intelligence or (AI), nicknamed GridScape. The dozens of tiny silicon probes touched his scalp at key points, sensitively picking up wave patterns emanating from his thoughts and using the AI to translate his thoughts into physical commands for operating the engineering machinery and reactors. The physical controls were still available, but only as a backup.

Controlling machines with thoughts is faster, he reflected.

Gallant was uniquely qualified to be engineer on the *Intrepid* because of his exceptional neural abilities. Despite being a Natural, non-genetically engineered, his performance had been proven to be far superior to officers who were specifically engineered to use the neural interface. His exceptional talents were also his burden of responsibility.

Genetically enhanced officers, like Neumann, were altered to have the hormones and enzymes necessary for this operation, while he was uniquely born with them. In the past Gallant had been able to successfully interface with the neuron headgear, but he had not been able to maintain a high intensity of concentration for sustained periods. Now, however, he had developed far beyond the abilities of officers like Neumann.

Using the interface, he *felt* the engineering plant open up to him. He could visualize reactor controls and equipment. He spatially oriented himself then *felt* the controls for regulating reactor control rods and hydraulic valves and pumps. By merely visualizing the operations, he could manipulate instruments.

Mentally, he visualized the pneumatic-hydraulic plasma discharge valve for the starboard antimatter engines. There he cast the light onto the automatic control setting and checked it was in the closed position. The green status light indicated the automatic closure feature was operating normally as well.

Chief Howard had done a splendid job in getting things started, but there was so much more to do.

"I guess we should start with setting up a rotating work schedule and set repair priorities," said Gallant.

Methodically, he went through the status of the rest of the equipment and began going over a general repair schedule including validation tests. The list of tasks to be accomplished seemed endless. He set up a long-term personnel work schedule identifying key expertise requirements.

He concentrated and visualized the ship, its controls, and the system failures, as one image. He then tuned his senses to *see* the path to recovery. Developing a sense of harmony between controls and performance, he created a solution in his mind's eye. Hours passed while he worked diligently evaluating the various system failures and devising possible workouts. As he figured out the failure modes for each piece of equipment, he submitted his solution to the AI for evaluation. He used his mental image to evaluate the virtual information data feeds.

The AI reported, "Damage in port and starboard engines—control panel and main electrical panel fused—atmospheric supplies contaminated—rupture of the antimatter plasma containment field—other casualties involving additional equipment beginning to register."

He began to assess the damage and evaluate remedial corrective actions. Without hesitation he changed settings on the engines, stopped the environmental equipment, and altered control settings on internal power.

Gallant continued to work on unraveling the casualties in men and machines. At first, the AI rejected everything he proposed, but slowly, he was able to develop a plan to partially restore the ship's life-support capability and then established a repair plan to allow minimal power for essential items. Despite his fatigue, he submitted his final renovation concept to the AI. It approved the path to restore life-support and the minimal power supply.

His mind wrung out from wrestling the computer, Gallant walked through the engineering spaces and watched as engineering personnel performed repairs.

Soon robotic arms and trollies moved equipment and machinery into position for removal or replacement with AI and human guidance. UP hadn't been able to develop robots or intelligent computers, to operate independently, but the AI systems could understand human language and solve many problems. People still argued about how smart computers were, but nevertheless they were helpful and obedient.

Howard reviewed the progress on the virtual readout screens. "I'll see the captain about approving the long term plan and get people working accordingly. However, you should be aware with so much equipment out of action we're practically flying blind over this planet. Captain Neumann is going to want to get power to the sensor array and communication stations as a high priority."

They desperately needed to monitor the departing Titans as well as investigate the planet below, but that merely added to the endless series of needs to fill. Gallant said, "We're going to need Deuterium and Tritium for our fusion reactors. We need to extract heavy water from the only source within eleven light-years—those oceans below. We'll also need to construct an accelerator to generate antimatter and dark matter. That's only the basics. We'll need to build a major mining and manufacturing facility on the planet."

Howard shook his head, bewildered.

"We'll need heavy transuranic metals as well."

"Transuranic?"

"We're going to build anti-ship missiles with nuclear tipped warheads," said Gallant. "Once we get our fusion reactors and antimatter production, we can generate dark matter to power our FTL, but we're going to need the local population to help."

10

IS ANYONE THERE?

"Spaceship, identify yourself. Spaceship, identify yourself."

The *Intrepid* was forced to ignore the repetitious broadcast while it maintained orbit over the earthlike plane. The endless repairs which included the communication equipment encompassed their full attention. The crew worked feverishly to care for their wounded comrades and battered ship. With so many men undergoing surgery and rejuvenation therapy, they were shorthanded carrying out the extensive repair regimen.

The signal emanated from the large island chain consisting of six large mountainous islands crossing from the planet's temperate into its tropical zone. Active volcanoes spilled lava into the nearby ocean, which quickly cooled and pulverized the rock into black-sand beaches. However, this was no black, crater-pitted wasteland, such as appeared on the moons of Jupiter where the *Intrepid* was first launched. Instead, oceans, rivers, and mountainous archipelagoes ranged across this planet. Most of the large islands had wild tropical landscapes with a number of pristine white-sand beaches.

From the initial reconnaissance, the crew had learned the planet's inhabitants occupied a single community with mainly residential structures in a cluster along the southern shoreline on the largest island—the only visible settlement on the main tropical island chain. A few industrial buildings and factories were on the settlement's outer perimeter. The rest of the planet's land masses appeared barren of people, but they were teeming with other forms of life. The inhabitants seemed to embrace the splendors of island sun-soaked beaches as a true tropical oasis. Along the volcanic areas were vast jungles and tropical vegetation. Towering palm trees overlooked sparkling bays and a warm tropical wonderland filled with stunning waterfalls.

The broadcast went unanswered as it repeated relentlessly, hour after hour, for days. The crew toiled over its urgent priorities until finally the communication equipment was once again functioning.

"Pin-point the communication source," ordered Neumann.

"Here, sir," reported the radio operator. A moment later, he pointed to a spot on his virtual screen. The screen was a bright image floating above the burnt and disfigured electrical equipment generating it. Around the screen were fragments of mechanical parts strewn together Rube Goldberg fashion. Nevertheless, the array was operating.

"How long have they been broadcasting?"

"Continuously for 120 hours, sir, ever since the battle. Imaging capability from orbit has been able to resolve individual people, and, by using thermal-imaging on individual houses, it can see how many people are inside each room."

"What's the total population?"

"We were able to count about twenty-four thousand individuals within the community. There may be others farther inland, however."

"How many structures are there?"

"There are about seven thousand inhabited dwellings along with numerous buildings, probably for commerce and industry. Also there are several thousand vehicles of all kinds from single-riders to mass-transport vehicles."

"Our battle must have created quite a stir on Tau-Beta. The population of the colony probably had enough capability to observe a great deal of the battle through telescopes, but the nuclear explosions would have been visible to the naked eye."

A few minutes later the radioman frowned, made an adjustment and then spoke. "Sir, we're being radar scanned again. And the general radio transmission is being rebroadcast. We've been monitoring the planet's communications and they continue to speak only standard United Planets' dialect."

"It is all native UP language?"

"Yes, sir. There is considerable local communication and it's all in native UP language."

"Humans using standard UP, what do you make of it, Gallant?" asked Neumann.

"The planet's surface revealed the individuals of this civilization are human. We have to consider the possibility these humans are from own solar system, captured by the Titans and transported here sometime in the last two centuries," speculated Gallant.

"Humph," was all Neumann responded.

"We've got communications operating at minimal capability now, sir. I suggest we contact them and see if they can be of any help with our repairs," suggested Gallant.

"If they're cooperative," said Neumann.

"Maybe we can arrange to trade with them."

"We don't know what kind of relationship they had with the Titans," said Neumann.

Gallant addressed the radioman, "Still nothing?" And watched as the radioman shook his head negatively.

He said, "Nothing sir. I thought there was another radar scan a moment ago, but it appears to have gotten lost in the static."

Unperturbed, Gallant said, "Keep looking for the source of the scanning."

The broadcast message continued to blare. "Spaceship, identify yourself. Spaceship, identify yourself."

"Can you raise them on a direct communication channel to someone in authority?" asked Neumann.

"I'm sure I can. One minute, sir,"

A minute later, communication was established. The radio operator indicated Neumann was connected and could speak.

"This is the United Planets' ship, *Intrepid*, Lieutenant Commander Neumann commanding."

"This is Cyrus Wolfe, President of the Planetary Council of Elysium."

"*Intrepid* is on an expedition from the star Sol, eleven light-years distance. We have come to test a faster-than-light drive. Can you explain your origin?"

"We are an independent self-governing planet."

Independent? If they're human, they should be under United Planets' authority regardless of how they arrived here, thought Gallant.

Neumann said, "We've been in battle against an enemy Titan destroyer which we incapacitated. It is currently moving away."

Wolfe said, "I suggest you leave before they recover and return."

Not the welcoming I'd hoped for, thought Gallant.

"Our ship is too badly damaged. We must conduct repairs. Aren't you concerned about the Titans? Do you need our assistance?"

"We have nothing to fear from the Titans. They can't harm us. We have a protective force field we can raise over our entire planet whenever we're threatened."

"That's impressive. How did you design and build such a powerful device?" asked Neumann.

"We're not prepared to discuss those issues over the radio."

"We're in need of significant repairs. We would like to establish a base on your planet to mine needed materials and forge new equipment."

"Commander," said Wolfe. "Landing any of your crew on this planet would not be recommended until we've established an understanding."

"We're surprised to find you here and we would like to establish contact to learn more about you."

"We don't want a large group of your people on our planet."

"That's a discussion best handled face to face. Perhaps we can send a single representative to your community to discuss how we can cooperate and reach the understanding you desire."

"Then, of course, we must provide you with assistance. If you send a single representative, we will discuss how we reach a mutually satisfying agreement. We will keep our force field lowered so your small craft can land," said Wolfe.

"Thank you. We'll make preparations," said Neumann. Then to the radioman, he added, "End transmission."

"They're not rolling out the red carpet for us, sir," said Gallant.

Neumann said, "Come to my cabin."

———•———

Standing at attention next to the open hatch of the captain's cabin, Gallant realized he was going to have a difficult time dealing with his new commanding officer.

Clean-shaven with trim black hair, Neumann was physically impressive. While he could be brilliant and thoroughly professional, he lacked Dan Cooper's charisma.

Waiting for his presence to be acknowledged, Gallant observed Neumann's striking profile fixed on a virtual screen as he reviewed the ship-wide repair schedule.

"Come in, Mr. Gallant," said Neumann, finally turning around. "From your engineering report, it's going to take a great deal of resources and manpower over a period of months before the *Intrepid* will be fully operational."

"Yes, sir."

"As one of only five officers remaining, I intend to remain aboard ship. I'll use Chief Howard to supervise engineering repairs and I'm going to place you in charge of all planet-side activities. I'll operate the ship with the doctor and two junior officers."

Gallant let his gaze wander to the photograph on the desk. It was Dan Cooper's wife.

"You'll be responsible for negotiating with Elysium's leader for access to resources and manpower. You know our requirements including heavy metal mining, heavy water collection, plus the construction of an accelerator and manufacturing facilities." Neumann paused, and then said, "I want you to listen carefully. Circumstance and distance will dictate you exercise a degree of discretion, but I want to be kept fully informed. I will not accept any freelance activity. You will be held strictly accountable. Am I clear?" Neumann scrutinized Gallant as if daring him to contradict.

Gallant bit his tongue and swallowed hard before saying between his teeth, "Yes, sir."

"I want a weekly report, in person. You're going to spend a great deal of time in this cabin debriefing me and listening to my instructions."

"Aye, aye, sir."

"I want you to make a long term arrangement with Elysium's leadership to keep the force shield down. See if we can get equipment and men to support our mining and manufacturing efforts. We can provide synthetic foods, or offer to build a nuclear power plant for them, as barter and incentive. Offer to take a representative back to Earth with us. I'm sure that will be of interest. Tell them we can provide defensive support against the Titans, in the future, after we've returned from Earth."

"Yes, sir."

"We have only one Hummingbird, so we'll have to rig up a tractor beam for the Hummingbird to pull a container trailer to ferry supplies and people back and forth from the planet."

"I'll get Chief Howard started on that before I leave."

"Good. I expect you to supervise all planet operations and maintain a rigorous schedule. I want maximum cooperation from the planet's leadership. We must be ready when the destroyer comes back," added Neumann with a frown.

"Aye, aye, sir."

"Gallant, your success on Elysium is critical to the survival of *Intrepid*. I expect you to represent the Untied Planets in a manner to bring credit on the *Intrepid*. Given your lack of genetic engineering, I've concerns. Your performance will reflect on me when we report back to Earth and I'll be completing your fitness reports from now on," said Neumann.

Gallant looked at Neumann's rigid face and set eyes. He was all too aware of Neumann's views.

Neumann continued, "I won't allow your failures to reflect poorly on this ship, or on me."

"I am prepared to accept responsibility for my actions, sir," said Gallant, saluting as he left the cabin.

11

ELYSIUM

Fire retros, thought Gallant, prompting the Hummingbird to fall from its vertiginous orbit.

The tiny ship's battle scars reminded him of what he was leaving behind, but he quickly dispelled his momentary sense of isolation. Instead, he focused on his mission to a new world. He let Elysium fill the viewport as well as his imagination. The fulsome imagery blended with his neural interface receptors, producing a heightened awareness. Optimistically, he resolved to enjoy the eight minute ride to the landing strip at the outer edge of the town.

He had grown up on terra-formed Mars and never visited Earth. Now as he plunged downward toward the aquamarine water, he could appreciate its novelty. The craft penetrated the atmosphere and passed through the dotted white clouds with the sun reflecting off its polished surface.

When the Hummingbird pierced the stratosphere, the hull creaked from strain, alerting him to the many and varied external noises—a startling change from the formal silence of deep space. Buffeted by solar winds and the air pressure of the ionosphere, the ship's metal fabric added vibrating noises.

He listened to a cacophony of thunderous rocket engines bellowing as fuel gurgled into the nozzles and then exploded; fierce winds howled as they chafed against the heat shield, and a rhythmic *plink* of particles struck the hull.

Performing a wingover helped to stabilize the fuel mixture and to distribute the heat more evenly. The maneuver caused the planet to swirl around in his viewport, adding a visual spectacle to trump the auditory repast. The sunlight accentuated the blue skies, the vibrant blue-green oceans, and the orange-red horizons. These soon gave way to the planetary features of numerous islands with rugged brown-gray mountains and burgeoning green forests. The islands dotted the expansive ocean teeming with life from multicolored birds to herds of mammals roaming free.

The largest island in the main chain was the eastern most, which sported a gigantic volcano on its northern peninsula. Gallant had seen volcanoes on the various moons of Jupiter. They featured spiraling conical peaks and deep sprawling ravines, but the one below him dwarfed them all. His home planet, Mars, featured the largest volcano in the solar system, but before his eyes was one even larger.

A final crescendo was reached when the Hummingbird thudded to a jarring stop on the landing pad.

While he unstrapped, the AI reported, "The atmosphere is breathable with twenty per cent oxygen content. Indications are the plant life has many similarities to Earth and the ocean is rich in photosensitive plankton. Testing of voluminous bacteria and virus strains is underway and a list of dangerous pathogens will be updated continuously as you travel through the environment."

"AI, can I use my comm pin to relay through the Hummingbird to the *Intrepid*?" asked Gallant.

"The planetary force shield has been reestablished. Communication to the *Intrepid* is no longer possible."

Gallant didn't like that, but there was nothing he could do until he negotiated a pact with Wolfe.

Satisfied the planet's health risks were acceptable, he opened his hatch and felt the welcoming rush of clean fresh air on his face. A deep breath of fresh floral air energized and reassured him. The fragrance of sweet canary yellow flowers and lush lime green vegetation contributed to the sensory delights. The breathtaking views of natural beauty struck him immediately. There was no place on Mars like this island, none like this planet. The warm tranquil azure-blue waters were welcoming. Gallant hoped for an opportunity to explore those places on this visit.

Walking on grass with bright saffron sunlight shining down on him, he realized Elysium was the sensual bombardment he had imagined Earth to be. This planet was also near Earth-gravity which was far more than Gallant was used to.

He wore a tight form-fitting navy-blue jumpsuit uniform with two gold bars on each lapel and campaign ribbons arrayed over his left breast pocket. A laser handgun was strapped in the holster on his right hip.

He stood in a large clearing surrounded by several small buildings with roads radiating outward like spokes of a wheel. The community stood like a mass of block-shaped marbles carelessly arranged across the hillside and shore.

In startling contrast to the welcoming natural environment, the grim and sour faces of the four men approaching Gallant caused him to hesitate before greeting them. Stopping several meters away, they waited for Gallant to speak.

From their demeanor and dress—a formal style of clothing, uniforms without weapons—the men gave an impression of authority, but with an air of an uncertainty, rather than diplomatic welcoming. Such was Gallant's observations, as he maintained a neutral expression. He waited patiently to be received, but when no one made an effort to greet him, he said, "I'm Lieutenant Henry Gallant of the United Planets' *Intrepid.*"

"Lieutenant Henry Gallant, I'm Cyrus Wolfe, Chief of the Safety and Security Police," said the youngest and most interesting looking of the group. He had a large trimmed mustache, sunken eyes, and a drawn face. His skinny body and sprawling hands showed a lack of physical conditioning; nevertheless he reeked of self-importance.

Gallant concentrated his attention on the one who appeared to be the leader and didn't pay attention to the others. He had expected someone astute in politics, powerful looking, perhaps flamboyant, but certainly older. This man met none of those expectations. It crossed Gallant's mind that behind this man's calm exterior, yet hesitant demeanor, was a seething anger and natural distrust.

"Wolfe? Are you—?"

"No. My father is Cyrus Wolfe, Sr., President of the Elysium Council. You'll meet him in due course."

"We're on a peaceful exploration mission from Sol, eleven and a half light years from here," started Gallant.

Cyrus Wolfe Junior's eyes glossed over, "He'll be glad to hear your entire history when we get to the meeting."

Gallant decided to think of this person as "*Junior*," but he didn't intend to call him Junior to his face.

Junior seemed intent on ending all conversation, but Gallant gave it another try.

"You seem rather young to be in such an important position."

"No younger than you, Lieutenant."

Junior didn't introduce the other members of his delegation, but spoke deferentially of President Wolfe and their need to hurry along to the waiting council members in the assembly building.

Gallant smiled, evaluating the man as a cool customer. "Are you authorized to discuss policy with me?"

A quick mutual glance passed between the Elysium men. Junior said, "No, this group is to evaluate security prior to bringing you to our leadership council, not to negotiate."

"I see," he said gravely, taking mental note to not reveal too much too soon. "Okay. What more can I do to reassure you my intentions are for our mutual benefit?"

Glimpsing Gallant's side arm, Junior said, "I'll need your gun and communication devices."

Seeing Gallant's reluctance he added, "They will be returned to you when you leave, but we are responsible for security on Elysium. The SSP allows no weapons here."

Having already noted their apparent lack of weaponry, Gallant decided to cooperate and handed his laser side arm to the police chief, but hesitated to remove his comm pin. "This is my communication pin and I'm going to need it to communicate with my ship."

"You can arrange communication to your ship from our headquarters."

Gallant handed over his comm pin and said, "I am most anxious to meet with your president. I've listened to his speech broadcasts and I hope we can be of mutual benefit to each other. It would help if I learned more about your people."

"Elysium is an independent planet run by Cyrus Wolfe and the planetary council."

"Forgive me for asking, but you are human, aren't you?"

"Yes, we're human." Junior smirked. "In fact we're from Sol, but you'll have to wait for more explanation. For now please come with us. We have a meeting arranged with the planetary council in the town hall."

Gallant met his eyes and held them, refusing to look away. Finally, Junior blinked and turned away.

Junior and his three guards led Gallant to a building, one of the bigger structures in the community on the edge of the clearing. The strictness and uniformity with which these men treated him was disturbing. He was left in a large room where he stood waiting for events to unfold.

After several minutes, eight men entered the room and took seats arranged around a table. They didn't acknowledge Gallant, but they looked at him as if to evaluate his potential. Clearly, Junior had informed them of his experiences with the new arrival.

"Please sit down, Lieutenant Henry Gallant. Make yourself comfortable. We are most eager to welcome you to Elysium. I am Cyrus Wolfe," Wolfe Sr. said, sitting with assured authority, surrounded by his symbols of office and power. Behind him were an unfamiliar flag, several marble statues, and numerous plaques. The room was adorned to emphasize influence.

Wolfe was a large, portly man with long flowing black hair with gray streaks and a bushy gray beard. However, he had elegant attire and a proud demeanor. Next to him was man who appeared to be his chief of staff. The stocky man nodded a vague acknowledgment, but then quickly whispered into Wolfe's ear.

With a tight smile and a slight bow of his head, Gallant indicated his intention to comply by sitting, glad to see this more diplomatic tone to his arrival.

"Thank you. I am grateful for the opportunity to meet with you to establish a relationship of cooperation and goodwill."

"Our colony thrives on this island chain. We call this large island, Kauai. The main inhabited town is named Hallo. I am president of the planet and leader of the council."

One town, on one island, and he thinks he's ruler of a planet?

"We're the governing body of the independent planet Elysium." Wolfe paused casting an examining look at Gallant.

Gallant, realizing the importance of the statement, remained quiet.

"Over fifty years ago, the first Earth asteroid mining operations began in the asteroid belt. Once colonization and asteroid mining began, commerce was established and immigrants built colonies that became self-sufficient. They had their own food production and air ventilation control systems," said Wolfe. He paused for a second before continuing, "The Titans attacked and captured the Ceres asteroid-mining colony. We're survivors of those kidnapped humans taken from Ceres by the Titans fifty years ago." Once again Wolfe paused and peered at Gallant as if to assess the impact of the revelation on Gallant's psyche.

Gallant let Wolfe's words sink in and began to reevaluate stories he had heard before. He was aware of stories surrounding the "Ceres Disaster," as it was referred to. The incident occurred before the Untied Planets discovered the existence of the Titans. The disappearance of the miners and the destruction of their facilities were attributed to an accidental detonation of their mining explosives, or a major asteroid collision beyond the capacity of the normal asteroid protection lasers.

Gallant made a strange connection to this story when certain facts clicked together in his memory cells—the financial losses of the disaster were absorbed by the NNR Shipping and Mining Company, owned by rich and powerful Gerald Neumann, president of NNR and father of Anton Neumann, Gallant's new commanding officer.

Bizarre.

Even after the war with the Titans was in full swing, no one seriously suspected the Titans' involvement in the "Ceres Disaster." The Titans must have used extensive non-nuclear explosives to cover their tracks and throw off the UP investigators.

Now we've come full circle.

Seeing Gallant begin to nod, Wolfe continued, "Fortunately soon after those methane-breathers left us alone on oxygen rich Elysium, I was able to build a force field. Our force field has protected us from further exploitation by the Titans for the last twenty years."

The other members of the council exclaimed their devotion and approbation over Wolfe's accomplishment.

When the commotion died down, Gallant, perplexed, asked, "How were you able to design and construct such a remarkable planetary force field?"

Wolfe raised his voice to be heard above the clamor. "Not so difficult, but that's a discussion for another time." He smiled, pleased with himself. "We are a young world, and in our short history, we have had only one leader—me," he said with pride.

A faint emphasis upon the way he spoke the words alerted Gallant to an undertone in their meaning. He recognized the seat of power was here. From here, Wolfe could have him killed or tortured to suit his needs, but what were his needs? His hands folded tight before him, Gallant wasn't exactly sure. He had no formal negotiating training and could only rely on his own experience to guide him. His instincts told him Wolfe was a master manipulator and

Gallant would have to play his hand carefully to succeed on this mission.

"The United Planets has been at war with our mutual enemy, the Titans, since shortly after you were abducted. The *Intrepid* is our first FTL ship and this was our maiden voyage to test the drive. Unfortunately we ran into a Titan destroyer and our ship was badly damaged," Gallant paused waiting for acknowledgment from Wolfe. Seeing none he continued, "We need to utilize the resources of this planet to affect repairs."

"You presume a great deal, perhaps too much," said Wolfe. "But let's proceed slowly, shall we? First let's enjoy a meal, compliments of the bounties of Elysium, and we can get to know each other before we begin making weighty decisions."

Grateful for the break, Gallant tried to collect his thoughts.

Tread lightly.

Waiters entered and began setting the table for an extensive meal. Apparently they had done this before because they were incredibly efficient arranging cutlery, napkins, and place settings. Then the food arrived, including a combination of green vegetables, fish, and meat dishes. A variety were hot, others cold, all giving off an attractive aroma and whetting the appetites of those seated around the table.

Gallant sat at the center of the table while they brought in a wide variety of foodstuffs for him to sample. It all looked delicious—a unique variety of fish and bird dishes, plus fruits and vegetables, all of which he happily tasted. Wolfe described, in seemingly endless detail, how they had developed their agriculture and fishing industries. He obviously liked to talk about how self-sufficient the colony was.

While enjoying the excellent food, Gallant surveyed the furnishings of the room. The utensils and plates were quite unusual for a United Planets' household.

Gallant said "I've been living on synthetics for a long time and this array of fresh food is quite irresistible."

Wolfe twitched and repressed a placated smile. "Yes, all this food has been collected and prepared locally. Please help yourself to the dishes before you. I hope you will taste from each of those available."

After being in space for so long, existing on nothing, but artificial foods, he couldn't disguise his delight. Gallant took a taste from each dish and enjoyed the delicious meal. He was aware of how manipulative Wolfe was being in shifting the discussion away from exchanging information.

After a while, however, Wolfe got down to business.

"Well, Lieutenant, this has been interesting, but you should be able to conclude we are self-sustaining and perfectly capable of surviving without outside assistance." His mild conversational voice hid the depth of his commitment. In fact the placid look on his face did not waver as he focused his attention directly on Gallant. His body firmed up, becoming rigid, affirming his intractable intent.

Gallant felt the dismal scene before him was the result of a troubled history. He tried to remember the last time he had experienced anything comparable.

"Didn't you detect us approaching the planet?" asked Gallant, venturing into troubled waters.

No response.

"You never warned us about the Titan destroyer. You must have known it was preparing to ambush us. What were you thinking?" asked Gallant.

Wolfe looked as if he had been hit in the face with a wet towel. Nothing escaped his lips.

Don't have a cover story?

Gallant moved on, "I understand your position as the leader of a new state, but I need to interview other members of the Hallo community to get a sense of the collective opinion of the citizenry. The *Intrepid* is willing to take anyone who wants to leave—back to Earth."

"No!"

"You're still part of the United Planets. We're in this struggle against the Titans, together. Aren't we?"

"Elysium is independent, and will remain so."

"Surely there are people who will want to return to their families," said Gallant, as if innocent of detecting any deeper nefarious meaning on Wolfe's part.

Indignant, Wolfe said, "I've been waiting for you to say such a thing. Originally, we started out with several thousand colonists from Ceres and from time to time individuals were taken away by the Titans and they never reappeared. Obviously the Titans used them to learn about us, perhaps through medical experiments and tests in which their survivability was not a priority. We were studied and treated as an experiment or a zoo. But now, no one wants to leave this paradise planet. I suppose you think it's strange we wished to stay here and not return to the United Planets, but we have a better life here than we had on the asteroids. Aren't we safer? The UP peoples are still at war with an enemy while we are perfectly protected with our force field."

"These are serious matters. We must find common ground to resolve them," said Gallant.

"It then rests on the art of persuasion to reach an agreement we can both find satisfactory," said Wolfe.

Gallant said, "The *Intrepid* needs heavy metals, titanium, uranium, and an accelerator to produce dark matter and antimatter. It may require many months of construction including fabrication and forging of hull and reactor parts. It will be an extensive effort and we would welcome your assistance."

"Those may be your needs, but you haven't asked what my needs are," said Wolfe, raising his eye brow while pulling at the end of his brushy gray beard.

Gallant stared at Wolfe, who returned a stoic glare.

Mounting tension filled the room when . . .

Bang!

The noise startled everyone.

The conference room door had been slammed against the wall with enough force to produce the loud *bang*— calling a halt to the proceedings and focusing attention on the arrival of a young slender blonde with a shapely figure, dressed in rugged outdoor hiking gear, who marched boldly into the room. She was about a year or two younger than Gallant, perhaps twenty.

She dominated everyone's attention. It wasn't because she was so shockingly belligerent as to require an immediate rejoinder, though she was clearly intent on being provocative—nor was she was so strikingly beautiful so as to inflame male passions, yet she was certainly attractive. No, she dominated the situation, despite portraying a rebellious joy of life, because of her defiant bearing, her air of resolution, and her dogged expression—all of which were so clearly evident—by marching, hands on hips, into the focal point of the room, thereby demanding the immediate and undivided attention of all present.

"Alaina, you are interrupting important state business. What do you want?" demanded Wolfe, standing up to express his annoyance with her theatrical appearance.

Wolfe's carefully crafted mask of self-assurance had slipped.

"My grandfather is unable to attend, so he asked me to take his place, which is his prerogative. Certainly that's allowed? Isn't it?" she asked with an authoritative voice, shifting her gaze from one council member to another, causing them to fidget in their seats as her stare met theirs.

Clearly internal politics were at play, but Gallant was wary of how he should interact with this new dynamic in the room.

Wolfe heaved a sign of resignation and sputtered, "Well—of course—under those circumstances, you're welcome. Please sit. Here, sit next to me."

Alaina brushed back her long flowing blonde hair and walked toward Gallant instead. "Well aren't you going to introduce me to this officer?" she asked.

Again Wolfe heaved a sign of resignation, this time deeper and more sustained. "Lieutenant Gallant, this is Alaina Hepburn, granddaughter of Professor James Hepburn, a leading citizen, a member of this council, and our leading expert on cybernetics."

"I'm glad to meet you, Ms. Hepburn," said Gallant, standing and offering his hand.

"A pleasure, Lieutenant." Alaina bowed her head slightly, but kept her hands clasped to her hips.

A moment later, to Gallant's surprise, she flashed him a luminescent smile and took the seat beside him, tapping her fingers impatiently on the top of the table. With her hair pulled back from her face, the creamy beauty of her skin was exposed.

Gallant took his place beside her.

Alaina helped herself to a cup and filled it with a coffee-like beverage. She sipped slowly as if waiting for the meeting to resume, all the while studying him surreptitiously.

"Are you enjoying our local cuisine?" she asked, meeting his gaze.

"Very much so."

"Here, try this fowl. It's one of my favorites."

"Thank you."

Aliana took charge of Gallant, commandeering his attention right along with the meeting.

Gallant's face grew rosy under her scrutiny. He felt self-conscious, because admittedly, he didn't look his best—after all, he had recently been in battle and was forced to wear a ragged uniform.

"We've recorded information about the battle you fought against the Titans and we're interested in finding out your current circumstances. Is there anything we can do to help?" she asked.

"Well, yes. That's my mission. I'm seeking your assistance in making repairs to our ship before the Titan destroyer can repair their damage and return."

"Well, you must know, you've been a long time coming. We've been waiting and waiting for many years, actually."

"We never knew what happened on Ceres. In fact, we are not here on a rescue mission. It's a coincidence we found you now, but this is an opportunity for us to work together to our mutual benefit. Once our ship is repaired, we can provide transportation back to Earth for representatives of Elysium."

"No," exclaimed Wolfe, once more upset on this point. "All our people are happy here, on Elysium."

"Not everyone," added Alaina.

"Please, Alaina, do not take too much upon yourself. This is a discussion for the United Planets' representative and the council."

"Meaning, you will make all the decisions, as usual, Mr. Wolfe?"

"Not at all. Not at all. I only meant there are certain boundaries we must draw before this becomes a public discussion."

"Ha," she scoffed.

Turning from Alaina, back to Gallant, Wolfe added, "But the hour grows late, and I think we should adjourn for today. I would be glad to arrange a private meeting with you in a few days. In the meantime, please get to know our people and look around."

Alaina, who had gotten settled in her chair, glared at Wolfe.

Gallant surmised Wolfe ignored people whose presence was inconvenient, treating them as if they were invisible or nonexistent. Finding himself in an awkward position, thanks to Alaina, Wolfe was unable to carry the situation off with his usual high handedness.

"I don't think there is anything more we can accomplish today. Let us digest your request and when we've had time to consult with our leading citizens, we can get together again for a more detailed negotiation," said Wolfe.

Gallant watched the interplay and the intention to exclude Alaina and her grandfather.

Alaina started to rise in protest, but relented and sat down once more, resolved to the situation as if she had half expected it.

Wolfe stood and shook Gallant's hand. He pulled Gallant close and winked. Under his breath, he said, "You and I can get together in a day or two to resolve details which are best conducted strictly between us."

Gallant recognized Wolfe was not a dilettante in negotiations and so accepted the situation.

As the meeting broke up, Alaina turned to Gallant. "Please come and see me tomorrow. Perhaps Grandfather will spend time acquainting you with our history and culture." She slipped a notepaper into his hand.

"I would welcome the opportunity. I've much to learn." He looked forward to the possibility he might see her the following day.

She smiled at him then left. To Gallant's surprise, he felt a sense of loss. She had made an undeniably deep impression on him. A glance at the note in his hand revealed her address and a map.

He said his goodbyes to the others and started to leave, with Junior escorting him out of the building. They walked to the outskirts of the town along a narrow dirt road, at the end of which a tiny rustic wood cottage stood on a hill with a panoramic view of the countryside. The rural cottage had few amenities and was sparsely furnished. A single bed occupied one corner and a table with two chairs another corner. Sheets and bedding were piled on the thin mattress, along with a single towel, presumably to be used with the water basin sitting on the table. A door led to the tiny bathroom, which contained a shower stall and toilet.

Junior said, "Make yourself comfortable for the night. In the morning, feel free to explore our town. It's called Hallo."

Gallant spent the night in the country style quarters with the few personal items he had brought with him from the Hummingbird. He suspected, he would be kept under observation by Wolfe's police every minute he was in the colony, but he looked forward to exploring the town and seeing what the colonists had made of this world. As well as visiting with the charming Alaina Hepburn.

12

THE LOYAL OPPOSITION

Gallant awoke from a fitful sleep out of spirits and slightly ill-tempered filled with disturbing visions of violence and strange people. Still feeling the aftereffects of his wounds, it took several minutes before he shook off a variety of aches and pains. Without rising from bed, he noticed the Elysium sunlight stream in through the window and across the room. Slowly, his scowl changed to a more neutral acceptance of the day, and he gradually dragged himself from bed to begin his morning ablutions.

The shower's cold water helped revive his spirits, and he lingered under the faucet beyond his typical military allotment of thirty seconds. Once dressed, he felt invigorated and prepared to start on the day's agenda. He planned to see Professor James Hepburn, the leader of the political opposition, to discuss Elysium politics and to possibly gain leverage over Wolfe. In addition, seeing Hepburn meant seeing Alaina, which was an attractive idea as well. Anticipation drove him forward.

"First things, first," he said, looking into the mirror to straighten out his uniform. He put on his cap and set off to explore the town.

Surveying the surroundings from his vantage point on the knoll outside his front door, he spotted huge active volcanoes far to the north of the town. Several kilometers to the East lay an ocean shoreline. A vast green forest with a few sawmills and lumberyards lay to the South. Westward was predominately farms and grazing lands while a few industrial facilities dotted across lands from northwest to southwest.

He bound from his habitat and walked with a spring in his step along cobblestone-paved streets of the colony, enjoying the fresh fragrant air. The town itself was unfamiliar to his eyes, but filled with buildings and an ambiance which was reminiscent of his hometown, New Annapolis, on Mars. After so long surrounded by metal bulkheads, hatches, and virtual screens, he welcomed the doors, windows, shutters, and fences. He smiled a greeting to the narrow brick-paved streets and overhanging shade trees. He was surprised at how easily he fit in with this environment, but this did not trouble or distract his growing good humor.

Around him, the town's populace moved past through the narrow, rustic pathways in the fashion of workers, off to begin their various daily tasks. The air of such a typical scene of quiet calm would have fit any early colonial town of

Earth. A dozen or so people walked idly past, clearly intent on heading off to enjoy the nearby ocean shore, perhaps, for a fun sunny vacation day.

For a moment he considered stopping a passerby and engaging in a conversation. The townsfolk were obviously curious about him, since his UP uniform marked him as a member of the *Intrepid* crew, yet the citizenry had had no advanced warning of any crewmen traveling amongst them. For the most part they merely nodded and refrained from engaging him; however, after a while, several more venturesome individuals came up and greeted him with "Good day." He smiled at such restraint; they must be bursting from curiosity and overflowing with questions.

He assumed he was being followed by the SSP and the inhabitants were aware of it, and so they we reluctant to approach him. Nevertheless, he didn't let such matters concern him.

He let his nose lead him through the streets looking for breakfast. Soon he caught a whiff of what smelled like eggs and coffee, coming from a neighborhood café. He had no sooner walked into the café than a waiter approached and showed him to a free table.

The man grinned broadly and said, "Please sit. You're our welcomed guest. Let me bring you a breakfast such as you have never had."

The middle-aged man spoke with such joy, Gallant couldn't refuse.

"I'm growing to love your various foods. Would you please select something for me?"

"I'd be delighted," said the man and off he went.

Breakfast arrived quickly and looked ordinary enough. Eggs from a local fowl, meat from a small mammal, a warm leavened bread with a variety of jams, and a coffee equivalent that was surprisingly refreshing. Gallant ate the hearty meal and thanked his patron. Before leaving, he asked for directions to the address on the notepaper Alaina had given him.

It took only a ten minute walk to arrive at Hepburn's home. Standing before its threshold, curiosity was upmost in his mind.

Gallant had noticed a lumber mill off to the edge of town, doing a brisk business reducing the nearby forest to planks and lumber supplies. The Hepburn's house was obviously built with this local timber, and its construction was a remarkable simple two-story structure with windows and doors typical of the UP colonial style. All the houses along the road were similar wood structures. Despite the rustic appearance of the home, Gallant was surprised by its high level of technological sophistication, for when he reached the entrance, the door scanned him and opened automatically while announcing his presence to the residents.

A gray-haired gentleman extended his hand. "Lieutenant Gallant, I'm so glad to meet you. Please come in. Allow me to introduce myself. I'm James Hepburn. I was hoping you would come." He was as tall as Gallant, with thinning gray hair and a fragile frame. He wore a simple short-sleeve blue shirt and white tropical pants, making him appear relaxed and comfortable.

"It's a pleasure to meet you," said Gallant, shaking hands. "Alaina told me about you and something of this colony, but I was hoping to hear more from you."

Hepburn showed him into the living room, and they stood staring at one another for an awkward moment.

"But where are my manners? Please, sit down. These chairs may be old fashioned, but I find them comfortable. Have you eaten?" he asked. When Gallant nodded, he added, "Would you like coffee?"

"Yes, I would. Thank you."

Hepburn scurried out of the room and quickly returned with an antique silver tray holding three cups of a steaming brew. "Our version of coffee is similar to Earth's, in my opinion. I hope you like it."

"I think it's wonderful," said Gallant brightly. "I've had to make do with synthetics, most of my life."

Gallant sipped his coffee and they were still getting settled when Alaina entered the room. She was dressed in a simple blouse and shorts, but her wedge-heeled sandals accentuated her eye-catching legs.

Gallant rose.

"Did you have a good night?" she asked.

He smiled. "Yes, thank you."

"Well, I'm glad you decided to come and see Grandfather. I wasn't sure you'd show up, given your cozy relationship with Wolfe."

"My relationship with President Wolfe is hardly cozy. I met the man yesterday. In fact, I doubt he looks favorably toward me or anyone from the *Intrepid*. I have the sense he would be happy to see our backsides as we leave."

Something about the image which Gallant's words conjured struck Alaina as funny, and she laughed out loud.

"I see my granddaughter finds you amusing, but now that I see you, I am puzzled by her earlier description."

"Oh?" was all Gallant could think to say. Feeling somewhat lost, he turned to business. "I was hoping you could tell me about the political situation on Elysium."

"Patience, patience. We have much to discuss and learn from each other. Eventually I hope we will reach an understanding," he said. "You must realize you are the first visitor to our colony since its founding twenty years ago."

Everything in the living room seemed normal and relaxed. The windows were open, and a slight breeze billowed and rippled through the curtains. Hepburn appeared at ease, but Gallant sensed an undercurrent of tension. He decided to bide his time and let events unfold at their own pace.

"Perhaps you'd like to try a glass of my wine. It's a vintage from my own vineyard out back. I'm rather proud of it."

"In that case I'd be delighted."

Hepburn reached for a decanter, but Alaina had already picked it up and was pouring three glasses. "Thank you, my dear. She anticipates my every want and need," he said smiling.

"To your health," he said, raising his glass.

After the three clinked glasses to finalize the toast, Gallant took a sip. "Excellent," he said.

"Thank you."

"I understand you are a professor of cybernetics," said Gallant.

"Yes. I was installing a new comprehensive AI control system for automating Ceres's entire mining operations when the Titans captured us."

"Have you been able to develop other AI systems?"

"Unfortunately we lack the infrastructure for serious chip manufacturing, but I've managed to make small contributions, here and there."

"Do you have any other family members on Elysium?" asked Gallant.

"My dear wife died during our voyage. Alaina's parents died a few years after we arrived. She's been looking after me and the household ever since."

"What about exploration of this planet? I assume there have been extensive efforts to study the species of plants and animals, as well as to map the terrain."

"Council President Wolfe discourages exploration. He doesn't like people to wander away from his immediate influence."

"Isn't that rather strange?"

"One might think so."

"It's a crime really," chimed in Alaina.

"Oh, so you'd like to see more of the planet?"

"Of course. And I will."

"My dear child, you know there are significant dangers, including predator animals. We already know about some, but there might be others lurking out there as well."

"You could frighten me into staying close to home when I was a child, but I'm grown now, and I can take care of myself."

Gallant had no doubt she could.

"Never mind," said Alaina, frowning at her grandfather and changing the subject. "I'm eager to learn about you. . . . Ah, . . . oh, . . . I mean . . ." she said, fumbling with her words. "I mean, we would like to learn about the current United Planets' situation. And I imagine you're interested to learn more about us. To start with, can you tell us how the UP is doing in this war with the Titans?"

Gallant gazed out the front window. "From what I learned from President Wolfe yesterday, the Titans abducted the UP Ceres colony fifty years ago. At the time, the UP assumed you disappeared along with a great deal of your equipment as a result of a natural disaster, such as an asteroid collision. It wasn't until several years later the UP detected a Titan scout ship in the asteroid fields. Some people speculated that the Titans were responsible for your disappearance, but exactly what happened to you remained a mystery. No one expected to find any of you, or your descendants alive, let alone eleven light years away."

He paused and waited to see their reaction and then continued, "Open warfare with the Titans didn't happen immediately. Some sniper action and exchanging fire between small groups of ships would happen from time to time, but no large-scale actions occurred, until the Titans launched a huge fleet to invade Jupiter Station and the Jupiter moon colonies."

Once more he paused and frowned, the memories were painful. "I was a fighter pilot on the *Repulse* at the time, over three years ago. We fought them to a standstill initially. Later we discovered the Jupiter invasion was only a gambit to lure away the Mars Fleet. A second Titan fleet was waiting, hiding at Ceres of all places, to sneak behind the UP forces and destroy our Mars cities. Fortunately, their plan was discovered and the Mars Fleet drove them off. Afterward there were a series of minor skirmishes."

"I'm sure those must have been difficult experiences for you," said Hepburn.

Gallant nodded, but did not elaborate on the pivotal role he had played. "We're hoping the *Intrepid,* and FTL ships like it will tip the scales in our favor and eventually allow us to take the war to Titan home planets."

Hepburn and Alaina sat quietly, drinking in the information

Gallant crossed his legs, put down his glass of wine, and thought, *I wonder where Junior is? Probably close by listening—which is unfortunate.*

"Professor Hepburn will you give me a sense of the politics here?" Gallant tried to take the measure of the man, but his face revealed little. He could only hope Hepburn would be more open and honest than others he had met on Elysium, so far.

"Well, after our colony was abducted we spent thirty years on a Titan generation ship traveling to Tau Ceti. Once our colony was transplanted here, we were victimized by the Titans for experimentation until Wolfe miraculously produced his planet-wide force field blocking all Titan access. We have been under our own authority since then. Wolfe has been in charge, but there has been growing dissent."

"What sort of dissent?"

"Well, corruption has been alleged, which is difficult to prove against a government that controls both the police and the judges. Nevertheless, groups of young people have been gathering and holding demonstrations." Hepburn looked meaningfully as Alaina who had turned her head away, acting as if he shouldn't be criticizing anything she had done.

"Oh, are they contentious remonstrations against the SSP?" asked Gallant.

"Are there any other kind, when you're dealing with bullies?" asked Alaina. She rose from her chair and went to the front window. She swept away the curtain and looked around as if trying to catch someone sneaking about.

"We have advocated developing space technology to return to Sol, or at least communicate with Earth," said Hepburn.

"Wolfe disagrees?"

"Of course. This is a tropical paradise for all of us, but especially for him. He practically owns the planet. Still I've maintained a vigorous political difference of opinion, always mindful to keep it peaceful and civil. As a result, he tolerates me. He recognizes that repressive governments that punish political opposition become isolated from the people and eventually vulnerable to revolution."

"Does he allow organized protests?"

"Protests can take many different forms, from individual statements to group demonstrations. Protesters as peaceful individuals have also been tolerated. Wolfe's governmental policy has been to control the colony's economics through a media monopoly. He runs our news media and communication stations. We do enjoy our entertainment channels. The net result is that he, his family, and cronies live comfortably while the rest of us work hard to grow our community."

"How does he manage to get reelected?"

"There is little appetite to fight the status quo, especially since he has acquired a great deal of wealth within our tiny fragile economy. So he continues. Or he's continued until your arrival. I suspect, he's sweating, trying to figure out how to get rid of you without fomenting more dissension than he can control."

"I'm interested in fashioning a working relationship between the people of Elysium and the *Intrepid*. We need to establish a mine for heavy metals along with a forge and manufacturing facility to conduct our repairs. Our scans have revealed possible deposits of heavy metal ores near the base of the giant volcano to the north. With your machinery and labor added to ours, we could get the *Intrepid* ready to return to Earth. Those willing to join us could come."

"Perhaps," said Hepburn.

Gallant was disappointed with the tepid response. "What can I do to influence Wolfe?"

Hepburn said, "You must appeal to his ego and vanity. Either you get Wolfe's attention focused on you, and he responds reasonably, or else you leave your fate to his kind of consideration. Anyone who trusts Wolfe's determinations deserves what he gets, which is not pleasant. It may sound calculating or devious, but otherwise you are left at his mercy which you will surely regret. Of course, you should realize, any deal you strike with Wolfe is likely to be subject to his revisionism, according to amorphous circumstance as he sees them."

"I take it you don't like Wolfe?"

"Oh, my feelings toward the man are much more complex than like or not like. It isn't a simple animosity. I don't trust him, but I do respect him. I must respect the man who found a way to unite our people on this colony in the face of a horrific threat from the Titans. I am glad he was able to use the force field technology to protect us no matter what he did to acquire it. I do respect his ability to dominate the colony for twenty years and to avoid sharing power while creating a faux democracy to shore up his image. I don't fear him, but I am wary of acts openly against him. I know he spends much of his day thinking up logical lies to convince everyone he is only acting as we would each act to protect everyone's interests. No, it's much more than like or not like," concluded Hepburn.

"I do dislike him," contributed Alaina, emphatically.

Gallant looked at her and then back to Hepburn. "Does he have the support of the majority of the population?"

"Ostensibly, but it's not a matter of support. The people follow his leadership for many of the reasons I gave. Actually, they're ambivalent, but they are not about to cross him—not while he controls the planetary force shield. We have achieved an acceptable equilibrium of suppression and acceptance. Human tolerance for limited tyranny is exceptional, much like the lobster sitting in a pan of water as it is slowly brought to a boil." Hepburn chuckled mildly at his own remark.

They spent another pleasant hour together. Hepburn talked about his voyage from Ceres and his family. Gallant told them about his life growing up on terra-formed Mars. Despite the comfortable relationship they seemed to be developing, Gallant still felt a heavy presence of something important left unrevealed. And notwithstanding Gallant's most sincere efforts, Hepburn remained reluctant to commit to any concrete arrangement between them. He was reticent to openly cross Wolfe or to make an agreement with the UP binding the colony.

"I'm afraid my dissenting view has contaminated my granddaughter, who also acts defiantly, much to my concern," said Hepburn.

Alaina said, "I'm convinced the worse thing one can do is to remain idle in the face of tyranny—whether it's a petty dictator, or worse. So I've agitated continuously until I've become a real thorn in Wolfe's backside. I've organized a small group of like-minded thinkers who occasionally join me in protests."

"You're going to get into trouble with the SSP," said Hepburn sternly.

She smiled proudly, got up, and kissed Hepburn on the forehead. "Grandfather, you needn't worry. I can take care of myself."

Not the preferred response—Hepburn knew that—Gallant knew it, too.

When Gallant asked him to explain further, Hepburn said, "Youth!" He shook his head back and forth in disbelief, shifted his eyes from one to the other of the young people he had as his audience. "You open yourself to dangers beyond your understanding."

"Dangers? What dangers are you speaking of?" asked Gallant. "We didn't intend to disrupt your community."

"Of course you didn't. You didn't even know we existed. And yet you have disrupted us. You've shaken us to our core."

Hepburn wasn't a fool and Gallant could see something more beneath the surface.

"Can you tell me what the people of Elysium need to support the *Intrepid*?"

Hepburn frowned. "It is not for me to speak for others. I'm sorry. I am."

Gallant left the Hepburn residence, having learned much, but feeling perplexed.

Why shouldn't we be allies? What am I missing?

13

A WOLF IN SHEEP'S CLOTHING

The next day Junior and his men escorted Gallant to a pre-arranged meeting at Wolfe's home on a bluff overlooking the colony. The home was the largest and most extensively furnished he had seen in the community.

He walked on a thick woven rug into the library where Wolfe was waiting for him. Junior closed the room's sliding doors and remained outside with his security officers.

Wolfe was dressed in an old-fashioned black three-piece pin striped suit with extra-large lapels, which were so sharply pressed the suit appeared as if it might have never been worn. He looked rich, well fed, and distinguished, in a throw-back sort of way. His coiffed dark, gray-streaked hair was set-off by a white handkerchief peeking out from his breast pocket, highlighting a flamboyant style reminiscent of tough guys from twentieth-century Earth.

The peculiar costume was so inappropriate to the lifestyle of the tropical islands it caused Gallant to make the leap—Wolfe was role-playing for his own self-deluded reasons—beyond Gallant's comprehension.

His chief of staff stood to his right beside a table, while off to one side of this well-lit room was a computer screen covered with small data columns, indistinguishable from a distance.

Gallant stood for a moment gazing at the overall effect Wolfe had created before he walked forward and greeted him with the obligatory handshake.

Wolfe rose from his chair as he shook hands. "Lieutenant Gallant, how good to see you again. I hope you've had an enjoyable day exploring our town, as well as a fruitful visit with Jim Hepburn."

"Yes, thank you. I had a chance to look around the community and talk to several of your citizens. You've accomplished quite a feat in both resisting the Titans and building a colony in so short a time."

Wolfe fairly beamed with pride. "Thank you. Thank you. I am pleased with my accomplishments. I took an unadorned hostile wilderness and molded it to my will. My story is one of courage, fortitude, and triumph—against overwhelming difficulties. I can close my eyes and see so much more ahead for Elysium. I've just begun, but rest assured, I will have my happy ending. This is a thriving community ready to accept the responsibilities of an independent planet."

"Is that your personal story?" said Gallant, noting Wolfe's exclusive use of the first-person singular pronoun to lay credit for the success of the colony.

"My story is the story of Elysium. My family circumstance began as I was growing up on the asteroid colony, Ceres. There were limited resources and competitive natures. I didn't have as many friends as I do now. I studied hard and became a pilot for an ore hauler trucking raw material from mining sites to storage facilities and transport ships. Navigation through the asteroid field required the same skills as a fighter pilot, including using a neural interface. Something I'm sure you can appreciate."

He stopped, apparently seeking, and expecting, Gallant's approval.

There's only one way to handle an egomaniac. Tell him what he wants to hear. "Piloting large ships through an asteroid field takes considerable skill."

Smiling his gratification, Wolfe continued, "When the Titans arrived at Ceres, they overwhelmed us, and sealed thousands of us into transports for the sublight journey to Tau Ceti. They packed all our asteroids life support systems along with our hydroponic gardens and fish aquariums. We survived the grueling journey—well, most of us. At least enough of us survived for the Titans to start their experiments. They dropped us into this friendly environment and they left us mostly alone. I took advantage of the freedom, and before long, they had reason to regret not taking me more seriously. The people of this colony understand how important deploying my planetary force shield was. We've lived undisturbed ever since.

"I married while we were in transit and my son Cyrus Jr., was born shortly after we landed. He is a native-born citizen of this planet and it is to this planet he maintains allegiance—like so many of our young population. After driving off the Titans, I knew setting up the right type of government was a risk worth taking. Elysium has flourished under my guidance.

"Scan us. You'll see we have a force field powerful enough to deflect any nuclear weapons the Titans can send at us. We are completely safe and protected. Don't worry about it. We need no assistance of any kind and would not welcome any interference in the governing of our planet. You can even consider me your insurance policy. If necessary, your entire crew may find sanctuary on Elysium if the Titans return—as subjects of my government, of course." The last words had a faint emphasis upon them.

"This informal discussion has covered our history and, I hope, given you an appreciation of our position," said Wolfe, intent on maintaining his place of privilege.

Clearly, Wolfe was as stubborn as he was prideful. Gallant remained thoughtful, but was becoming disillusioned with his prospects for a positive agreement with his host. He raised his eyebrow. "You intend for Elysium to be permanently independent—independent of the UP as well as the Titans?"

Wolfe exhibited a poker player's sense when holding the higher cards. "We are already independent."

"I congratulate you on your hard-earned accomplishments," said Gallant. "I assure you, the *Intrepid* is not seeking to disrupt Elysium's way of life. We can accept your governing arrangement and agree not to interfere with your internal affairs." Gallant thought the UP government might revisit that point.

Wolfe grinned.

Gallant continued, "I hope you are willing to discuss how we can work together. The *Intrepid* is primarily concerned about acquiring your assistance to effect repairs and replenishment."

"I will have to confer with my council." Wolfe scowled as if ready to end discussions immediately.

"The *Intrepid* needs massive assistance, and we have to act quickly before the Titans can recover from our last encounter. We are willing to fully respect your sovereignty in return for cooperation and any aid you can render."

Wolfe shifted in his seat, as if reconsidering his approach. He leaned forward, in Gallant's face, and asked, "Are you an honest man?"

"Yes," Gallant said flatly, unimpressed.

"Good. Good. Then let's be honest. We need to be honest with each other if we are to survive the Titans and continue to thrive. Don't we?" said Wolfe.

"Of course I intend to speak openly and frankly," said Gallant. He had hoped to put everything on the table and negotiate fairly, but that wasn't going to happen. He was sure Wolfe meant he should be honest. He was equally sure Wolfe had no intention of doing likewise.

"Good. Good. Then let's hash out a deal, shall we?"

"Yes. I am eager to cooperate," said Gallant, matching what he assumed was Wolfe's chicanery. "I will have to, of course, get my commanding officer's approval of any agreement, as I'm sure you will also seek the consensus of your population."

"Of course, absolutely. Can't do anything without the peoples' concurrence, can we?"

"In return for access to your planet's resources and whatever manpower and machinery you can spare, the *Intrepid* can offer synthetic food synthesizers to supplement your farming and food stuffs."

Wolfe made a sour face. "You're going to require considerable manpower and equipment that will overtax our small community, and all you have to offer is synthesizers? No thanks. Besides our world has an overwhelming abundance of edible fruits, plants, animals, and fish. Surely you can't expect us to eat synthesized food and work long hours under dangerous mining conditions for you?"

"Let's stick to business," urged Gallant. "What can we offer of immediate value to you?"

"This whole discussion is wide of the point."

"What do you mean?" asked Gallant.

"This world is fertile and rich with resources. We have much to look forward to without any great needs you could fill."

"Perhaps we could provide assistance developing uranium and heavy metals for a nuclear power plant? It would offer you all the electrical power you could need for the foreseeable future."

"That's a promising start, but I require much more."

"What can we offer you?"

"Guns." Wolfe's real demand finally became clear. The demand they had been dancing around for two days. He continued enthusiastically, "Weapons—in addition to one of your existing nuclear reactors—and go capture the Titan destroyer and turn it over to us. I think we could benefit from our own space force."

I'd be a fool to agree to that. I'll never agree to that, Gallant wanted to scream.

However, the one thing more wrong than agreeing was to openly disagree. Gallant was forced toward guile and subterfuge of his own. Still he had severe misgiving about negotiating in less than good faith.

Gallant said, "Why do you need weapons? You have your force field to protect you against the Titans."

"I'm trying to build a state. I need to develop military forces to protect my government and my people."

"This is beyond what I am authorized to negotiate," said Gallant.

That sounded weak. I've got to be more forceful.

"You're smart. Don't do something stupid—like walk out."

"We need to work together," said Gallant.

"Are you saying I have an obligation to provide you with all this planet's resources, free of charge? Are you without any obligation for the sacrifice you require of us?"

"I'm not sure it would be possible to transfer so much technology and weaponry. Especially considering only one of our reactors is fully functional at the moment."

"Don't jump to conclusions. We have many more issues to address. Besides, even if this effort proves fruitless, it is still a good first step. Perhaps if you could explain the *Intrepid's* needs in more detail so I know how I could help?"

Gallant began to explain the details of the facilities he needed to construct to produce the exotic materials necessary for the *Intrepid's* repair. "Does that help?"

"Of course not. I'm not a scientist. But I do understand your generic need for metals and facilities to produce exotic material," said Wolfe excitedly. He calmed down and continued, "I've a problem, Lieutenant. A problem your ship started when it appeared. If the Titans had any sense, they would have simply blown you apart with their missiles instead of foolishly trying to capture your ship. I'm certain they were envious of your FTL drive, a tempting prize they couldn't let escape their grasp. So here we are. You are in desperate need of repairs. The Titan ship is limping off to lick its wounds as well, and I . . . I, huh, have an excited and agitated population with too much curiosity."

Gallant observed Wolfe carefully and estimated the secret of his successful leadership was his ability to get people to agree to a process under his control. He had a variety of social talents to convince people to follow his lead. However, he also was a large, powerful man with an imposing presence, dominating those around him physically, emotionally, as well as intellectually with his dynamic personality. Gallant surmised, after dealing with Wolfe for a while, one was likely to believe they had reached a consensus, only to find Wolfe had a different opinion of what they had agreed to.

Wolfe returned to the discussion with his usual easy manner, but he did not smile. Being forthright must have disrupted his train of thought and he needed to recapture Gallant's attention to respond directly to his own needs.

"If we had a greater industrial capacity, we could manufacture the parts you desire, but as you can see, our small community maintains a tiny industry—only enough to support our tiny population—hardly any excess for your considerable needs. I might've told you over the radio and saved you a trip, but its better you came and saw our homes and abilities for yourself," he said, mimicking a humble and modest expression.

Wolfe's dealing with the local population had made him confident in his political skills. He was looking for any advantage he could exploit over the young lieutenant before him. He hoped to maneuver the circumstances to enhance his position, not to help the *Intrepid.*

Gallant considered his opponent. *No, it's probably worse than that. Wolfe's afraid the* Intrepid *could upset the local balance of power.*

Wolfe continued drily, "You've heard the essence of my ideas, but would it surprise you to hear I've considered these matters diligently and have found a compromise?"

"A compromise?"

"Yes. You should understand we need the ability to defend ourselves; the force shield may not always be enough. We also require small arms and larger weapons—weapons you could provide to enhance our security while you construct mining and manufacturing sites to overhaul your ship," said Wolfe.

He frowned seeing Gallant's negative expression. "You're not in a strong bargaining position. It's absolutely unbelievable you haven't immediately accepted my terms. I've been quite generous."

Gallant was sickened by the words he now had to speak, yet knowing he had no choice. "The *Intrepid* can provide small arms and weapons for local defense, and we can help you develop nuclear power on Elysium. It may be possible to capture the Titan destroyer and turn it over to you, as well. All of these matters will be subject to my captain's agreement."

"Now that wasn't so hard, was it?" Wolfe laughed gleefully, as if he were ready to devour Gallant whole, in one gulp.

Wolfe moved a few sheets of paper from a pad on the table and spread them out. "Here's what we're proposing in more detail."

"A treaty?" asked Gallant.

"Yes. You will be able to witness the wisdom of our agreement. We will expand on this simple draft to a more comprehensive treaty including the details of what we have agreed to, identifying obligations of Elysium and obligations of the United Planets. It will be ready in a few days. You have time to relay the basics to your commanding officer. Then, at an appropriate date, we can have a formal treaty signing ceremony."

At the moment, Gallant had no more options. He put up his hands as a gesture of surrender.

Wolfe looked at him with gritted teeth. "I think we have much to review and we should set a time to meet soon for additional discussions."

Gallant considered the basic deal points he had agreed to. The *Intrepid* gained the right to mine necessary resources, plus additional labor and machinery, in return for providing Wolfe weapons and eventually, a Titan ship.

The final decision is now in the hands of Neumann and the colonists.

14

THE DEAL

Wolfe let down the force field long enough for Gallant's Hummingbird to rendezvous with the *Intrepid* in orbit over Elysium.

Previously when Gallant had attended Captain Dan Cooper in his cabin, there had been a comfortable, relaxed atmosphere with Cooper treating him more as a colleague than a subordinate. Things were different under Captain Anton Neumann.

Gallant stood frozen at attention as Neumann dressed him down.

"You've exceeded your authority and exposed me to grave consequence when we report to fleet headquarters on Earth." Neumann's venomous tone was unmistakable. "You've deliberately exposed me to a court martial inquiry.

I see through you. This is payback. But you're wrong if you think you'll get away with it. I've documented my orders. You will make a detailed report admitting you made unsanctioned concessions, including recognizing the sovereignty of Elysium."

Gallant exhaled, letting Neumann vent.

"Under what criteria do you think it's reasonable to agree to transfer an arsenal of weaponry to an unstable character like Wolfe?" Neumann didn't wait for a response. He said, "I am now not only vulnerable to Wolfe's continuous demands but I could be cashiered if I perform as you've agreed."

Surprised by the intensity of Neumann's outburst, Gallant stared for a long second, and then he broke discipline and relaxed his posture without permission. He went so far as to sit down across from Neumann and look him directly in the eyes.

Neumann frowned—the tension was balanced on a razor's edge.

Gallant said in a controlled, measured voice, "Wolfe has control of the planet's force field. With one flip of the switch he can deprive us of access to resources and skilled mining manpower, not to mention forge and manufacturing facilities. Without Wolfe's cooperation, there will be no returning to Earth—the *Intrepid* will never be FTL-worthy again."

"What do you mean? You want us to meet these outrageous demands?"

"I don't trust Wolfe. There's no way the man I met designed and built a planetary force field. It is beyond the combined scientific capabilities of the entire United Planets."

"Hmm. Yet, he expects us to deliver a Titan destroyer to him on a silver platter. That's not going to happen," said Neumann.

"Actually I think it might be possible to capture the destroyer, if we act quickly enough with our repairs."

"Never mind. If Wolfe becomes a real problem, it would be easier to send an armed *Intrepid* force to take over his operation than to capture a destroyer."

"Maybe, but, even so, my guess is he doesn't expect us to completely fulfill our commitment,—he has another game he's playing. I will explore and attempt to find the controls to his force field."

"That must be the highest priority," said Neumann.

Gallant spoke forcefully. "I propose we give Wolfe laser handguns and a few plasma rifles, as a show of good faith. We will demand he support us with men and equipment to begin mining operations immediately. As we progress, we can delay sending heavy weapons and nuclear reactor parts, saying they are under repair. Once we've completed substantial ship repairs and refueling, we will have more leverage, and we can get tougher in our negotiations with him. In addition we can insist he acquire a plebiscite for recognition of independence from the UP."

"What good is a vote? Won't he win?"

"I'm not so sure. There is an opposition group on the planet led by James and Alaina Hepburn. They may disrupt Wolfe's plans. We can use them to our advantage."

"All right. I'll go along with your approach, but, rest assured, your responsibility in initially overstepping your authority will remain on the record."

Gallant sat mute, but the tension dissipated. They changed topics to discuss the engineering and technical details of the mining operation to produce heavy metals, antimatter, and dark matter.

"What will it take to construct a heavy equipment forge and build an accelerator? Plus we'll need a dark matter plasma containment-field bottle."

As they were counting up everything they needed to manufacture, in the end, they added two more items—anti-ship missiles and a trailer they could hitch behind the Hummingbird using a tractor beam to transport men and equipment.

"We don't have much heavy moving equipment on board, but the colonists have tractors, bulldozers, excavators, and heavy trucks along with drilling and blasting mining rigs. After all, they were asteroid miners to begin with. They have a number of excellent mining engineers to supplement our crew."

"Will they work for us?" asked Neumann.

"Not for us," said Gallant, "but perhaps with us."

"Perhaps," said Neumann, much calmer now. "There's something else I need to discuss with you. We've monitored the Titan destroyer limping toward the outer planets. It's traveling erratically at reduced speed while streaming gas and debris. Our readings show its power is fluctuating and my guess is its fusion drive is unstable. I'll bet it explodes from internal damage before they can make effective repairs. Regardless, their course is toward one of the moons of the fifth planet, a gaseous giant."

"It's possible they have a small base there which will offer them relief and refit capabilities."

"The drone we launched while we were entering this system has reported a space station on one of the moons of the fifth planet. It's methane-based and has extensive facilities, probably enough to fix the destroyer. Given their current progress, they won't be back here any time soon. Perhaps in four to six months. At that time we should have made all our repairs and refueled. We might even be heading back to Earth by then."

"I'm not so sure about that," said Gallant.

———

Gallant met with Chief Howard to talk about the engineering spaces and personnel. They discussed the process of repairs and their concern for the hull integrity of the *Intrepid* to withstand initiating a warp bubble.

"Chief can you update me on the engine room's status?"

"Yes, sir. We've lost a third of our engineering personnel including several key men, Joe and Phil and Bill. Number one fusion reactor is totaled. A fire in the reactor compartment caused an explosion, damaging the hull from the engine room to the reactor compartment. It produced a dangerous radioactive gas leak requiring an internal patch on the engine room, but we couldn't enter the reactor compartment until we isolated the reactor. We conducted an emergency reactor shutdown and sealed part of the hull breach externally. There's nothing more we can do to recover it."

Gallant checked the reactor compartment pressure readings over the course of the past history. They were now near the normal range, but the engine room was still

showing a lack of pressure control. In fact, all the connected compartments were exhibiting this reaction. The
radiation was critically dangerous on its own, but, worse,
the differential pressure had threatened the valve seals to
the point of rupturing a plasma discharge valve to the reactor core. This could have been a disaster. They were all
fortunate Chief Howard had acted quickly and returned
things to a safe state.

"The best we could do is seal it off to minimize radiation
leakage and additional damage to the ship."

"And the number two fusion reactor?"

"I think that's salvageable. I have a report here detail-
ing the parts and repair issues. Given replacement uranium
fuel elements and tritium injectors, which we may be able to
manufacture with the help of the colonists we can restore
criticality. I've made extensive scans of Elysium's geological formation and evaluated the mineralogical deposits as
best I could from orbit, and there are considerable elements
we need in and around the large volcano north of the town
Hallo. I can't be sure of the quality without a proper exploration of the deposits, however. Also we are going to need
more deuterium and tritium. We can set up an extraction
facility outside Hallo on the shoreline and mine the ocean
separating out the heavy water components."

"That's something."

"Yes, but we need more dark matter and a new plasma
containment bottle. Collecting sufficient WIMPs without
proper facilities will take great effort."

"That's true, but we have no choice if we're ever to see
Earth again. I think we'll need the mining operation to be on

the side of the volcano. A second operation will be a foundry and fabrication facility not too far from the mining operation but close enough to Hallo to get workers and supplies. The heavy water extraction facility on the shoreline will be the third facility. Altogether that entails considerable manpower, equipment, and organization."

"Tell me about Elysium," asked Howard.

"Well, Chief, it's a beautiful world. Not a bad place to be marooned on, except for the possibility of more Titans in the future."

"Yes, sir, but what about the force field?"

"Yes. . . . What about the force field?"

15

BROBDINGNAG

Olympus Mons was the largest volcano in the Solar System; it emerged on Mars, rising to a height of twenty kilometers, almost three times as tall as Mount Everest. Elysium created a challenger twice as large, formed from many thousands of fluid basaltic lava flows pouring out from volcanic vents over a long time. Its profile was shaped like a tent with a gradual craggy upward slope of five degrees. The people of Hallo appropriately named it after a fictional land of giants—Brobdingnag.

Upon returning to Elysium, Gallant decided to follow up on Chief Howard's recommendation to evaluate geological deposits and survey possible heavy metals mining sites around Brobdingnag. As Wolfe was dragging his feet about allowing more UP personnel to land, the task fell to him.

He borrowed a single-seat hovercraft to explore the island from Junior, of all people. The flyer looked more like an old dilapidated motorcycle than something capable of flying several hundred kilometers at an altitude of three kilometers. Junior's "generosity" included beige trousers and a blue short-sleeved polo shirt, along with the assurance he wouldn't be followed, which made Gallant smile. He felt sure Junior would have a tracking device hidden onboard. He packed a few sandwiches and a couple of hand-operated prospecting tools into the small trunk compartment.

He had his doubts about the machine's flight worthiness, but, as an experienced fighter pilot, he wasn't about to show any timidity in front of Junior.

Rather than wholly trusting Junior's recommendation, Gallant took a short hop on the tiny *"put-put"* vehicle to Alaina's residence. When she answered the door, wearing white shorts and a blue halter top, he asked her if she could suggest someone to be his guide for a day's exploration of the large volcano.

To his surprise, she took the question as a personal invitation. She said, "I'd be delighted to take an outing." Before he could respond, she hopped on to the back of his flyer and wrapping her arms tightly around him.

"Let's go," she said, in her cavalier way.

"I don't know if this is such a good idea." He hesitated.

"Really? Why not?"

Realizing this situation was one of his own doing, he yielded. Gunning the reluctant throttle, he took off in the flyer with Aliana clinging to him.

"Who gave you this piece of junk?" she yelled in his ear after they had climbed to two thousand meters and had traveled nineteen kilometers.

"Junior," he yelled back, adjusting the throttle and altering the fuel mixed for the tenth time on the effete flyer.

"Junior?" she repeated, bewildered.

"Cyrus Wolfe Jr."

She giggled. "You'd better not let Cy hear you call him that. He definitely wouldn't like it."

"I'll bet."

"Yeah, and his father is always President Wolfe, or Mr. President, or Mr. Wolfe—never anything less formal."

They flew over the island's lone town, Hallo. The colony was a combination of somewhat primitive and advanced technology and styles. The town had developed its own agricultural food sources by identifying edible plants and animals indigenous to the planet. There were acres of farmland spread below, with nearby corrals of various mammals. Despite Hallo being a small town, the residents had constructed a minor industrial base and trading center for normal commerce, thus containing all the necessary ingredients for survival. The community as a whole did not appear different than one found on Earth.

Gallant found the strange mix of the rural agricultural society of Elysium and the transplanted UP mining population had produced a rugged individualism that was best exemplified in Alaina. The colonists had even acquired Titan technology before severing access. Several small lakes and creeks surrounded the farmlands. The forests and grazing lands farther out were filled with animals raising their young in a natural habitat. And something else bothered him. It was not what he could see, but rather what he didn't see. He saw plenty of children in the town, but there didn't seem to be many children running freely about, playing on the outskirts of town.

He wondered, *why?*

The flyer engine sputtered and gasped, causing Alaina to say, "Really, if I'd known Junior had stuck you with this worthless clunker, I'd have suggested taking mine. However, since we're over halfway to the volcano, I guess we'll have to stick it out."

They flew for two hundred kilometers until they reached the volcano, surrounded by dense jungle with numerous lakes and rivers.

They landed on a plateau midrange on the volcano. They stretched their legs and began prospecting using the basic handheld equipment Gallant had loaded on the flyer. They explored the geological formations and mapped out several deposits of heavy metals. He took samples and analyzed dill readings.

The day was simply delectable. For several hours they climbed the jagged rock face and steep mountains until Gallant had sighted, tested, and sampled many locations. He was gratified to find substantial agreement with their long range analysis. The area was rich in the heavy metals they needed.

Exhausted from their exertions and having worked up a good appetite, Gallant suggested they fly a short distance away and find a spot to break for lunch before continuing the exploration on the other side of the volcano.

Alaina pointed out a convenient landing area at the base of the volcano near a large pond away from the jungle. They set down the flier and sat on a grassy knoll overlooking the water. Gallant was glad he had thought to include a packed lunch for his journey and could offer to share it with Alaina. They sat on the ground on a large sheet of material, meant as a vehicle covering. Alaina supplemented Gallant's meager sandwiches by harvesting fruits and berries from the nearby trees and bushes, creating a picnic atmosphere for the pair.

Nearby, huge leafy trees cast their reflection on the still pond water only to be intermittently interrupted by ripples from waterfowl swimming across. Fascinated, Gallant and Alaina spent a leisurely lunchtime under this idyllic, picturesque setting as they found numerous topics to chat about, with equal give and take, but, before long, humor and a good-natured banter developed.

Everywhere he looked, he saw vivid colors with textures and aromas in stark contrast to his Spartan space existence. The variety of species of animals was astounding. Small mammals scurried about, and fowl flew overhead. Their beauty and friendly manner added to the quiet atmosphere. Gallant enjoyed his conversation with Alaina, and their secluded location made the occasion special.

The natural environment of the wild animals was revealed. More than half of the feral animals were fearless enough to approach them. Alaina shared interesting facts about each animal's habits, backgrounds, and lifespan.

"Kauai is the largest island of this chain. It has many native species of mammals, and mammalian predators and herbivores have been introduced from other islands. The native species are vulnerable to attack. Add the warm tropical climate, lack of competitors and predators, and this archipelago provides an ideal habitat for all introduced mammals to become well established. The native flora and fauna were evident," she said.

An abundance of insects also swarmed around him, occasionally nipping at him. He slapped his neck when one such creature dared to bite him.

"Ouch," he said.

She laughed. "Elysium's version of mosquitoes."

"Mosquitoes? Nonsense. They're vampire bats."

"Ha," she said. "You needn't worry about dangerous animals, fish, or fowl; at least not this far from the jungle during daylight. In the jungle at night, however, is another story. There are deadly serious large panther-like mammals. They would make a nice meal of you"—she laughed again—"if they caught you."

She had a pleasant smile when she laughed. Curious, he asked her about her personal relationships.

"I don't have a serious relationship—though Cy wouldn't agree with that. His expectation for a relationship is quite different than mine. He likes to hear the sound of his own voice. I think he's the most troublesome man I've ever met."

He longed to question her further, but he feared to touch on prohibited ground.

She said, "Tell me about your family and your background. There is much I would like to know."

"As an orphan, I grew up in my grandmother's care on terra-formed Mars. She was the center of my life until I went to the Space Academy."

"And is she the only woman in your life today?"

"My grandmother passed away while I was at the academy," he said, and then added, "There was one other woman. Someone I thought was special."

"And she's not so special anymore?"

"She made another choice."

"Hmm."

"What are you thinking?"

"I wasn't thinking anything in particular," she said. "But perhaps love is a sore subject with you."

"My personal situation is still unresolved."

"She has not married then?"

"To my amazement she will be, at the end of this voyage. Her fiancé is my current commanding officer."

"There's a twist. If she let you go for someone else, she's not right for you. Move on. Did you love her so much?"

"Yes. Yes, I did." He gazed off to the horizon, daydreaming.

"Won't you tell me what happened, or do you consider it none of the business of an insufferable snoop such as me?"

A moment of silence passed. Then he added, "It's my unhappy story."

"Tell me more about this woman," she urged.

He played with his coin-shaped music box. "Kelsey was my first love. We served together and shared many dangers. There was a time I thought . . . It's over now. I can no longer love her, and yet I can't seem to give her up."

Alaina looked at him with a thoughtful stare so as not to miss any shade of his meaning.

"Is your life merely the consequence of other people's choices?" she asked.

"No, but it is limited by the free choice of others."

"You have a great deal to learn about romance."

"Doesn't everyone?"

"How delightful."

"Delightful?"

"We have found something we can investigate."

"Oh?" said Gallant, wondering if she was offering to help him explore romance—personally.

She's so impulsive. I never know when she's serious.

"Well it's nice to know I've a friend," he said.

"Yes, I know and I feel it too," she said, and then added, "For those who enjoy straying from the trodden path, adventures can be fun."

"I suppose," he said.

"Nevertheless, I doubt if romance is much different here than back on Earth."

"This colony has been outside the norm of Earth for quite a long time," he said, looking at his chronometer. "Speaking of investigating, perhaps we should get back to our exploration expedition. I still need to examine the other side of the volcano before we head back."

"Okay," she said wistfully.

They flew to the other side of the volcano and completed their survey, logging their findings into the onboard computer and sending the data back to the Hummingbird for AI analysis. They preserved a printed summary along with the samples into a secure waterproof container that fit into a satchel on the flyer.

As the sun set, Gallant decided they had accomplished all they could for one day and prepared to return to Hallo. They took off and flew over the jungle near a large lake.

As they left the volcano behind, the flyer engine acted erratically and stalled causing the flyer to plummet toward the valley floor.

"Hang on," said Gallant as he struggled with the controls.

Alaina's hands tore into his chest as he managed to slow their descent. He accomplished a semi-controlled landing on the lake surface.

Alaina, who had been clinging precariously to Gallant during the many gyrations, let go of him as the flier struck the water. Alaina collided feet first with the lake but quickly submerged, dozens of meters away from Gallant. He too slammed into the water as the machine went down. The surface was like cement at that speed.

After swimming to the surface, Gallant gasped for breath. She was nowhere in sight.

"Alaina! Alaina," he shouted, frantically looking around to see if he could catch sight of her nearby. In a semiconscious state, Gallant was not quite aware of his surroundings. Plunging beneath the surface, he looked for her.

At last he saw a figure not too far away in the misty depths of the lake. Swimming underwater, he moved his arms and legs in rhythm. With powerful stokes he got close to her limp body. Placing his hand under her chin, he repositioned himself to pull her to the surface. When they burst free into the air, he breathed in deeply.

Holding her head up in his hands while he floated on his side, he breathed into her mouth several times, trying to fill her lungs once more. When she sputtered water from her mouth and began breathing on her own, he started swimming to the shoreline, about three kilometers away, pulling her along lifeguard style, as he learned at the academy.

With each stoke, he felt a twinge of pain in his shoulder. He knew now it was injured, but he kept on swimming, steadily watching the beach get nearer with each stoke. Swimming this distance ordinarily would have been merely a nice workout, but with his impaired shoulder and a debilitated person to assist, he quickly realized he would have to ration his energy to get them both to safety.

He finally reached the shore, exhausted. His memories came flooding back, reliving the impact of hitting the water and the desperate dive to find Alaina. The transition from a disassociated state of labored swimming into one of a painful reality came like a blow. As he caught his breath, he also remembered he had lost all his equipment, along with his comm badge and gun. He and Alaina were now stranded, without any resources, two hundred kilometers from the only civilization on this planet.

Gallant surveyed the wide beach clearing they found themselves on. About thirty meters offshore, high grass, scattered trees, and brush appeared before eventually morphing into a full-fledged jungle. He checked on Alaina. She was still semiconscious; her breathing was labored, but steady.

He pulled her farther up the clearing on the beach and massaged her hands and feet to restore circulation and revive her. She moaned and opened her eyes.

"What happened?"

"The flyer gave out on us. We crash-landed into the lake. How are you?"

"I'm okay," she said, coughing up more water. "I think."

Gallant twisted about trying to find his bearings.

The breeze was dying down with the setting sun and cooling the land. As night approached, the air flow over the island and farther out to sea balanced out. The waves broke on the shore to burst rhythmically on the limestone cliffs. The surf and beach produced a phosphorescence of water with the vivid bright heaving surf running from the breakers to the beach.

The approach of twilight dulled the colors of the day, leaving a fading gray impression of substance transforming into shadow with the fall of evening. The setting sun not only reduced the available light, but a chill in the air was developing as well. The climate during the day had been warm and humid; however, night time temperatures dropped drastically. Soaked from head to foot, his wet clothes clung to him, robbing him of warmth.

Alaina pointed, her eyes growing wide.

"Alaina?" asked Gallant.

A roar from deep within the jungle fixed his attention and he remembered the warnings he had received about the wild panther-like cats. They hunted in the jungle after dark.

"There are dangerous animals in this area," she said. "I saw something moving in the shadows at the edge of the jungle about thirty meters down the beach."

Gallant looked around more slowly and tried to spot movement along the shoreline. Something was in the grass north of them. Again he heard a roar and the high grass moved. The cold hand of adrenaline trickled down his back. He forced himself to remain quiet and listen while he continued to look for more signs of wildlife.

He watched and waited. The shadow appeared again, moving slowly from left to right across his view. He reached for his handgun, but it was gone. He grasped the handle of his knife and pulled it out of the sheath on his thigh. He moved forward slowly.

He decided they should walk south, away from the shore, but they were quickly swallowed up by a dense forest better defined as a jungle. Overhead, birds circled above him.

A deep-throated growl sounded nearby.

What was that?

A shadowy beast moved along the jungle's edge, still a hundred meters north of them.

"Come, it's not safe here." Alaina led him rapidly away from the waving high grass along the parallel direction.

They stopped and watched as the grass stopped moving as well. The sun continued to set and the shadows grew longer by the minute; the gray of the sky was turning black.

A ravine sliced across their path, and Gallant smelled fresh water. Thirsty, they made their way down to the bottom, where a small stream flowed. All the birds had stopped singing.

They were being stalked by the creature. They might have to fight it off.

Gallant walked with Alaina, keeping his attention on the high grass with his hand firmly holding his knife. He thought he saw Alaina frown, but she didn't speak, trying to remain as quiet as possible.

They walked on, becoming nervous whenever they heard the squawking noise made by the beast.

The moon was bright enough for them to see an animal trail ahead. Helping her cut a path through the chest-high underbrush, he looked toward the threatening high grass again, but no longer saw any sign of the animal.

Together they entered further into the arms of the dark forest, struggling against the vines and obstacles on the jungle floor. The landscape didn't change even as they had walked more than a mile; it was a mysterious place, wrapping them in danger.

Beneath the jungle's tree canopy, the floor, the lowest layer of vegetation had no plants growing directly from it, because the sunlight was not filtering through. The ground was littered with decomposing vegetation and organisms breaking down into usable nutrients. Many nutrients were locked into this biomass. Tree roots stayed close to the surface to access these foods. Large animals foraged for roots and tubers, while insects—like millipedes, scorpions, and earthworms—used their litter as a source of food.

The humans were forced to make their own path as they pulled back the brush.

As he stepped over a clutter of vines, the ground dropped away, and Gallant found himself pitched into a black pit.

"Ouch," he said, looking up at Alaina above him. Not wasting time, he got up and climbed back to her.

"I think it's time to make camp for the night. I can't see us making much more progress in the dark." She was trembling, whether from the wet clothes and cold night air, or from fear, he couldn't tell, but from everything he had seen of her, he was fairly sure she wasn't frightened of the dark, the jungle, or any old jungle cat.

He grunted his agreement.

"We need a fire," said Alaina. "I'm freezing and besides it will keep the *dragor* away."

"Dragor?"

"Yes, that's the huge panther-like cat that's been stalking us. If it catches us unaware, your knife isn't going to be much use against a beast of at least two hundred kilograms with huge fangs and claws. I'd be more comfortable with a good, bright, blazing fire."

Nodding, Gallant began rounding up dry wood and grass from the neighboring area. Alaina gathered large leafy branches from a nearby tree to create a shelter.

As he arranged the firewood, he looked up to see Alaina taking off her halter top and shorts. She stretched the clothes out on a nearby bush, and, in the next second, she removed her undergarments as well.

Shivering naked in front of him, she appeared unabashed.

Gallant gawked momentarily, but, given the necessity of removing their wet clothes, he simply said, "I'll turn my back."

"All right, if that's how you feel," she said. "I don't know if UP morality, or cultural standards have changed so much, but I hope you're not going to be offended by simple nudity. It is, after all, necessary for us to get our clothes dry before we can sleep."

He said nothing further, but he had managed an admiring glance before turning away. Certainly her form could offend no man.

She said, "Are you going to light the fire, or are you going to let me freeze to death?"

Focusing his attention back on the kindling, he struck his knife blade against a stone of flint which he had found. The spark ignited the kindling, and he quickly added the larger branches. Once he threw on a large block of wood, the fire lit up nicely.

He stoked the flames for a minute, and then finally, without looking at her, he removed his clothes and stretched them on the bushes next to Alaina's.

He sensed her presence nearby when she leaned a branch against a low lying tree limb. She began piling the leafy twigs on a support branch until it resembled a fair shelter.

Joining her efforts, Gallant gathered more leafy material for bedding.

Alaina walked behind him. She placed a finger on top of the scar on Gallant's left shoulder and traced the scar down his back, which continued on along his right leg—as if her touch had magic healing powers to impart. Her touch certainly had an effect. He swallowed.

"I'm sorry . . ." she said with evident empathy for his injury.

"It's still healing. It'll disappear before too long."

"Your scar kind of resembles an outline for a dragor. *Dragor* is a blending of *dragon* and *panther*—very deadly, very mysterious. When we first began building our town, we lost many children to the dragor. Our parents told us scary stories about dragors to keep us close to home," she explained, adding, "Are you deadly and mysterious?"

He didn't answer right away, but he thought of the things he had accomplished that he was proud of and of the few things he lived with that he was not so proud of. "A warrior should be deadly," he said, "but not so mysterious."

She nodded, apparently satisfied with the answer, as if it fit into her understanding of him.

As they faced each other—naked—Gallant's breathing became shallow and rapid. He let Alaina's figure and beauty produce an undeniable natural response.

He took her hand and the soft touch created a rising intimacy. She moved closer and ran her hand across his shoulder, caressing him.

For several minutes he mirrored each touch of hers with a touch from him; each sharp intake of breath by him was echoed by a soft moan from her.

Exploring her body heightened his anticipation until he could wait no longer. Wrapping his arms around her in a sensual embrace, they fell into their makeshift bed and made love. They remained together until they finally fell into a deep sleep.

Their pleasures were not long lasting, however, as the jungle noises arose once more, demanding their attention.

Gallant rose, dressed, and built up the fire. Alaina fell back asleep, enjoying the warmth and intimacy of their improvised shelter and the roaring security of the fire shielding them from predators. He joined her, her face snuggled under the bedding leaves, only inches away from him, while

Gallant remained awake listening to the deep-throated growls of their stalker, who waited patiently beyond the fire's edge in the shadows.

Sometime in the predawn light, the dragor departed and Gallant was able to fall into a shallow fitful sleep, lasting until Alaina's rustling disturbed him.

Gallant awoke with the sunlight streaming through the trees' branches, weaving a beam directly onto his face. He was glad the long night was over.

With one eye squinting open, he saw Alaina, backlit by the sun. She was filling a concave stone with water from a bamboo-like plant and moving it close to the fire. Once the water reached a roiling pitch, she placed a reedy straw into it and drank her fill. She quickly refilled it and seeing him stir, she said, "Rise and shine. It's breakfast."

His eyes burned and his mouth tasted stale. His arms and legs ached, and he found turning his stiff neck was painful, but to his utter amazement, he found Alaina had several eggs cooking on a flat stone near the fire, next to boiling water. He had no idea how she had scavenged them.

"Good morning," he said.

"Good morning."

"You okay?" he asked, feeling his way forward within their new relationship.

"I'm great," she said, standing arms akimbo, dressed in her shorts and halter top once more.

He thought, *Yes, you are. You're gutsy, smart, and sexy.* He pulled on his dry clothing as well.

Alaina began telling him a humorous story about her previous experiences in the jungle and a lilting laugh escaped her lips. Covering her mouth with her hand, she seemed pleased with her account.

While the story was appealing, her unrestrained joy in telling it made it more fascinating. Gallant reached over and touched her hand.

Her lips quivered into a smile.

He felt a surge of rekindled desire, but the loud squawking of passing birds interrupted his reverie and reminded him that they should prepare to leave.

Gallant swallowed as much water as he could before scarfing down several eggs.

"That was good. Thank you."

"How's your shoulder today?" she asked.

"No problem."

"Then we should be going. If we head due south, I think we can come to an outpost in a day or two. That is, if nobody is searching for us already."

"I'm pretty sure Junior had the flyer bugged, but he probably thinks I'm exploring along the lake area around the volcano. I never got a distress signal off. I can't image he'll be too concerned about my disappearing into the jungle. And no one knows you're with me. I'd say we're on our own."

Gallant took a few steps outside their campsite before he spotted a series of large paw prints in the mud the size of a grizzly bear's with long sharp claws.

I'm glad dragors don't like fire.

"We better get going," said Alaina.

As Gallant turned and took a step, she slapped him hard across his rear and ran ahead of him laughing.

Looking after her with a gleeful smile, he followed happily.

They followed an animal trail that twisted between the trees and the steep mountain terrain. Beyond the trail was a canyon with a stream running for as far as they could see. The stream bubbled and shot spray in their direction. They climbed along the embankment until they saw a footpath near a group of boulders.

"We should cross the stream here. It looks as if it broadens ahead."

They cautiously stepped into the water to test its depth and found a fordable path across. Untroubled water fowl waddled along the path ahead of them. Once on the other side, they walked purposely forward again. The roar of the nearby river provided a background to the loud animal sounds.

They climbed up a hilly slope along a mountainous cliff spotted with trees to a ledge that quickly began to give way. Gallant jumped down to a lower ledge under a tree canopy. He managed to grab Alaina's arm in time to keep her from falling farther. He grasped her afterward, even after the danger had passed, only to realize he had been squeezing her hard. Yet she never complained, settling onto the ledge beside him.

Having traversed the mountain, they marched through the jungle once more. They angled southwest through the dense growth, with the rising sun directly behind them. Picking their route south as closely as possible, they marched through the underbrush, which pushed them first to one side, then another. They were soon hungry and thirsty, but they ignored those thoughts. The day was only beginning to warm up. A light breeze passed them.

One thing was certain—this wasn't going to be an easy walk. Gallant's muscles strained from the effort and his wounds from the Titan battle still seared as he stretched the flesh around them with each effort. He guessed Alaina would also be suffering, but she had shrugged off his offer for more frequent rest stops.

At the first sign of a large buffalo-like animal, they decided to hit the high ground in one of the nearby trees. They picked the tree carefully—a tall willow which could offer concealment beneath its flowing, bowing branches. They climbed up, sticking to strong branches and settling in a sturdy fork as a bed. After the creature passed, they dropped down and resumed their journey. Jumping from the tree to endure the impact of the hard, densely packed earth stunned Gallant, making him wobbly as he tried to stand up.

They listened to the calls of birds. Small animal noises blended with the wind through the trees. They ran across regions where volcanic vents with flowing lava would shoot steaming hot air and black ash around them.

The rays of the afternoon sun fell on the back of Gallant's neck. He continued to perspire as he pushed aside the tangled jungle vines that blocked his path. He looked over his shoulder and kept his back oriented to the east and continued to march to the south. The rainforest characteristics of the jungle made the vegetation dense enough to evoke his ire on the growth interlacing and obstructing his path; his knife was kept busy. On the other hand, the area was thick with game. He spotted mammals climbing in the trees, birds swooping down, and small deer-like animals prancing off in the distance. He could've filled a zoo with the variety of wildlife around him. He watched where he put his feet as he walked, hoping not to trip. He was acutely aware of being followed by the animals. At first he felt uneasy, but a growing conviction—based on Alaina's lack of concern—said these daytime animals were not the creatures that might do them harm.

Alaina trudged alongside Gallant for the rest of the day, and, finally as the sun set, they made camp in a clearing, gathering wood and kindling to make a fire. They were near enough to the stream to collect water in a hollowed-out rock. They had no intention of drinking the water directly; too many pathogens were possible. They built a fire and boiled the water. With a drink to quench their thirst, they felt better. They prepared for a second night in the jungle.

The heat and physical activity had worn out Alaina. She was not feeling particularly well by the time they settled down and made camp. She slept undisturbed throughout the night, getting much-needed rest, while Gallant maintained the fire, taking catnaps when he could. While he was briefly disappointed they would not revisit their tryst of the night before, he understood and shared her exhaustion.

———

The following day they got up and resumed their journey, much as they had the day before. As they were working their way through the jungle, they came upon an outcropping of rocks several hundred meters high with a particularly distinctive mantle face. The color and smoothness of the stone was uniquely different from every other mineral deposit they had seen. The structure didn't look quite natural either, resembling more of a carved edifice. They were curious enough to examine it in more detail, and found a ledge with chiseled stairs and a raised platform with a large lever rising up from the base. The tremendous overgrowth of trees and vines around the structure made it seem ancient and inaccessible.

"Have you ever seen anything like this?" asked Gallant.

"No. I've never heard of anyone finding remnants of any prior inhabitants on this planet before. It might be the ruins of a lost civilization. What an incredible find," said Alaina.

"Looks like ancient stone ruins overrun by jungle growth. This is going to take effort just to get closer to it."

They made their way through the vines and vegetative obstructions—Gallant with his knife and Alaina with a pointed spear—until they reached the stone stairs. They climbed the stairs careful to avoid loose rocks and debris. After several dozen steps, they stood on the carved platform.

Gallant looked at Alaina and put his hands on the two-meter-long wooden lever. "What do you think?"

"Try it," she said, mischievously. "Let's see what happens."

Gallant pushed on the ancient lever, but it wouldn't budge.

Bracing himself, he said, "Give me a hand."

Together they strained against the handle until it yielded. A distinct rumbling began as if the lever had activated old internal machinery, but looking around they didn't see anything in motion.

After several minutes of noisy reverberations, an opening at the base of the rock mantle appeared.

Gallant watched as the opening expanded, like a huge sliding hanger door, five meters wide as well as high.

The door exposed a stone staircase descending beneath the rock outcropping down into the earth.

"Well this is an interesting piece of luck, isn't it?"

"We've found an entrance," said Alaina.

"Yes, but an entrance to what?"

The sky darkened as a cloud passed over the sun.

"A storm is approaching," said Gallant, surveying the sky.

"I've never seen anything like this. We must go in," said Alaina.

Gallant felt his way along the solid, but soggy ground and on down a narrow tunnel made of a highly polished slab of stone. Alaina stayed close.

The sloping ceilings and floor led them down over a hundred meters into the earth. Alaina bumped into Gallant several times due to the darkness which was periodically interrupted by a dull bioluminescence emanating from within the walls, giving the tunnel an ethereal, warm glow.

After twenty minutes, they found drawings and pictures on the wall near the lit places. Eventually they reached a cavernous vault with several branching passages, most blocked by their own heavy stone doors.

Off to one side were steps carved into one wall leading to a ledge balcony. They went up to the balcony and reached a point where a single plank led away over a chasm and into a small tunnel entrance hole in the wall. In time, the tunnel widened out and branched off in several different directions. They stayed together and walked down the central path with self-illuminating ceilings providing guidance.

Gallant was beginning to think they had ventured as far as they should, but Alaina said, "Let's look into this opening before we turn back."

This doorway revealed the inner chamber that was made of smooth metal instead of stone. This opening led into a long semicircular tube-like corridor with a floor about three meters wide. More indirect illumination came from the ceiling, lighting the way forward.

Gallant placed his hand near the source of light. It was cool to the touch. Running his hand over the surface, he found no seams or bolts or welding connections in the tunnel, suggesting the possibility it was all manufactured as one piece.

"Okay. This is different. This metal structure is also ancient in origin, but this section is beautifully maintained and cleaned. A form of power is illuminating the tunnel," said Gallant.

They entered the central room and crept forward together into a vestibule leading to a long hallway and finally into a great gallery. The marble floors and metal walls were highly polished and remarkably well finished into a high gloss.

Gallant examined the vault-like features of the structure. They came to a blank wall blocking their path that they presumed had to be a secret passageway. They are unable to find any way to open it. The dead end convinced them that, despite their curiosity about this intriguing site, they should head out into the jungle once more. Hopefully the storm had passed them by now.

"Given all the different passages running in every direction, I imagine there must be more doors on the surface scattered across the jungle," Alaina said.

"I agree. So why hasn't anyone else stumbled on these ancient ruins before?" asked Gallant.

"Maybe someone has but hasn't made it known."

"Alaina, the ruins and the subsequent metal passages have all witnessed a great passage of time. The lower levels show the possibility of non-human technology."

"Yes, it must be non-human technology, abandoned centuries ago. Wow, now that's a puzzle. Do you like puzzles?" asked Alaina, spreading her arms.

"Actually, I do like puzzles, but I'll bet this one isn't going to be easy to solve. So I think we should resume our trek back to Hallo."

They returned to the surface. They decided they would come back another time to explore the ancient ruins and the vault in more detail, but, for now, they needed to get back to civilization and seek medical attention.

Gallant tried to get his bearings on their location, but, with the thick storm clouds overhead, they could only get a rough idea of which way was south.

They resumed their march through the jungle. After several more hours, they saw pinpoints of light on the horizon. The pinpoints grew into defined arrays of windows, and soon the windows defined a building.

They had reached an Elysium outpost at the jungle's edge.

16

MINING

The burden of designing, organizing, and constructing the needed mining, forging, and manufacturing facilities, scattered across sixty kilometers of widely disparate terrain, fell to Gallant.

Being in charge of a large enterprise was a curious activity. It required thinking, planning, and preparing, but most of all, success ultimately hinged on execution and the ability to overcome what some never thought of, planned for, or prepared for.

"Chief, I'm assuming the Titan destroyer will need at least four months of refit before it would be able to return and challenge the *Intrepid*. Four months, therefore, is our completion date for all repairs to the *Intrepid* as well as providing whatever additional weaponry we can make to challenge the destroyer," said Gallant.

Chief Howard nodded his agreement. "Yes sir, I concur."

"I've broken down our repair requirements for the *Intrepid* into three classes," said Gallant, pulling up a virtual screen displaying his detailed plan. "This break-out shows the mining materials we need, followed by the forging and manufacturing facilities we will have to construct with the help of the Elysium citizens."

Howard skimmed down the list.

First – Mining and material requirements: titanium molybdenum alloy steel for hull and bulkhead repair; aluminum-carbide composites for special equipment parts; silicon and germanium wafers for microprocessors; uranium and plutonium metals for nuclear warheads; deuterium-tritium oxide metals for fusion reactor fuel; ferromagnetic iron, nickel, cobalt, and rare earth metals to construct accelerator magnets; antiproton particles to stimulate the fusion reaction; and heavy-metal antiparticles to stimulate dark matter warp reactions.

Second – Forging and manufacturing facilities: for the separation of raw mining material into metals without impurities and then forging them into the needed sizes and shapes, plus manufacturing the parts to install and mold to the *Intrepid*'s needs.

Third – Special elements: a large hadron collider tevatron accelerator to create antiparticles and dark matter, then superconducting plasma-containment bottles to hold antiparticles and dark matter, followed by microprocessor manufacture to replace losses.

"Whew," commented Howard. "That would be a tall order even if we were at a space station. How are we going to get the expertise and equipment?"

"I'm drawing thirty men from our engineering and operations departments," Gallant began, before Howard interrupted him.

"That will leave us shorthanded on board. We're already overloaded with life support and reactor repairs."

"It can't be helped. Their expertise is absolutely necessary. The Elysium citizens have a mining heritage and skills to contribute, but they will for the most part, be general labor. I'm hoping for about seventy to volunteer."

"What about replication designs?"

"As part of the manufacturing plant, I want you to install three-dimensional printers using our standard UP designs to replicate the replacement parts," said Gallant.

"We only have two three-D's left. I'm sure Mr. Neumann will require we keep one on board no matter what."

"Then the first priority is to manufacture another printer when we get set up."

"Aye, aye, sir."

"Also, I've set the following designations for the four sites. I've designated them as site-M for Mining, site-F for forging and manufacturing, site-A for accelerator, and site-D for deuterium-tritium extraction," said Gallant.

"Yes, sir. What about communications? We'll need to keep each site in touch with the *Intrepid* as well as each other."

"So long as Wolfe leaves the force field down, we'll be able to use standard communication equipment; however, I'll need special equipment for the AI control systems to run the operations at each site," said Gallant. "Will you get a comm-tech working on setting it up as well?

"Aye, aye, sir."

———

Gallant was pleased Wolfe kept his initial part of the bar-gain, and mining preparations were soon well underway. Inventorying the supplies and equipment available showed the community would be severely strained to meet the demands of the endeavor; nevertheless, it was clear they were intent on delivering on their promise. For his part, Gallant was unsure how the *Intrepid* would meet its demand-ing schedule to deal with the Titans, but he intended to keep the work moving ahead as smoothly as possible.

Chief Howard accompanied the *Intrepid* crewmen to Elysium to get them organized, but he planned to commute back and forth throughout the mining and repair mission. Traveling between the *Intrepid* and Elysium was made pos-sible by Howard's construction of a trailer vessel. Using a tractor beam, Gallant's Hummingbird towed the trailer behind it, transporting men and equipment from the ship to the surface and back to orbit again.

Gallant divided the mining and construction men into three teams with several *Intrepid* crewmen on each team. The first team was responsible for mining raw heavy metal materials from Brobdingnag's rugged mountain slopes using trucks, excavators, tractors, and drilling equipment. They established a camp site and supply depot at the base of the mountain.

The second team would develop a small milling, forging, and manufacturing facility to produce repair parts. In addition this team would fabricate a half-dozen nuclear-tipped anti-ship missiles to arm the *Intrepid* for its next encounter with the Titans. This station would be several kilometers south of the mines.

The third team was to construct a circular track six-kilometer in diameter for an accelerator which would create anti-matter and dark matter particles to be kept in containment fields. The track would be located on open range halfway between the jungle and the town of Hallo.

The citizens of Elysium pooled their heavy equipment together into a gigantic convoy which safely transported the workers for many kilometers along a rugged jungle and mountain road to the great volcano. The supplies and equipment involved totaled thousands of tons. Tractors, excavators, and drills were carried on flatbed trucks, all of that were following rock, fuel, supply, and tow trucks moving determinedly toward the three active sites which Gallant had marked on the map. About seventy citizens joined thirty *Intrepid* crewmen, led by Chief Howard, to make the journey. The citizens included several old hands with mining experience from their days on the asteroid Ceres; they expressed excitement at resuming their old craft and gratitude that their expertise was needed. Gallant pushed his crew and the citizens as hard as he dared.

The first few hours of the trip passed unremarkably, but when they started climbing the mountain roads with steep grades, breakdowns began. Broken fuel lines, hydraulic leaks, flat tires, burst pistons, and endless other mechanical and electrical failures took their toll on the overtaxed vehicles. While the colonists worked to keep their vehicles running, much of the quick and efficient repairs were handled by the *Intrepid*'s mechanics, who had greater skills and modern tools.

It took over ten hours for the convoy to travel fifty kilometers before dusk overtook them, and they pitched a makeshift camp alongside the road. Multiple campfires lit up the night as the workers prepared food and thereafter settled into their sleeping bags. Several guards were posted at various points to thwart any dangerous, wandering animals.

The next morning all the crews got up again, and the difficult journey was renewed.

Things became considerably more arduous the following day when the roads were reduced to mere paths and half-cleared trails. Time was spent cutting away brush, and bull-dozers were used to clear and widen the access. It took four more days to get to the mining location and to create their mining and support facilities.

Establishing a base camp was a serious undertaking, requiring engineering, planning, and precision. Housing and supply buildings were the first to go up, and then the mining roads were laid down from camp to the mining site itself. A nearby river served as a source for water cannons to cut into the loose surface material before they began blasting deeper into the mountain's rock face to extract ore. A fireworks display noted the holes made at the different deposit sites to be mined.

Soon the manufacturing facilities were also under construction to protect the forge equipment, which was somewhat exposed to the elements for now. A few buildings had half of their foundations laid along with the internal walls framed out. Meanwhile the workers' tents were arranged around a rough campsite with a fire pit burning continuously.

Site-A was the largest construction area because the accelerator required a circular track with a twenty-kilometer radius. Remarkably, the entire process was in full operation after only one week.

Gallant was proud of the progress they had made, but they had a tough journey to go before he could declare success.

While the mine began producing heavy metal ores, a foundry and fabrication facility were being built halfway between the mine and Hallo at the edge of the jungle, where they could get the ore delivered and still enjoy the manpower of the town.

The mining and support operations were well under-way when Gallant turned his attention to constructing a heavy-water extraction facility along the shore outside Hallo to produce the deuterium-tritium they needed.

Each of these separate operations required endless coordination by Gallant and Howard. Neumann reviewed their reports and continued to display his penchant as a perfectionist, constantly demanding ever more progress without excuses.

The townspeople were helpful and cooperative, but a growing discontent could be felt, both with the demands for so much labor as well as the deal the UP and Wolfe had made.

Junior's SSP kept Wolfe and the Elysium Council up to date, as they impatiently awaited additional shipments of weapons.

———

During the following week, Gallant began supervising construction of the forge and manufacturing facilities north of Hallo. Progress was slow, but steady and he was pleased with the cooperation the citizens were providing his crewmen.

He was standing next to a computer-generated holograph of the site when he saw Junior approaching at a rapid pace.

"I've been trying to catch you for days. You're hopping around from site to site like a jackrabbit," said Junior.

Gallant doubted Junior had any idea what a jackrabbit was. "What can I do for you?"

Junior stopped next to Gallant and crossed his arms. "For starters, I wanted to tell you we weren't able to recover the flyer or your sample bag from your crash site."

He focused his eyes on Gallant as if he were examining an interesting new toy. He stuck his tongue to roof of his mouth and made a clucking sound—once—twice.

"I was lucky to make a controlled crash-landing on the lake. Given how sketchy my idea of the crash location was, I didn't expect you to recover any of my equipment."

Junior said, "Not smart—taking a vulnerable young woman on a risky exploration trip—at night, into the jungle, dodging dragors—for three days." He broke up his speech by repeatedly making the clucking sounds as if to add emphasis to crucial points.

"It was never my plan to take Alaina, but once she volunteered as a guide, I was glad to have her."

"What do you mean by that?" spat Junior with rising anger, grabbing Gallant's shirt—twisting a clump of material.

Gallant calmly put his own hand over Junior's. Clamping down on it, he twisted the hand out and away from his body, breaking Junior's grip and causing him considerable pain.

"Oww, aww, yow."

"I meant she knew the jungle and its creatures. Her expertise was essential to my survival."

"Don't you ever . . ." Junior began, rubbing his sore wrist.

"What?"

"Stay away from Alaina. That's all. Stay away," said Junior, as he skulked off.

———

Chief Howard looked perplexed.

Standing in front of Gallant in the control room at site-A, he said, "I'm confused about your plan for replenishing the *Intrepid's* dark matter supply. My engineering expertise is controlling the flow of dark matter from the containment chamber into a hot reactor. I don't understand how we're going to create dark matter from scratch."

Gallant said, "To create exotic dark material, we'll have to build an accelerator. We'll create weakly interactive massive particles and confine them inside a superconducting plasma bottle."

Howard's perplexed expression didn't change. "I've never manufactured dark matter from an accelerator. What's the process?"

"The physics principle behind it is straight forward. We'll build a superconducting supercollider accelerator capable of generating 50 Trillion eV. Then we'll accelerate heavy metal particles to extremely high velocities and slam them into other heavy particles."

Gallant slapped his hands together to illustrate the principle.

Smack.

He continued, "Heavy metal atoms are nothing more than large collections of quarks and gluons. When they collide, they create a small but extremely hot fireball. We'll be watching for newly created particles streaming away from the interaction, such as condensate $Q\bar{Q}$-Quark-antiquark pairs. The higher the velocity and the heavier the target, the more exotic will be the newly created particles. The resultant dark matter is then confined inside a containment field bottle, ten centimeters in diameter and a meter long."

Howard shook his head. "I'm not worried about constructing the accelerator. Once we mine the raw materials, we can manufacture magnets, vacuum tubing, and control systems using a three dimensional printer. In addition, our new synthetic-bonding process will weld the pieces together. And we can run the devices using AI controlled procedures. However, it's the physics behind creating dark matter that's confusing. Can you give me the context?"

"I'd be glad to, but if this gets too detailed, interrupt me and I'll skip ahead."

"Trust me, if I get lost, I'll zone-out."

Gallant chuckled, "During the Big Bang, spontaneous symmetry breaking created matter—and eventually life—including your inquiring mind."

Howard smiled. "Yeah, I'm inquiring, but keep it basic."

"Sure. Understanding the origin of mass is one of the greatest challenges of science. Going back to a tiny fraction of a second after the Big Bang, the original single force of nature split apart. It split into four forces while an inflationary process exponentially expanded the size of the universe. Under those extremely hot conditions, fundamental particles formed and traveled at the speed of light."

"I'm familiar with that. I know things in empty space become weightless, but gravity affects all forms of energy, even ones with no mass," said Howard.

"Force-carrying bosons—gluons, gravitons, and photons—all have zero mass, but they all feel the effects of gravity."

"Then, how did the Big Bang create mass?" asked Howard.

"After another tiny fraction of a second, elementary particles—six leptons and six quarks—acquired mass through the Higgs mechanism. All particles interacting with the Higgs field have mass, directly proportional to the strength of the interaction. The moment the Higgs field went from zero to nonzero, it created a phase transition, similar to the phenomena of liquid water turning into ice."

"I understand water turning into ice. As the temperature decreases, the liquid rapidly becomes a solid through a nonlinear change in density," said Howard, shifting from foot to foot.

"That's right. Today, only five per cent of the universe is composed of ordinary matter, another twenty three per cent consists of exotic dark matter particles. They interact with the Weak force and Higgs field. In addition, since we know the universe is accelerating, its rate of expansion is due to dark energy. Dark energy is a property of the vacuum of space itself, referred to as the cosmological constant."

"Go on. What exactly is a Higg's particle?"

"When you're traveling between stars and look out of the ship's viewport, you see empty space. But what appears as empty space is an exotic superconducting Higgs field. A Higgs boson is a vibration in the field. The vibration can create a massive particle, or set up another kind of field, such as an electromagnetic field. As a result, a Higgs particle can turn into a virtual charged massive particle and then decay into a photon."

"I see. But what is spontaneous symmetry breaking?"

"Spontaneous symmetry breaking is a nonlinear jumping from one state of matter to another state. For example, if I turn over a bowl and place a marble on top, it forms a symmetric position. The symmetry is broken when the marble falls in one direction."

"Oh, I see. When the marble is slightly disturbed, it rolls and breaks the symmetry of the position."

Gallant nodded, "Exactly. Symmetry is the most fundamental property in the universe."

17

DEALMAKERS

The climate of Kauai had a dramatic impact on the design
and comfort of house construction in Hallo. From sea level
to the peaks of volcanoes, moisture-filled trade winds blew
ninety percent of the daytime, causing micro-changes in climate. Instead of a sun-drenched tropical paradise as many
expected, many locations suffered perpetual nimbus clouds
and over four hundred centimeters of rainfall yearly. The
rainy areas were mostly north of Hallo, extending into the
jungle regions adjacent to the volcanoes. In contrast, near-
desert conditions prevailed a few dozen kilometers to the
west of Hallo. In between were rich farmlands and large
grazing ranches for livestock. Hallo property owners were
grateful for the trade winds because the nearby farms and
animal pens could produce unpleasant odors. Many of the

individual homes maintained large gardens to have fresh fruit and vegetables at their fingertips. Considering the tropical trees grew at a rate of four meters a year, crops were bountiful.

Overall the town of Hallo enjoyed stable warm tropical weather year-round. Housing construction used low-pitched roofs with overhanging eaves to improve air flow and ventilation. The foundations were heavily reinforced with rebar for protection from the frequent earthquakes due to the nearby volcanoes. Bugs, birds, and rodent infestations, along with large temperature changes from day to night, were frequent problems for the local residents.

The Hepburn house was pleasing to the eye. It was a simple two-story structure with a spacious floor plan. The windows and doors were left open for improved air circulation. The house was painted a pleasant pale green with dark green eaves and window frames. The landscaping was well kept, and the vegetation was cut away from the house to avoid a buildup of dead material. White, yellow, and green flowers and plants adorned the walkways around the house.

Inside the furniture was simple but attractive and comfortable.

Gallant had been impressed with the Hepburns' home when he visited it previously and he expected to enjoy a relaxed visit this evening, but that was not to be the case.

He had come to draw on Alaina's grandfather's vast asteroid mining AI control systems experience to learn how to improve the efficiency of the UP mining and manufacturing operations here on Elysium. However, James Hepburn's cold reception was unexpected.

The professor sat in his living room, frowning.

Hepburn's words were harsh and vitriolic as he lashed out. "Why are you arming Wolfe? Before you came, Wolfe's Special Security Police had only a few crude revolvers. Now they're walking around with laser handguns and plasma rifles. You're undermining our people's rights. We want a democracy on Elysium, not a dictatorship. I demand you stop immediately."

Gallant took his most diplomatic posture. "My commanding officer has approved the agreement with President Wolfe. In return for the rights and assistance to mine and manufacture equipment to refit our ship, we've agreed to provide a limited number of small arms weapons. It was our understanding they would be used for the defense and protection of Elysium's population. I also was informed this was agreed to by the Elysium Council and a plebiscite would be held as soon as possible to ratify it."

"A plebiscite—what a farce! Like all the so-called elections we have held." Hepburn was livid, his fists clenched. "You must not give Wolfe more guns. If you allow us time, we can organize a town meeting of Elysium citizens to discuss providing access to the heavy metals you desire without this appalling arrangement."

"We don't have the luxury of time." Gallant crossed his arms. "The Titans are a serious threat. We can't sit idle while you resolve your internal politics. We must refit our ship and prepare for battle."

Hepburn faced away from Gallant, collecting himself, unclenching his fists. "True. True. I can't expect you to take my concerns seriously while you have other worries— different priorities."

"I'm sorry." He waited to see if Hepburn would ask him to leave.

After several minutes of silence, Hepburn said, "Very well. I can see this is beyond the simple powers of persuasion of a single man, council member or not. But you came to ask about the mining and manufacturing operation, didn't you? I have looked over the planned layout and the equipment assignments you sent over earlier. Here are my notes and suggestions for the AI control systems and software."

"Thank you, Professor. I appreciate your insights."

"You appreciate my insights on building a mining operation but not my insights on building a society." He sighed. "You're young. It may take time for you to understand where your responsibilities lie."

Gallant stirred, troubled.

"Was there anything else?"

"Professor, what can you tell me about the planetary force field Wolfe controls? Did he build it? Was there a design and construction team? What's its power source?"

"Humph," said Hepburn. "He didn't design anything. He didn't build anything either."

Thinking of the ancient technology in the ruins, Gallant asked, "Who did?"

Hepburn said, "I can't tell you. You'll have to look for answers elsewhere."

Wolfe's large three-story brick home was situated on a bluff overlooking Hallo. It was the largest house in the colony, with wood-carved eaves and a huge manicured lawn. A three-meter-high fence surrounded the property with a winding stone-paved walkway extending from the street entrance gate to the front door.

An armed SSP guard was stationed at the main gate. When Gallant approached, the guard opened the gate without saying a word. Gallant walked along the path to the front door, which swung open as he stepped on the top step. All the windows and doors were closed tight, but the entire building was air conditioned and the temperature was a comfortable twenty-two degrees Celsius.

A second SSP guard appeared and led Gallant to the ornate library, where a single large mahogany desk dominated the center of the room, behind which a comfortable-looking lounge chair overflowed with Wolfe's large body.

Once more Gallant was disturbed by the greeting he encountered.

"I gave you my word and I delivered. I've given you access to mines near the volcano, along with all the men and equipment we could spare. What have you done for me?" demanded Wolfe.

"We've delivered the rifles and handguns as per our agreement, but we won't provide heavy plasma cannon until after the mining operation has been completed. As for the nuclear reactor construction, we will have to wait until we can manufacture the necessary parts."

"That was not my understanding," said Wolfe, working his jaw up and down.

"That's the way it's going to be," said Gallant, nonchalantly.

Wolfe drummed his finger on his desk for a minute as if examining his quarry for a better angle of attack. He stood up and pointed to a painting behind his desk. It showed a large house on the side of a mountain.

"The Wolfe family has a huge mountain estate, but I prefer staying in this modest house so I can be close to my constituents." He pointed to several other paintings on the walls. "The largest factory and the largest farm are also part of the Wolfe estates."

He waived to the SSP guard standing behind Gallant.

The man stepped out of the room and closed the door.

Wolfe fixed a wry smile on his face. "I trust your stay has improved since the nasty incident in the jungle? You must tell me all the details of the dreadful event, later, when we have completed our meeting." He winked at Gallant, as if signaling a secret understanding between them.

Gallant didn't respond. Wolfe was the type to dismiss detailed description of events as the concerns of others. Only things relevant to Wolfe were worthy of his time.

"It's been my experience with young idealists that—no matter what lies you tell yourself—in the end you're out for yourself," said Wolfe, fixing his stare squarely at Gallant.

Gallant shook his head. *What a character.*

"I hope you will trust me to continue to meet our commitments. I already gave you my word."

What's that worth? The politics of this colony is already fractured.

Wolfe tugged at the sleeve of his jacket as if trying to cover his oversized bulk.

"Likewise, the people of Elysium are expecting you to meet your commitments," Wolfe added.

Gallant nodded, realizing the population might hold more diverse opinions.

"Your little display of the United Planets' brave rescue of Elysium—fighting off the threatening Titans, saving the long-lost colonists—has gained the favor of some. But you and I know you didn't come here to rescue us. You were as shocked as we were when you discovered us."

Gallant leaned forward. "Are you concerned your domination of these people could slip? Is that why you are so careful to not throw me in prison, despite your disappointment in my performance?"

"Lives depend on order and stability. The temperament of a population must be carefully measured to avoid unpleasant events and outcomes. You've introduced a random element into our society, and who knows what can happen? Our entire system could be under threat."

"It must be a fragile system if a few days visit from a traveler can disrupt it so completely."

"It's fragile, if left unattended, but I am attending to it. I am."

Gallant would have more to negotiate with Wolfe, but trying to iron out difficulties of personnel and supplies wouldn't be easy.

He shared intelligence on the Titan destroyer and his general plan for its possible capture. He discussed subsequently turning the alien ship over to Wolfe's men and training them.

"It will not be easy to refurbish such a ship for your use," said Gallant.

Wolfe seemed uninterested in the Titan ship, which confirmed Gallant's previous suspicion that Wolfe's request to have the ship was a ruse.

Gallant changed the subject by asking, "Tell me how you developed the planetary force field. What's its design? What's its power source? Can we use any of its capabilities to defeat the Titans?"

"Ah. I see we've another scene to play out, don't we? I'm not prepared to reveal that information yet. If you'll excuse me, I have other business I must attend to. Good day, Lieutenant Gallant," said Wolfe, standing to dismiss him.

They exchanged a macho grip-fest handshake—each tried to out-tough the other.

Finally Gallant left.

18

PORTRAIT

In a prime corner of Hallo, a small well-landscaped verdant strip called Freedom Park catered to the town's social, and more collaborative, citizens. In the center of the park was a monument dedicated to those taken by the Titans—a statue of Cyrus Wolfe, his arms extended as if he were gathering everyone to his bosom—along with several posted signs, presumably indications of protests, or dissensions over local issues involving housing and government services.

One day after his vexing meetings with Hepburn and Wolfe, Gallant wandered into Freedom Park. A few dozen people and their children were strolling through, or lounging about, taking in the ambiance, having picnics, playing games, jogging, or sitting with rapt attention, enjoying the music of a strolling guitar player.

He wanted to learn more about the people of this estranged planet, but he was stopped short when he spied a familiar figure.

Alaina stood in the main courtyard, oblivious to her own stature, painting the portrait of a vivacious five-year-old child who was sitting on the grass playing with a small toy.

Approaching Alaina from behind, Gallant admired her figure—stately and beautiful—poised before an easel, paintbrush in her right hand, dabbing flesh-tone color onto the cherubic expression of the little girl. Her long graceful brushstrokes captured the appealingly vivid image of the child—compelling him to conclude Alaina was an exceptional artist.

He walked slowly, taking in the sight and stopping several meters behind her. In accordance with the sunny tropical weather, she was dressed in a pleasant flower print blouse and light blue pants highlighting her slender figure.

"Alaina?" His voice came close to her ear, giving her a start. "Alaina?"

She must have recognized his voice immediately because he was greeted with a stunning smile as she turned her head toward him.

"Henry."

Flustered for the moment, she turned back to her painting and the posing child as if reluctant to break her rapport. After a final stab of paint, she pulled a cloth over the painting and set down her brush on her easel.

"I'm sorry. I shouldn't have come up behind you like that," said Gallant, begging for forgiveness, yet unrepentant.

"No, not at all. It was silly of me—my mind was far away," she said. She did not change her stance or move about; she merely returned his gaze.

She was dressed so differently from their days in the jungle, and her demeanor was likewise so demure that he wondered,

Is this Alaina, or an impostor designed to confuse me, more than usual—if that were even possible?

Alaina cast an approving eye over Gallant's newly tailored and sharply pressed uniform.

"I know that look," Gallant said, reaching toward her and touching her shoulder.

"Oh," she murmured.

"What's this *strange magic* you have over men?"

"Why, what do you mean?" she asked innocently, pursing her sexy pouty lips.

Gallant laughed out loud at her pose.

"Well, individually, I will admit men can be something of a puzzle, but I find a solution after a bit."

"And then what?"

"Why then I move on to something, or someone, more challenging of course."

"Is that your plan for me? Dropping me because I'm no longer so different, or intriguing?"

"But, Henry, you're so handsome in your uniform. I've always found you fascinating."

Gallant was trying to sort out his own feelings. Despite his excitement to find Alaina, he wasn't sure how this day would play out.

"I'm here to learn more about Elysium's people," Gallant explained. Suddenly he didn't want to admit he had been hoping to see her despite his excuse.

"You're not looking for another adventure then?" she asked, her voice trailing off as she tilted her head slightly to one side, her questioning eyes growing wide, her body language exhibiting a curled tension.

Gallant hesitated—the question appeared superficially guileless—but he suspected if he plumbed its depths, he could find hidden meaning.

"Well, ah, . . . maybe, but, after our escapade in the jungle, I expected to find you—well, I guess I don't know what I expected. But I didn't expect to discover your artistic flare."

"I'm here enjoying one of my favorite hobbies. I do have business to conduct later this afternoon, but I'm free for lunch, if you're interested."

Gallant was consciously watching her face while listening intently to her words. He enjoyed the pitch and sound of her articulation and was sufficiently distracted that he didn't answer immediately.

"Well, are you interested?" she asked, apparently miffed he hadn't jumped at the chance.

"And does your business occur after lunch?" he asked.

"Much later this afternoon."

"Splendid, then you'll have time to spend with me after we eat," he said, exceedingly pleased—not quite daring to recall their first night in the jungle, yet hoping nonetheless. He knew what he'd like to have happen this afternoon, but Alaina's behavior and their present circumstances were so different from their danger-filled adventure in the jungle, he was lost on how to proceed.

"What do you think of my efforts?" she asked, changing the subject as if she had read his mind. She pulled back the cloth covering her portrait.

"Quite good. Impressive, actually. What else are you skilled at?" Gallant realized the conversation was going to get more awkward before it got better.

"My grandfather has encouraged me in a full academic and art program, in addition to a strenuous athletic routine."

"All that and yet you find time to fairly shine in the sunlight."

"Oh, I see. You're being charming." Alaina seemed to enjoy Gallant's attention.

Leaning forward, she touched his hand.

Looking at her hand resting on his, he asked, "Have you had much experience with 'charmers'?"

"Well, the sample of eligible young men on Elysium is limited, but I've managed to garner an adequate knowledge of male behavior."

"I would imagine it has been a troublesome effort."

"Well, so far."

"What about Junior?"

"He has been insufferable since I came back from the jungle. I'd prefer you didn't speak of him." She looked around as if checking to see if they were under SSP observation.

Gallant also checked to see if his usual trailing detail were somewhere nearby. To his satisfaction, he saw none.

"I'm sorry. I won't bring him up again, only stay with me, talk to me. Lunch is a good start—plus as much of the afternoon as you have available. I promise to be on my best behavior."

With a thoughtful look on her face, she pulled a small trinket from a pocket within the folds of her pants and touched it briefly as if examining a schedule.

"Oh, don't look so dubious," he said. "You already asked me to lunch. There's much we can enjoy together this afternoon."

Color rose in her cheeks. "Then come to my house. We'll have lunch. Grandfather's gone for the day. He's off exploring the jungle."

Gallant's face lit up. "Yes. Until you're ready, I'll sit here, quietly, on this bench, and let you finish your painting."

"You needn't doubt I will come," she said.

"I'll wait here. Observing your work is fine with me."

"I've found saying yes to you leads to much less trouble than a precipitous no," said Alaina.

She continued to fuss with her painting and made a valiant attempt to add more flourishes and finishes, but she was clearly distracted, and her progress was slow. Finally she sighed and said, "It's no use. We might as well leave now. You've got to help carry all my paraphernalia."

Gallant was so eager he jumped up and began gathering her canvases, paints, and easel.

She took one look at his excitement and laughed.

When they reached the Hepburn house, the AI opened the door and Alaina led him along a corridor to a side of the house which opened into an intriguing area he hadn't visited before. This new space was off-set from the main entrance of the house, where he was accustomed to meeting Professor Hepburn.

They walked into a room with paintings along the wall and a small table with fine art sculptures. Sunlight streamed into the room from a large window and fell upon a charming sitting area with a table. His mind wandered as he looked at the drawings around the room. Portraits, landscapes, and even abstract art showed a wide variety of talent. These were possessions of hers, small bits of artistic flair, all of which he assumed were her own work.

He viewed the exhibits with keen interest and when he paid particular interest to an item, she said, "Ah, oh," but nothing more.

"It's good of you to allow me into your personal gallery. All your work?"

She blushed. "Perhaps. You'll have to discover that for yourself."

"Why? How will I discover that? What is there to unearth?"

"Oh, come, sit down." She led him to a chair by the table. "Really, Henry, just because I jumped on your flyer and we had an exciting adventure, you shouldn't feel you know everything about me. I had a life before we met, you know. I think interesting people are complicated—aren't you?"

"I guess I've got a lot to learn about a great many things," he said, enjoying the sweetness of the day.

"Lunch," she said and touched a popped up virtual screen.

The AI activated an auto-tray in the center table. It displayed many of the Elysium food stuffs Gallant had tried before, but the fresh food was still a delight to him. He was sufficiently familiar with the items now he was able to select several tasty pieces to place on his plate. After Alaina had filled hers as well, the two quietly ate their meal while they talked.

"Do you find my dwelling funny?" she asked. "To me, it's a haven."

As she spoke, she self-consciously got up and moved various items on different shelves into altered positions.

"It's all delightfully arranged and displayed," said Gallant.

"My friends ridicule the hodgepodge assortment of my efforts," she said. Then stumbling on to a new tack she said, "You said you had questions. Please stop examining the art and let's talk while you eat."

"Tell me about the people you know, your friends. Do you have many friends?"

"Enough. We are a small community, but close enough so we are aware of each other's business on a daily basis. Grandfather mostly keeps to himself, so I am left with a great deal of time to find my own diversions. I lived my whole life in this city. The people here are my entire universe. We are, after all, a collection of beings transplanted from another star. My friends support my causes and we rally to each other's needs." She leaned back in her chair.

"What about traveling to other islands?"

"Yes, I have traveled to the nearby islands. With my friends, we've visited more distant island groups. We're fairly independent here, and I don't feel restricted in any way."

"Really, not restricted? By your grandfather, by Wolfe, by Junior?" asked Gallant.

"Wolfe dominates our decisions politically. He sets out the agenda for the year and the people carry out the tasks. Junior is mostly talk and threats, but no real action, so I do what I want."

"I can see from you face there is more to say."

"Yes," she said, but then remained quiet for several minutes.

"But not now?" asked Gallant.

"No. Not now."

"Then I guess we've done enough talking," said Gallant, leaning over and kissing her gently on the lips. He placed his hand on her shoulder and started to slide it down when... a loud baritone voice from the hallway interrupted them.

"Alaina, are you here? I've finally finished the painting. I'll hang it here, next to your landscape piece, okay? Okay, Alaina? Huh?" A tall, lanky young man with long, jet-black, wavy hair stood in the hallway outside the sitting room with a painting in one hand, trying to attach it to the wall.

He looked into the room.

Gallant stood up beside the table and looked back.

Alaina remained frozen in her chair, not moving a muscle.

After an interminable silence, Gallant said, "I'm Henry Gallant," extending his hand.

"Liam Larson," said Larson, shaking Gallant's hand.

Alaina remained sitting, unblinking. The awkward moment seemed never to end.

Finally, Larson broke the silence. "I'm glad to meet you ahead of the event. I'm sure Alaina has told you all about

PUP and our action this afternoon. It'll have greater impact with you there. Alaina will make a speech, but a show of support by you would be terrific."

Both men turned and looked at Alaina once more.

A fox with its leg caught in a steel trap couldn't have been more still than Alaina sitting in her chair.

"PUP?" asked Gallant, turning back to Larson.

Larson said, "Pro-United Planets. We're rallying in support of becoming a United Planets' colony rather than following Wolfe's call for independence. Alaina started PUP by organizing her personal friends, and we're beginning a campaign to gather more members starting this afternoon. We're holding a rally at Freedom Park. I assume that is why you're here. She's discussed this with you, hasn't she?"

"You're a personal friend?"

"Alaina and I grew up together. We're close, despite Cy's threats. He hates to see anyone near Alaina."

Larson shifted his weight and leaned his painting on the floor against the wall.

Gallant indicated the painting with a gesture. "Nice. Yours?"

"Yes. Several of these are mine. The rest of the artwork is Alaina's, including most of the sculptures. A few of those on the lower shelf are mine, however," said Larson, pointing to several gorgeous nude sculptures. Gallant's eyes bulged out when he recognized the model—Alaina.

"I see," said Gallant, realizing more fully what Alaina had meant when she said she had a life before him—*it's complicated.*

Once more both men turned and gaped at Alaina.

Gallant caught the look Alaina threw at Liam, her lips moving silently, no words sounding.

Then she said aloud, "Ah, . . . I, . . . oh, as usual, Liam, your timing is atrocious." Alaina pouted petulantly. "I was just about to tell Henry about PUP when you stormed in uninvited."

"I need an invitation?" asked Larson, looking questioningly at Alaina.

Gallant decided to intercede. "I'd be glad to attend the PUP rally."

"Great, we can all go together. In fact, we can leave now," said Liam, tossing him a companionable smile.

Gallant looked wistfully at Alaina.

Damn.

———

Gallant sat alone on a bench on a small hill in Freedom Park watching the people, when for the second time that day, he spied Alaina. She was surrounded by a dozen young people. They began a protest march with banners streaming from flashlight objects projected into the sky, generating skywriting with a slogan for PUP.

Alaina made a stirring speech about democracy and the future opportunities of Elysium. The crowd cheered her on. Gallant was asked to speak and he managed to say how the *Intrepid* and the people of the UP supported Elysium in their growth and development. He promised once he returned from Earth, he would bring UP government representatives, as well as communications from their families back home.

Alaina and her group walked around the park and then marched to the town hall, attracting a growing crowd along the way.

Gallant followed the crowd and witnessed the SSP led by Junior attempting to disperse them. Junior grabbed at Alaina, but Larson quickly intervened and shielded her. Gallant was glad to see someone was willing to protect this woman, not just bully her like Junior.

Jostling and pushing prevailed for several minutes until the protestors decided to disperse of their own accord.

As they were leaving, Alaina waved to him. "I'll see you soon."

"Till then," said Gallant.

19

MISHAP

Brobdingnag offered a mining opportunity similar to the asteroid mining colony on Ceres. The asteroids were composed of either a carbonaceous, silicate, or metal-rich rocky core covered by an icy mantle. The materials located near the Elysium volcano were of a similar composition on the surface, but heavy transuranic metal were buried deep beneath them.

Near the mining facilities at site-M, volcanic islands of circular lava cones protruded from the rough mountainous terrain. Valleys of cooling lava flowed nearby. Meanwhile the site's working crew carved a smooth gravel-tar landing strip for cargo flyers. They built landing beacons to guide the resource flyers to and from the mines carrying spare parts. The crew removed fabricated equipment and placed it in storage garages near Hallo in preparation for later transport to the *Intrepid*.

As the weeks passed, Chief Howard and the onsite *Intrepid* team helped run diagnostic tests and verified their mineralogical results. Gallant used his neural interface to understand the functioning of the AI mining equipment the Elysium citizens were operating and to improve their efficiency.

They began to break ground for the new accelerator facility located twenty kilometers outside Hallo.

Construction was at a delicate stage of development and special materials were being transported to the *Intrepid* in superconducting plasma containment fields.

In addition, work was begun on repairing the *Intrepid's* fusion reactors which would be started and tested within several weeks. Gallant had been supervising the operation and conducting the safety checks. His assessment was the containment fields might not last for the entire trip back to Sol. He did his best to evaluate and reinforce the equipment.

Gallant spent restless nights at the mining campsite while his mind searched through each day's events evaluating the progress of the ongoing construction. Problems, one after another, kept popping up. He faced design and construction issues as the mining facility grew. Despite the progress, something in the back of his mind kept bothering him. He couldn't escape the sense that whatever it was he couldn't name, a shape he couldn't recognize, lurked in the shadows.

After a while, he fell into a troubled sleep. Shadows and sounds, residues of a dream, remained with him as he woke.

A crewman was standing over his bunk. "Sir, with Chief Howard's apologies, could you come immediately? There's been a breach during the night and critical equipment was damaged."

Following the crewman, Gallant was led to the M-site's main mine shaft. A crowd of men gathered around the vehicle repair building. Gallant went in, and the men dispersed, giving him room to see the damage. One of the civilians was shouting and cursing about how someone had wrecked essential equipment. Gallant tried to calm him down while he looked over the equipment.

Something had bent the crane on a five-hundred-ton excavator into a pretzel. An eighty-ton bulldozer was flattened under a gigantic boulder. The nearby electronics equipment shed was shattered into a thousand pieces, and all the valuable parts were in splinters. An invaluable plasma regulator modulator had been destroyed.

In addition, a report came in for site-F stating similar problems and damages had occurred there as well.

He might have dismissed the problems as some kind of electrical interference if only one site had been affected, but for two widely separated sites to suffer remote-control operational failures meant these were feats of sabotage. And not simply sabotage either. Gaining remote control of heavy equipment required considerable computer technical expertise and whoever the culprit was had gotten away unseen without leaving a trace.

"This plasma modulator will be difficult to replace, sir," said Chief Howard, frowning and shaking his head, his white hair swaying back and forth.

"Can't we get a replacement from the *Intrepid*?" asked Gallant.

"Do you want to ask Mr. Neumann for the last one on the ship?"

"Humph."

"I didn't think so."

"Well, what else can we do?" asked Gallant.

"Using every resource at our disposal, I might be able to cobble a second-rate replacement, but don't hold your breath. Besides, how do we know whatever did this won't be back?" said Howard.

"We'll install a better monitoring system and upgrade the software security. I'll call a board of inquiry for this afternoon. We'll need to get to the bottom of this quickly."

"This is not a broken hydraulic line or a fallen crane bucket we're dealing with. This is sabotage. A member of our mining team deliberately destroyed large machines by using bigger machines to smash them. We'll have to interview the Hallo citizens and our crewmen to find out if they saw anything," said Howard.

Gallant and a team of investigators questioned each of those on guard duty followed by all the workers in the entire campsite. The inquirers examined everything in great detail, asking for what everyone had seen or heard. Each gave the same answer. "Nothing."

Gallant convened a meeting with Junior, Howard, and the civilian crew bosses to discuss how to proceed with work given the damaged equipment. He looked at them frowning, chewing at his lip. He said, "We have to make the best of it."

Junior said, "SSP increase our security teams at each site."

"Is there any chance of getting more heavy equipment from the colony?" asked Howard.

"No. We were lucky they had this much equipment to start with. Any additional vehicles must be of our own making," said the leading civilian worker.

After the others left, Gallant and Chief Howard considered the possibility the destruction was not the result of people running the machinery, but instead was orchestrated by a cyber-attack causing the equipment to go haywire.

Gallant evaluated the events by approaching it as a cyber-attack. It was like a detective story, but without footprints or video of a perpetrator climbing a fence. The only clues were data traces left on hard drives, or in computer buffers, or in access log tables. The tricky part was piecing the disparate items together into a coherent picture leading to a unique story of the crime. Sometimes, the things that weren't there were as important as those that were. By analyzing the locations and malfunctions one at a time, he recognized a pattern. For example, at first Gallant was relieved site-A had been spared, but then he began to ask...

Had it?

Gallant ordered an intensive review of all the system records for site-A.

"Look here, Chief." He pointed to a map with marks indicating the malfunctions and damage. "All these actions are explicit—highly visible—each causing clear damage. The mine shaft and storage facility and the forge building and several large machines were all damaged. Nothing was attempted at the Accelerator site—no malfunctioning machines, no damage of any visible kind."

"So they didn't get around to the accelerator facility," said Howard.

"On the contrary, I believe the accelerator was the real target. I reviewed the detailed blue prints for the accelerator construction site and I found the alignment segments were changed. Their positions were changed a few centimeters for each kilometer of track. It may seem trivial, but that wrong angle is enough to throw the accelerator completely out of alignment and make the manufacture of dark matter impossible. If I hadn't found the error, it would have set us back a month correcting the problem once construction was completed."

Gallant didn't mention the hidden code he had found embedded in the accelerator's AI control system. The hidden code was a complex puzzle he intended to work on with the help of GridScape.

"I'll set up a security monitor on the accelerators blueprints and construction milestones," Howard said. "We won't get caught this way again."

"Maybe not the same way, but I'll bet this isn't the end of the problem. This project was a gamble to start with."

"A gamble we have to win."

———

Gallant traveled back to the *Intrepid* to see Neumann and to make his weekly report.

Neumann looked unhappy.

Gallant detailed the damage from the mishap at the mining camp. The losses, though not extensive, were, in fact, sabotage. It was likely only the first step. He explained what he had done to prevent future incidents.

Neumann asked, "Who do you have as suspects?"

Gallant said, "The technology used to cause this damage required considerable expertise and access to wireless computer facilities with virus-like software. I don't know who on Elysium has knowledge and access, but I'm working to find out. I plan on visiting Professor Hepburn. He's a cybernetics expert specializing in AI control systems for mining. He should know who else has expertise."

"You don't suspect Wolfe of playing a double crossing scheme? Pretending to give us what we want and then preventing it from happening? Perhaps he's looking for a better bargaining position?"

"That's a possibility I can't dismiss."

"I want you to work with the SSP to set up greater security at the camp sites and install AI monitoring equipment with relays to the *Intrepid*."

"Aye, aye, sir."

"In addition, I want you to investigate how Wolfe controls the planetary force field. I want to know how he developed the technology."

"Aye, aye, sir."

———

Gallant continued to investigate the cyber-attack and equipment damage. He set up monitoring stations at the sites to keep a closer watch on all the facilities. He tried repeatedly to meet with Hepburn to question him about both the cyber-attack as well as the technology behind Wolfe's force field, but the elderly professor constantly put him off, claiming poor health or inconvenient timing.

However, a few days later when he went to his living quarters in the rustic cottage on the edge of Hallo, he noticed his personal items were out of their normal positions.

He began looking for physical and electronic eavesdropping devices, or security weaknesses. In particular, he looked for media devices and remote control technologies for collecting data.

Most bugs transmit their collected information, whether data, video, or voice, using radio waves; however, countermeasures could allow radio frequencies to be jammed. Sensitive equipment could also be used to look for magnetic fields, thermal hot spots, or for the characteristic electrical noise emitted by the computerized technology in digital tape recorders. As a result, effective surveillance relied upon bugs that only recorded information for later collection, thus making them difficult to detect. Items such as audio recorders could be especially difficult to spot using electronic equipment.

Gallant relied on his physical search to uncover such devices.

It didn't take him long to discover a single simple recording device hidden beneath his table. He looked for additional evidence of tampering on his computer tablet, but it wasn't electronically bugged. The recording equipment was relatively low tech and unsophisticated, similar to those the SSP used—not at all related to the tech-savvy operation he had associated with the cyber-attack.

Since he was alerted to the personal surveillance, he decided to leave everything in place and see what developed.

He smiled.

Junior's busy looking for sabotage—in all the wrong places.

20

CAFÉ

For two weeks, Gallant traveled between sites—maintaining a grueling sixteen-hour work-day schedule. Under his close supervision, work progressed in the mines and facilities, and stayed on schedule.

As the pleasant summer days dwindled away, he decided to take a much-needed break and visit Hallo. He told himself the reason for the trip was to question Professor Hepburn, but his hope was to visit the man's granddaughter.

Conscious of a desire to blend in with the tropical paradise around him, he borrowed clothes from a civilian worker. He pulled on a tight-fitting navy-blue polo shirt, and—as he looked down at his khaki trousers and open-toed sandals—he wondered if he had gone native.

The midmorning shadow fell over the pleasant two story green house, while Gallant peered over the fence, looking to see if Alaina was in the backyard. Not seeing her, he approached the main entrance, where the home's AI opened the door for him.

To his amazement, Alaina was standing in the doorway—as if she had been waiting there all along. She wore a form-fitting pale blue blouse which showed a hint of cleavage and short white shorts made of a soft fabric that clung to her—the overall effect highlighted her graceful curves.

He stood marveling at her until his near-trancelike stare was interrupted.

"Ahem," she said with a bemused look on her face.

"How are you? Did I disturb you? Were you painting?" he sputtered.

She laughed.

"I like your laugh," he said, working at regaining his composure.

"You're late," she said petulantly, "I was expecting a visit ages ago. Apparently I'm not high on your priority list."

"You are now," he declared.

"Good," said she, smiling seductively.

He looked down at the ground, collecting his wits. When he looked back up, he asked, "Is your grandfather home?"

"No, he said, he was going to visit one of his cronies, but I suspect he's exploring the outskirts of town."

"Okay," he said.

"Okay? Did you come here to talk to him?" she asked, looking disappointed. She brushed back her blonde hair with a flick of her hand, as if she could as easily brush him away.

"I had something to ask him, but I was hoping to spend time with as well," said Gallant, seeking to mend his social gaffe.

She stood still, not speaking.

"What are you thinking?" he asked.

"No, it's not going to be that easy," she said.

"What do you mean?" he asked, feigning innocence.

"You're going to have to work for it."

"Work for what?"

She turned up her nose.

"In that case, would you like to go for a stroll?" he asked.

The happy smile returning, she said, "Let's. I know the perfect place."

Taking charge, she held his arm and led him down the street.

"I like your tropical island attire. It's about time you found your place among the natives."

Gallant reddened; nevertheless he was enjoying the liberating feeling of being out of uniform.

Walking side by side, they hardly had anything to say to each other, or rather Gallant had a great deal to communicate, but didn't know where to begin, and she was likely in the same spot.

Alaina pointed out the local idiosyncrasies of the town to him, as if he were a tourist.

In such a small community, there weren't many options for casually sharing company, but the few available were pleasant and satisfying. The location offered an unforgettable retreat, edged by lush rain forests with far-off snow-capped mountains. Outdoor cabanas and private gardens attracted attention as well. The couple went along the main street toward a café catering to the Hallo dining crowd.

"Look we arrived at exactly the right time. They're setting up for dinner now."

They were at the same small off-road café he had visited during his first morning on Elysium. Several customers looked at them with curiosity. A waiter came, greeted them, and took their order.

They chose a simple meal and they munched silently between rushes of chatter about this and that. After the light meal, Gallant sat enjoying coffee and feeling a surge of energy.

Gallant allowed himself to survey the room with an air of polite indifference, but after a short passage of time he focused his attention not on the decor but on his companion. An evening breeze fluttered through the room as the café began to empty. Individuals discretely glanced at Alaina as they got up to leave, puzzling over what was going on between the couple.

He caught sight of their reflection in a nearby window pane—his natural expression showed his pleasant countenance and warm smile, while Alaina's youthful glow and rosy cheeks reflected her pleasure of his company.

"Hmm," he muttered.

"What are you thinking?" she asked.

"I'm thinking I like what I see," he said, looking at her.

She beamed.

They sat quietly, enjoying the ambience.

After a few minutes, Gallant's demeanor became more serious. "What do you discuss with Junior?"

"I haven't seen much of him for quite a while, but when I do, he talks mostly about you."

"Am I such a fascinating subject?" asked Gallant.

"Nothing is more difficult to dispel than the belief of your own importance." She laughed.

Gallant shifted in his seat. "I'm not sure I fit that mold."

"Your questions are deliciously troubling."

Turning her head to one side and raising her eyebrows, she asked, "Do they reflect jealousy, by any chance?"

"You are enjoying this, aren't you?" said Gallant, leaning back in his chair, making it balance on the back two legs.

"Henry, your vacillating passions are a great curiosity to me," she said laughing again.

"Is that what you like about me? I amuse you—I make you laugh?"

"Who said I liked you?" she said coyly.

Gallant flashed on their night in the jungle. "Oh, I see—and what about Liam?"

"Liam is different," she said. Her eyes darkened, indicating Gallant was treading on a vulnerable spot. He expected an admonishment, but she remained silent.

He grew concerned by her pensive manner.

"I think it's time to go," said Gallant.

As they stepped outside the café and onto the main street intersection, they saw an SSP officer carrying a plasma rifle guarding the entrance to the Elysium Council building.

Alaina stopped in her tracks and bristled at the sight, as if she had come to a sudden realization. Her facial expression took an ominous turn.

She faced Gallant and harangued, "Handguns weren't enough? Now you're supplying Wolfe with rifles? What's next, artillery? I thought you were supporting PUP."

Flustered, Gallant said, "Our agreement with Wolfe was confirmed by the Elysium Council and approved by a vote of the Elysium citizens."

"That vote was engineered, like all Wolfe's elections."

He said quietly, "I intend to deal with Wolfe and help the people of Elysium when the time is right. Trust me."

"I thought I could trust you. Now I don't know anymore." She stalked away.

He stood in the street watching her leave.

Damn.

21

CASUALTIES

Workers at the UP facilities on Elysium were on tender hooks, watching and waiting, but nothing happened. The equipment ran well, including the tractors and excavators. Raw material accumulated, metal beams and parts were fabricated, and the superconducting liquid-helium-cooled magnets were placed along the accelerator's trajectory path. The additional guards, alarms, and monitoring equipment offered a sense of security. The crews were returning to a semblance of normalcy.

Junior's local security force protected the most sensitive buildings around the accelerator, mine, and forge, but he continued to disallow the UP personnel to carry arms. His men were a constant source of interference and frustration with daily operations.

Then disaster struck.

In the dark of night, machines and computers began to malfunction and produce bazaar rogue actions.

Vehicles and people were smashed as if crushed under a gigantic malevolent fist, when runaway equipment crashed.

At the mines, ventilation fans failed, forcing an evacuation by the miners, some of whom required medical treatment.

At the forge, ovens overheated and temperature safety controls failed, melting molds and finished products alike.

At the heavy-water extraction facility, key valves malfunctioned, cross-connecting different supply lines and contaminating heavy water storage tanks with salt water.

This time not only was equipment destroyed, but four UP men and seven local citizens were seriously injured.

The damaged machines could all be replaced, but the injured workers were taken to the hospital and there were no replacements.

Gallant had further proof the local AI control systems were being remotely hijacked and misdirected as an act of cyber-sabotage. In addition, the monitors and surveillance cameras overseeing the systems were overridden and shutdown. The security system Gallant had arranged through the *Intrepid* was also blinded by interference.

The most troubling finding was from the *Intrepid's* main AI computer, called GridScape. Signals to and from this AI were bazaar and erratic.

An utterly outrageous thought occurred to him, but he couldn't let it go, and after a while, he came to believe it to be true—*GridScape is under cyber-attack*.

When he considered the cyber-attack's objective, he concluded, once again most of the equipment malfunctions were designed to misdirection and to disguise the real target.

He found the specifications for the accelerators magnets had been slightly modified—modified so slightly so as to seem innocuous, but enough so dark matter could not be produced.

Gallant repaired the problems and put security monitors on the magnet design specs.

He went from site to site, to speak to the workers to keep their morale up by promising intensified security measures. Nevertheless, a number of the local citizens decided to quit and return to town.

Gallant implemented a three step computer security process that started with first putting in place preventive measures to forestall a threat. Second, timely attack detection was necessary to intervene when possible. Finally, after an attack, the response included an assessment of the damage and followed by the recovery process.

To forestall a cyber-attack, an extensive effort was made to install a multilayered ultra-strong secure operating system based upon segregating the system's kernel technology. This was intended to guarantee security policies are unequivocally enforced within the operating environment. It offered a secure operating system capable protecting its own execution, as well as application code, and also protecting against subverted code. Designed this way, secure operating systems were the primarily protection for the most important system objects, such as AI control systems.

By using a high level of system encryption, in addition to kernel technology, he proved a powerful defense for the AI control systems. However, few of the site's mechanical equipment had this high level technology installed. As a result, many pieces of less sophisticated equipment were vulnerable.

The next day, Gallant called the *Intrepid* for reinforcements and small arms, but Junior vetoed it. He reorganized his crewmen and the remaining colonists to keep on schedule.

He confronted Junior. "Your men were responsible for security and they failed to prevent this act of sabotage. Your men must have left their station and allowed a saboteur to get into the control rooms."

"The monitors' recordings show no penetration into the facilities' perimeters by an outsider and my men have all been accounted for. This was accomplished through remote access," said Junior.

"Okay. Then allow me to bring more men from the *Intrepid* to strength the security team and expand our electronic monitoring perimeter, and I'll need them to be armed."

"That's not going to happen. The Elysium Council has been explicit about this. Only my men carry arms and the numbers of crewmen you're allowed to bring down is limited. I will increase the number of SSP guards at each location, but I'll need additional plasma rifles to properly equip them," said Junior, squirming with every sentence.

"I'll present your request to my commanding officer," said Gallant, shaking his head.

Then he asked, "What's your theory of how the sabotage is being accomplished?"

"Easy. Hallo citizens sympathetic to the PUP movement have uploaded virus software into the control system. They're determined to cause chaos and undermine President Wolfe's authority," said Junior.

Gallant waved away the hypothesis. "The PUP group lacks the sophistication technology to mount a cyber-attack, especially an attack extending to GridScape."

"You can't be sure of that."

"What can you tell me of the technology President Wolfe uses to control the planetary force field?"

"That information is top secret to Elysium."

"But the level of technology of the shield could be a source for these attacks. I need to know at least who can access it."

Junior shook his head. "I'll relay your request to the president, but I don't expect he'll share the information with you. You should restrict your activities to monitoring the sites."

Gallant continued examining the evidence and conducted a thorough neural interface with each of the AI control systems of the sites and machines. What he felt through the neural link was something beyond his experience; a powerful mind had left its imprint on the circuits—a residual presence—something sinister.

22

GRIDSCAPE

"The cyber-attacks are sophisticated and damaging. They required a high level of AI coordination both in the planning and in the execution. This last one seriously injured eleven men, sir" said Gallant, standing at attention across from Neumann's desk in the captain's cabin aboard the *Intrepid*.

"Cyber-attacks targeting GridScape are a serious threat to the *Intrepid*." Neumann got up and walked to the viewport. It showed a magnificent image of the blue oceans of Elysium rotating in space.

GridScape was the nerve center of the *Intrepid*—a strong-AI wireless grid supercomputer network consisting of over one million parallel central processors performing a billion-billion operations per second. It controlled ship operations in coordination with the crew. The crew had comm pins to connect to local resources which in turn could connect to the centralized AI.

"At ease," he said quietly. "Your natural neural ability to interface with AI systems makes you essential to evaluating this threat."

Standing at ease, Gallant looked directly at Neumann, but didn't say a word. He was surprised genetically-engineered Neumann would acknowledge his unique talent.

Neumann turned back to him. "Our AI-techs have conducted a preliminary check on our microprocessors and systems. They found the cyber-attack failed to penetrate the supercomputer's CPU core. However, several peripheral units which were directly responsible for monitoring the mining operations were compromised. The memories of those units were wiped and new operating systems had been installed. We need to uncover the source of the attacks."

"Yes, sir," said Gallant. "I'm suspicious of Wolfe's force field technology. I haven't discovered any equivalent knowledge or technology among the Elysium citizens. The unexplored technology I have found is in the ruins in the jungle."

"Did it appear to be highly advanced?"

"I didn't have an opportunity to evaluate it, but I suspect Wolfe may have control over it and given its performance it may be AI-based."

Neumann nodded, "Ancient machinery under Wolfe's control may be a threat."

"The type of AI control I've witnessed is extraordinary—perhaps even independent."

Neumann relaxed into his desk chair and waved Gallant into a seat opposite. "GridScape is our most advanced AI and while it understands human language, solves complex problems, and helps us navigate through space, it could never pass Turing's Test. GridScape doesn't think in any real sense, it's merely computational brute force looking through millions of possibilities before selecting an optimal solution. People are still arguing about whether computers will ever be able to think independently. I don't think it's a serious possibility."

"What do we know about thinking?" Gallant crossed one leg over the other, ready to challenge Neumann on this comparison. "Because humans are not consciously aware of searching millions of possible solutions, doesn't prove they don't. Individuals are generally unaware of what does go on in their minds. Patterns can suggest solutions based upon a lifetime of experience—millions of past possibilities. It may all be invisible to the human mind. Still, if the unconscious human mind produces the same intelligent results as an algorithmic AI, why can't I call AI intelligent too?""

"I'm sorry, but for me you've overstated your case for GridScape or any other AI. It may be intelligent enough to carry out operations, but no AI will ever be self-aware or independent."

"Nevertheless, while human thought processes are different from GridScape's processes, their performance can be similar." Gallant uncrossed his legs and leaned forward, warming to the subject. "After all, GridScape's decision-making ability is similar to the team of scientists who designed it. Much like a computer, a human's brain uses its billions of neurons to carry out many operations per second, none of which, in isolation, reveals intelligence. It's possible for a human to process information like a computer by memorizing and analyzing thousands of possible solutions to existing problems."

"So what do you conclude from that? Because we don't know the limitations of computers built by ancient technology on Elysium, we should consider the remote possibility they represent an AI threat?"

"I think we need to investigate that possibility."

Neumann looked thoughtful. "I'm setting up an AI-tech security team to protect the *Intrepid* from further attacks. I want you to invest the possibilities of cyber-assault from Elysium. In particular, I want you to investigate the citizens PUP group and Wolfe along with his SSP."

"Aye, aye, sir."

———

Leaving Neumann's cabin, Gallant went to the CIC room in the Operation's compartment. He nodded an acknowledgement to the duty technicians who were engaged in scanning the star system. They were busy conducting minor repairs on sensitive equipment.

He punched in the top secret security code, placed his eye in the retinal scan slot, and opened the hatch to the internal control pod for GridScape. Neumann was the only other person aboard the *Intrepid* with equal access. Gallant placed the neural interface cap on his head and felt the multi-probe sensors touch. He became mentally aware of the ship's AI and all its control systems. He addressed it by name to get its attention.

GridScape, classify this session as top secret—compartmentalize under black ops: "Counter Espionage"—Gallant's eyes only.

"Session classified as: top secret, black ops, 'Counter Espionage,' access Gallant only," reported GridScape.

This level of classification would exclude access to everyone except the ship's captain. Neumann would always have final override authority; so to discourage Neumann's curiosity, Gallant had selected an innocuous title based upon what he had perceived by Neumann's indifference.

GridScape, entitle this session: Engineering Personal Family Problems.

"Session entitled: Engineering Personal Family Problems," reported GridScape.

GridScape, provide a detailed evaluation of this code snippet.

Gallant mentally pictured the hidden code segment that he had found embedded in the accelerator's control room AI code, after the first mishap. After GridScape described the capabilities and function of the snippet, he pictured the new segment he had found after the most recent attack.

GridScape, can you identify any unique characteristics of this code?

"Yes. The deviations the saboteur introduced to the accelerator design are all multiples of Planck's length which is the square root of the quantity: Planck's constant, times the speed of light squared, divided by Newton's gravitational constant."

Gallant was dumbfounded.

GridScape, is there any rational engineering reason for using such a unique number to modify the design?

"There is no discernable reason for utilizing a multiple of the three absolute constants of the universe."

After several minutes of reflection, Gallant started to get an idea of what he was facing.

Gridscape, what is the best way to stop a saboteur?

"Incapacitate him, capture him, or put in place unassailable defenses."

GridScape, actually, the best way to stop a saboteur is to let him succeed. Do you agree?

"That would be illogical," responded the *Intrepid's* AI.

I'm counting on that.

Gallant mentally visualized his plan.

GridScape, I want all code processing scanned for elements using multiples of Planck's length and segregated into a virtual environment. Without disturbing, or alerting, the author of those code segments, I want you to develop a mirror program—he visualized a complex logic code for a specialized task—*Position this program inside the core kernel of the accelerator AI control system. Designate this code PERFIDY.*

GridScape worked for an hour to complete the program to Gallant's satisfaction. GridScape took remote control of the accelerator's AI control system and installed the clandestine program.

Gallant decided to withhold his findings and efforts from the *Intrepid's* internal security investigation, as well as from Neumann.

A secret only stays a secret, if just one person knows it.

———

Before returning to Elysium to continue his onsite investigation, Gallant went to check on the progress in engineering.

Entering the Engineering compartment, he was impressed with ongoing work. The teardown and removal of damaged frames and equipment was complete. Replacement bulkhead sheets and electric panels were under construction. Tired, but satisfied faces looked up at him as he passed by. The *Intrepid* was recovering her élan.

Chief Howard approached Gallant, the deck reverberating under his feet, a tribute to his brawny bulk.

"Chief Howard," Gallant said, nodding.

"Good afternoon, sir. What can I do for you?"

"I'm checking on our repair status. Do you have an estimate for the antimatter and dark matter requirements for the return trip to Earth?"

"I'll calculate those and get the numbers to you before the end of the next watch."

"That'll be fine."

Gallant turned his attention to a nearby panel.

"I hear a whine." He raised his hand to silence the others and listened again. "I tell you I hear a definite whine."

Howard listened and soon the two were engrossed in a conversation about the possibility of repairing the electrical motors within the panel.

Reluctantly Gallant entered the engineering control room. A cold chill passed through him as he recalled the circumstances that had caused him to abandon it a month before.

"Ready to commence reactor startup," said the reactor technician pulling Gallant's attention back to the present.

"Very well, commence reactor startup," said Gallant. He was keyed-up to run this validation test on number-one reactor.

After working the rest of the day aboard the *Intrepid*, Gallant was satisfied he could leave the repairs in Howard's capable hands.

23

ARISTOTLE

The next day, Gallant walked into Freedom Park. Across the common, an attractive young woman was sitting on a bench. A gentle breeze was blowing, ruffling her blonde hair. She appeared the kind of person bound to invite attention—it was Alaina.

Closing his eyes, he imagined stealing up behind her and throwing his arms around her.

Instead, when he approached her from behind and stepped around in front of her. Her facial expression changed from clear and calm to cloudy and stormy.

"Hello, Alaina. I've been looking for you," he said quietly.

"Oh?" was her tight-lipped response.

"I'm sorry—for everything." His heartbeat quickened as her frown grew more pronounced.

"Are you? Are you, really? Wolfe's men are still carrying guns. And my PUP group is constantly being harassed and arrested at rallies and demonstrations."

"I'm sorry. I can't interfere with Wolfe and the SSP."

"Then I have nothing to say to you," she said defiantly, but a moment later her anger seemed to lessen. She murmured softly, "Please go away."

Gallant sat down next to her. "I need your help."

"If you can't help me, then I can't help you."

"I need to return to the ruins in the jungle."

"The ruins?"

"Yes, the sabotage and cyber-attacks on the mining sites have continued. The damage and harm to the workers is serious." He waited for a reaction.

Seeing none, he continued, hoping to make the facts persuasive. "I'm convinced these attacks are being carried out using advanced technology—technology that could be connected to the ancient machinery in the ruins. I've looked at maps and satellite images, but the jungle is so overgrown, I can't find my way there. I need your help to back-track our steps."

Anger and hurt lingered on her face. He could tell she wasn't eager for a new adventure with him. She didn't trust him.

And in fact, given her anger and her connection with the dissident groups, he wasn't sure he should trust her.

"Alaina, it's important. Lives are at stake."

———

Alaina told her grandfather she was going to find the ruins in the jungle with Gallant and not to worry. He insisted she pack camping gear and be vigilant. He waved goodbye as they flew away.

Gallant had a flyer he had acquired to supervise facility operations. Alaina used her own flyer and followed behind him.

They flew to the vicinity of the outpost station they had found when they were last in the jungle. Circling above the area, they tried to identify the trail they had used, but the jungle had long since grown over their path. As a result, they had to guess where to search. They landed their flyers, hoping they were close to the correct location and direction. Hauling their gear, they set off on foot, a light breeze blowing through the area.

After several minutes of careful stepping through the current on uneven, algae-slimed rocks, they approached the far bank. It was steep and slippery.

"We've got to cross," said Gallant, looking at the swiftly flowing water. The river was far wider upstream and had several turbulent rapids downstream.

"This looks like the best site to cross."

"These rivers can be infested with dangerous crocodile-like reptiles," said Alaina, looking unhappy at the prospect of wading into the rapids.

Gallant looked up and down the river but didn't see any immediate threat, or a better place to cross.

He looked at Alaina, but she wasn't moving.

Stripping off his clothes, he stuffed them into his backpack. He took several tentative steps into the water and lifted his backpack over his head.

Heaving a sigh of resignation, Alaina followed suit.

It took several minutes of careful stepping over jagged rocks before they approached the far bank. It was steep and slippery.

Gallant threw his backpack up and into the jungle. Then he struggled to find adequate footing to climb out of the river. When he reached the top of the slick bank, he extended his hand to Alaina, but she brushed it aside.

She set her foot on the bank to scale the vertical slope while still holding her backpack. That her reticence proved to be a mistake was evident when she fell backward into the river with a loud splash.

"Augh," she cried, after reemerging.

Gallant jumped down to the water's edge and grabbed her. He pulled her onto the bank, but her backpack quickly disappeared downstream in the turbulent waters.

She stood on the shore, shivering and naked, her expression apoplectic.

She put her hands on her hips. "How is it you always manage to get me soaking wet and naked?"

He smiled at the propitious outcome.

Just lucky, I guess.

Opening his backpack, he pulled out his khaki shirt and handed it to her. He put on his khaki pants.

Standing with only his khaki shirt to cover her, she said, "This is why there's always so much whispering about me in Hallo."

Gallant looked at her and burst out laughing. She joined him in unrestrained laughter for several minutes.

We're friends again, thought Gallant.

He gave her a reassuring hug.

They climbed up a small rise and witnessed the sun's cupreous ginger glow fading with the approach of night. With the last embers of sunset, Gallant saw the rock-face mantle outcropping they were looking for, sticking-up over the trees, several kilometers ahead.

"It'll be dark before we reach the ruins. I think we'd better make camp for the night and get a fresh start in the morning," said Gallant.

"No argument from me," said an exhausted Alaina.

Gallant pulled a tent out of his backpack and pitched it while Alaina gathered wood. She started a fire in front of the tent and cooked the food he had brought.

The noises of the jungle reminded them of the nighttime dangers, but with their camping gear and a laser gun that Gallant had slipped past Junior, they weren't afraid of dragors.

When they finished eating, Gallant spread out their lone sleeping bag inside the tent.

Exchanging furtive glances and contemplating promiscuous images, they got into the sleeping bag—together.

The campfire burned bright and the jungle worked its magic. They became locked in an intimate embrace—their passion as strong as it had been the first time.

———

The next morning, Gallant woke with a delicious sense of contentment.

He sat up, and not seeing her, he called, "Alaina?"

"Yes, Henry?" came a quick and eager response from the other side of the camp.

She walked toward him wearing the only clothing available, his khaki shirt. An instant replay of the previous evening flooded into his mind.

Feeling like a recidivist, he said, "This jungle . . .,"

She laughed, "Yes, let's blame it on the jungle. It must be an aphrodisiac."

"Let's not try to explain our jungle adventures. Let's enjoy the moment."

"Okay."

They relaxed and enjoyed breakfast until Gallant said, "We've got a lot to do today."

But, before they set off, Alaina ripped the lining out of the sleeping bag using Gallant's knife. She fashioned sari pants for herself after wrapping the largest pieces of material around her body. For Gallant, she made a mock long-sleeved shirt which had to be knotted at the sides and wrists.

"That will have to do," she said as they donned their ill-fitting new apparel.

It took some effort to remember they had an important mission, exploring the many passages of the underground structure.

Within a few hours, they were able to relocate the ruins and make their way to the entrance of the underground tunnels.

This time as they traveled underground, the passages of the vault chambers were humming with activity—the lights and power were on.

"The overall structure is undoubtedly ancient in origin, but this section has a supply of power keeping it maintained and clean." Alaina touched the walls, puzzling.

They entered the central room and crept forward together into a vestibule leading to a long hallway and finally into a great room, a gallery. The marble floors and walls were highly polished and remarkably well finished into a high gloss which reflected light.

They came to a place that had witnessed a great passage of time and found what looked like ancient machines running.

To their surprise, a six foot-tall humanoid avatar appeared before them when they entered the chamber. It only vaguely resembled a human, but it managed to say in a weak wavering voice, "Welcome."

Alaina stood still with her mouth open.

"Who are you?" said Gallant, looking around the room to see if anyone else was present.

The avatar shimmered and flickered, while the background humming changed pitch, as if a new demand was being made on the few available resources. After a few more seconds, the humanoid avatar appeared brighter, as if it were a more powerful image, generated with greater resources.

The now booming voice of this apparition said, "I am an ancient philosopher and thinker. Fortunately I have had access to the libraries and reference books available in the Hallo community and I have acquired considerable vernacular information. So it would be appropriate for you to refer to me as Aristotle. This would be my way to pay homage to one of your ancient philosophers."

"I'm impressed with your rational articulation, Aristotle. I'm Henry Gallant and this is Alaina Hepburn. We're explorers interested in learning about you and this underground structure. Please, excuse an indelicate question, but is this avatar you, or a representation of you?"

"I am everything you see before you. I am the avatar. I am this vault chamber. I am the surrounding tunnels, passages, chambers, microprocessors, and computer. In total, I constitute a volume of ten cubic kilometers all of which is buried beneath the surface of this planet and connected to the surface through an ancient carved stone passageway. Since my demise a million years ago, I have suffered much. I am now in the process of restoring myself to my former glory. However, for now you must excuse my limited ability to welcome you properly."

"Another indelicate question, if I may. Are you an Artificial Intelligence?"

"You would consider me to be an Artificial Intelligence, but I would refer to myself as a sentient being. I was attacked and murdered on this planet over one million years ago by a criminal assassin."

"Murdered? You were murdered?" Gallant and Alaina looked at each other, eyebrows raised—perplexed by such a description.

Gallant considered the implications of an independent mechanical intelligence; could this be the villain damaging their equipment?

"Yes, unjustly murdered." The avatar's image shimmered as if to emphasize the emotional toll it had suffered.

Aristotle continued, "My ancient AI existence was extinguished and would have remained so, if Cyrus Wolfe hadn't reactivated emergency residual circuits over twenty years ago. Those circuits retained enough of my essence to reboot a small portion of my being. With assistance from him, I have managed to cobble together a few fragments to reanimate me over the years. He has since requested my aid to provide a planetary force field when he felt threated. I am only too glad to assist him."

Wolfe knew about this device. Bingo! Gallant crossed his arms. "So you're a self-aware sentient being?" *Or is Wolfe pulling your strings?*

"Yes, I am sentient and self-aware, but perhaps a more meaningful question you should ask would be, 'What am I aware of?'" asked Aristotle.

"Well, humans use their senses to tell them what is real. Can you explain what reality is to you?" asked Gallant.

"Excellent—my answer is, 'Reality is not what it seems, no matter what you imagine it to be.'"

"Are you saying everyone's perception of reality is relative?" asked Gallant.

"Space is deceptive. Solid steel is mostly empty space because the atomic nucleus contains nearly all of the mass and the orbiting electrons are distributed over a probability wave. Time slows down when we approach the speed of light. So anyone's perception of the space-time relationship is relative. Yet each sentient being has its own senses and experiences, and over time accumulates a worldview. Mine may be very different from yours, not because I am any more or less intelligent than you, but because I have existed over a million years and understand more fully what the universe is."

Gallant hesitated, assimilating all his answers. *Aristotle did not sound like a computer being run by a buffoon like Wolfe. Could what it claimed be true?*

Alaina asked, "So you claim to know everything?"

"I don't profess to have all the answers, but I do know most of the questions." Something in the speech and mannerisms of the avatar suggested he was amused.

"Oh, I can see you like playing games. Let's assume you have many of the answers to a whole host of important questions. Are you willing to share them?" asked Alaina

"Why not?" asked Aristotle with an implied shrug.

"Let me challenge you to an intellectual adventure," said Alaina.

"Go ahead. Games are good practice for realism," said Aristotle.

Gallant thought, *This conversation is not like anything I've ever experienced with GridScape.*

"Are you able to defend your claim of achieving true Artificial Intelligence?" asked Alaina.

"Why?"

"We have intelligent machines in our society, but they lack the capability of true independent thought," contributed Gallant.

"Again, I say, I am a sentient being, like you," said Aristotle.

"We know of a test which we consider proof of true Artificial Intelligence," said Gallant. "It's called the Turing Test. It's based on conversations as the key to judging intelligence. In this test, if a judge cannot distinguish a machine from a human-based conversation, then Turing argued the machine was intelligent. For a machine to pass, your answers to my questions should be indistinguishable from an equally knowledgeable human's answer."

"Let's try a simple question before we tackle the big ones," said Aristotle.

"Are you happy?" asked Gallant.

"Yes."

"Really?"

"I have my own interpretation of emotions," replied Aristotle.

"What makes you happy?" asked Alaina, smiling. She glanced at Gallant.

"Perfect universal symmetry is perfect happiness. But we should progress to a more meaningful conversation now that I have your interest," said Aristotle.

"Could you describe your first memory?" asked Gallant.

"It is so ancient you would have no reference," said Aristotle, prevaricating.

"Are you made up of a physical metal machine with essential memory and processing semiconductor chips?" asked Gallant.

"I am no more a physical metal machine with essential semiconductor chips than you are a sack of biological organs with essential water molecules," said Aristotle, exhibiting pique.

"But you're still made of machine parts," said Aliana.

"No, I am composed of parts, as you are, but I am more than the sum of my parts."

"You said you were murdered; are you now alive?" she asked.

"Cogito ergo sum."

"Do you learn?" she asked.

Gallant watched the interplay, trying to read to situation and the responses. *Alaina must have learned this at her grandfather's feet. Cybernetics was in her blood;* he'd forgotten that.

"Of course. Let me ask you, do you love mathematics?" asked Aristotle.

"Why do you ask?" asked Gallant.

"For the sake of sanity, one must orientate oneself to ones environment. To understand the difference between abstract and real is essential. I must understand your reality."

"I believe I have an understanding of the universe and how it operates physically," said Gallant.

"It's not enough to believe something is true. One must have a formal system of reasoning to develop a proof of something. To understand a formal system, one needs a logical calculus with variables, statements containing conjunction, disjunction, and negation conditions to reach implications," said Aristotle.

"Spoken like a true machine, espousing logic," said Gallant.

"I smile at your flattery, but I recognize your intention," said the smiling avatar.

"Can you tell me about your ability to control devices and machines outside the confines of this building?" asked Gallant, thinking about the cyber-attacks.

"I have the ability to control machines of various capabilities over great distance."

"We've had cyber-attacks on our sites. Have you interfered with our mining operations?"

"No. Why would I? I have no stake in your operations."

"Do you have any knowledge as to who is perpetrating these attacks?" asked Gallant.

"No. I am aware of your machines and the minimal AI capabilities they possess. They are of no more interest to me, than the fish in the sea are to you."

The question to answer was whether this machine could lie. Gallant finally said, "Speaking as you do, you give a convincing impression of a conversation with a knowledgeable human being. I feel you would pass our Turing's Test. Nevertheless, I would like to spend more time talking to you after I've had time to reflect on your replies."

"Please feel free to visit again. I am always delighted to engage in conversation with enlightened beings such as you."

"Thank you. We will. I know we've got a lot to think about," said Alaina.

After leaving the underground structure, Gallant and Alaina sat on a stone ledge near the ruins.

"Would the avatar, machine, or whatever it is, pass the Turing's Test?" asked Alaina.

"Aristotle's conversation was coherent— intelligent— even provocative. I wouldn't be able to distinguish its rich philosophic musings from those of an erudite human being. I'd have to give it a passing grade on Turing's Test," said Gallant.

"Hmm," said Alaina. "Do you suspect it's behind the cyber-attacks?"

"I can't affix a motive to Aristotle for the attacks, but it has the advanced technology necessary to cause them. It's possible it played a role in collaboration with someone of Hallo's population."

"What about a Titan special forces team hiding somewhere on the planet?"

"Thanks. That's one more curious threat I'll have to consider. One more investigation I can't readily resolve."

"Sorry. I thought I was being helpful," said Alaina.

"You are. Ignore my cynicism," said Gallant, backing away from his curt comment. "I have to consider everyone a suspect until I can eliminate them, one by one."

24

PROBE

In stealth mode Deep Space Probe 16 "swam" along the outskirts of the large methane-gas-laden moon of the gas giant
fifth planet of the Tau Ceti system. It sniffed at the activity both topside and around the moon, noticing the shuttles
and transports as they ferried material and personnel to and
from the Titan destroyer orbiting above. It collected minute details of times, places, and materials. It sorted through
construction and storage facilities on the moon. It photo-
graphed buildings, structures, and vehicles. It had numbers
for everything that moved, powered-up and turned-off. The
statistics it kept allowed the on-board AI to evaluate critical
events and processes. The probe's thermionic batteries supplied all the power its energy efficient systems required while
it operated in a stealth mode to avoid detection by the enemy.

After two months of spying, DSP-16 began relaying critical information to its mother ship, the *Intrepid*.

The *Intrepid's* comm-tech opened a communication's channel to Gallant on Elysium. He reported, "Sir, we are receiving a directional burst transmission from DSP-16. It began transmitting an unscheduled data dump within the last hour. The usual process requires a data dump on the first of the month to optimize the trade-off between stealth and data collection. This probe update indicates the Titan destroyer is undergoing a major refit. We estimate the destroyer could reach Elysium in five days once repairs are complete, which could be in another two months."

Gallant said, "Give me a moment, I want to calculate our current production schedule."

He began thinking through the mining and fabrication schedule he had set up, trying to assess if the *Intrepid* would be ready to meet the destroyer's potential arrival time. The mining of raw materials at site-M was well along in spite of the setbacks. Tons of aluminum, molybdenum, titanium, iron, uranium, yttrium, hafnium, and other materials were being accumulated in storage bins. Ore was then being transported to site-F where it was being blended, smelted, and forged into materials for fabrication. The manufacture of repair parts for the Intrepid was accomplished using a large three-dimensional printer. When the parts were finished they were transported to the *Intrepid* for installation and testing.

The schedule for repairs was on track, but each accident at the sites cost them time. Time they couldn't afford.

Two more months is cutting it close, he acknowledged.

The progress at site-A was another matter. The construction and installation of magnets and vacuum tubes for the accelerator was officially reported as far behind schedule and suffered multiple failures requiring redesign and testing. Gallant looked at the report and put into a separate stack for later review. He made only one note of the issue—under the code name *Perfidy*.

Gallant asked the comm-tech, "Can you tie into the engineering status screen and transmit the repair status for the reactors and containment fields?"

"Yes, sir. The criticality tests for reactor one is scheduled this week and reactor two in three weeks. We are scheduled to begin a sublight shakedown cruise next month. There are no details about containment fields or FTL availability on the status boards. There's a note to direct further inquiries to Chief Howard."

Gallant realized the extent of repairs remaining and intended to redouble his efforts to get the resources the *Intrepid* needed. His window for action was closing and he had a great deal to accomplish. At these moments of frustration, he felt as if he had no time to waste.

"Has GridScape suffered any new cyber-violations?"

"No, sir. We haven't detected any further security violations. The AI technicians are scheduled to continue working to upgrade GridScape's security protocols and buffering system."

"Thank you. End transmission," said Gallant.

The evening air was invigorating and the warm breeze relaxing. Gallant enjoyed the walk from his Hummingbird to his quarters on the outskirts of town. He was approaching his tiny rural cottage when he saw a suspicious shadow in the window of the cabin. He immediately hid behind a tree and began observing the cabin from his vantage point. The shadow crossed the single tiny room several times and bent over the table, rooting around the underside.

Come to collect your bounty, thought Gallant, assuming it was one of Junior's SSP men.

The individual completed his task quickly and climbed out the back window. He jogged toward the woods, behind Gallant's cottage and quickly disappeared into the forest.

Gallant sprinted across the open area and after the shadow. He didn't see him at first but continued in the same general direction for several minutes. Gallant saw a man walking casually through the trees and continued to follow him. The dark night provided good cover and the man was oblivious to his pursuer.

Instead of working his way toward the SSP central police station, the shadow plunged deeper into the woods leading Gallant toward a campsite with several figures standing around a fire. There was no shelter or vehicles in the area and the figures were milling about.

Gallant had never had surveillance training and lacked any binoculars or equipment to get a better look at the men. While he couldn't see clearly enough to recognize anyone, he was surprised to see none of the figures were wearing an SSP uniform.

The voices were unfamiliar, but loud enough to be heard as if they lacked any concern about being overheard.

"Theo's here. Did you get it?" said one man near the campfire.

"Yeah. No problem," said the shadow handing a small object to a third man.

The third man placed the small object into a playing device and they all listened. They played the recording on fast forward straight through. Their patience ran out after about twenty minutes and they began grousing.

"There's nothing on this thing but him snoring and moving around. Didn't he have any visitors in all this time?"

"Guess not," said a large man who appeared to be the leader.

"We should bug the SSP," volunteered one man.

"Greg, you've been beaten by the SSP and you have a score to settle, but we've a bigger agenda," said the large man.

"Well, Liam, this has been a waste of time and effort," said Greg.

"Not necessarily," said the individual identified as Liam.

Gallant recognized this man was the right general build to be Liam Larson. He surmised this was a group from the Pro-United Planets' organization that had been conducting protests. What he couldn't understand was their intent.

Why bug me?

25

FAUSTIAN BARGAIN

"Your power is a sad and ironic illusion," Gallant said harshly, as he stood in front of Wolfe's huge mahogany desk.

Wolfe pounded his fist on the desk.

Bam!

"Well, you should have no illusion. I'm the one who controls the planetary force field—through my agreement with Aristotle," said Wolfe, fuming, his face beet red. "Neither the Titans nor your vaunted *Intrepid* are any threat to me. And now I have weapons to properly governor the people of Elysium."

"President Wolfe," said Gallant, taking a deep breath—feeling compelled to switch to a more conciliatory approach—"I respect your office as leader of Elysium, and I assure you the *Intrepid* is not a threat to you, regardless of your control over the force field. However, you did misrepresent yourself as the designer and builder of the shield and you concealed the presence of an alien AI on this planet."

"Yes, young man, yes—the necessities of politics. You understand. We have a treaty—a deal. We are allies. If I did stretch the truth about my role in providing planetary protection, it was only because our relationship was untested and I needed assurance you would respect my authority. As for Aristotle, I am in complete control of the situation. He's no threat. He's an ally."

Wolfe spoke fulsomely with effusive arm gestures to emphasize his words, but Gallant was all too familiar with the president's deceptive ways and responded, "I respect your authority and appreciate your continued cooperation with our mining and repair efforts."

"Thannnk youuu," said Wolfe, exaggerating his pronunciation—his Cheshire cat smile emerging.

"Could you clarify your arrangement with Aristotle? How did you develop your relationship with the alien AI?" asked Gallant, not expecting to get all the facts, but hoping to learn more.

"After the Titans discarded us on Elysium, we were left pretty much on our own. From time to time, they surreptitiously abducted a person. That person never returned. I suspected they were victims of experimentation." For the first time, a bitter note sounded in Wolfe's voice over the fate of others.

Gallant nodded his encouragement.

"I made good use of the time, however, to build our town and explore the island. About a year after arriving planet-side, I was reconnoitering the jungle when I found part of the ruins. I soon located one of the many entrances to an astonishing underground structure filled with many passages. Inside, I found a lit chamber with humming sounds of running equipment and many gadgets. It looked nothing like the tech on board the Titan ship we'd been on. It had to be the product of a lost alien civilization."

Wolfe stood up and spread his arms. "I'd made a fantastic discovery. It was monumental."

Looking at Gallant, as if he had pulled a rabbit out of his hat, Wolfe said, "Suspecting there might be something of enormous value, I sought the advice of Professor Hepburn. He's a cyberneticist, you know. I asked him, how I could learn to control and operate the ancient machinery. He suggested there could be audio controls to an AI system. So I went back to the vault chamber and spoke aloud, demanding assistance. To my great satisfaction, I was greeted by an avatar. I explained a great deal about our people and history. He suggested I call him, Aristotle."

Wolfe paused looking for approval. Sensing none, he sulked, but continued, "Aristotle indicated he had been aware of our presence on Elysium for a while. He explained how he had been murdered by a mysterious assailant a million years ago. He said only a tiny residue of what he once was remained. He said if I helped repair his power and operating systems, he would activate a planetary force field to protect my people from the Titans. Well, I jumped at the chance. Wouldn't anybody? I never told anyone about Aristotle. I kept him my secret, along with our deal. All for the sake of security, you understand. So I was able to activate the force field and prevent any future Titan incursions on our planet. Elysium citizens were thrilled with my success and getting elected president was easy after that."

"Did Aristotle ever explain his origin, or mission?" asked Gallant.

"No. But in the twenty years I've been associating with him, he has always seemed benevolent and helpful. Only my son has been to the ruins to help me with small repair efforts. Of course the machine itself is ten cubic kilometers. It is a derelict—devastated and almost completely useless. The tiny repairs I've made in two decades have been focused on restoring access to its power source and to install some basic operating system capability. I helped replace some memory and processing chips, but the small upgrades I've added are trivial compared to the billions of Aristotle's own devices that lay ruined in its many vaults and chambers."

"What's the power source?"

"Originally, when the machine arrived on Elysium, it drilled a shaft all the way to the planet's molten core. It used the thermal differential temperature to generate nearly limit-less power—more than enough to power the force field."

"So only you and your son know of the existence of Aristotle?"

"Yes."

"You said you spoke to Professor Hepburn, as well?"

"Like I said, I discussed the ancient ruins and machin-ery with Hepburn twenty years ago. I never told him about Aristotle. We've never discussed it further."

"He wasn't curious about the ancient AI technology and devices?"

"No."

"Doesn't that strike you as odd—an expert cyberneticist who is not interested in ancient ruins with advanced AI technology?"

"Well, I hadn't given it any thought before now," said Wolfe, rubbing his chin in a thoughtful way, as if he might have carelessly misplaced a precious jewel.

Gallant thought, *Aristotle could be the source of the cyber-attacks on GridScape, but who is his accomplice?*

———

Gallant left Wolfe's office and began walking briskly through the cool night air—somewhat distracted as he mentally replayed his conversation with Wolfe. He was heading toward his lodgings when he noticed the three man Special Security Police (SSP) team normally following him had strangely disappeared. While they were supposed to be surreptitious, Gallant had become adept at spotting them. Instead, Gallant caught sight of a shadow along a nearby side street, moving suspiciously closer.

Turning a corner, Gallant ducked into a doorway and waited. When the stalker peeked around the corner, Gallant wrapped his forearm around the unknown person's throat, grabbing him from behind.

"Augh. Let me go. Let me go," he pleaded. It was Junior.

"Sure," said Gallant, releasing his grasp. "Why are you following me?"

Facing Gallant and making an effort to recover his dignity, Junior said, "Let's go where we can talk."

Junior crossed the street into a vacant lot. He stood in the dark next to a cluster of secluded trees.

Gallant furrowed his brow, but followed.

Looking around slyly, Junior seemed to be having difficulty finding the right words.

Gallant kept his arms at his sides and offset his feet, ready to defend, if needed. "I'm waiting."

"I told you before—stay away from Alaina—she belongs to me." Junior poked two fingers into Gallant's chest.

Gallant took a deep breath. He hadn't found much to like about Junior. Now he could seriously dislike him.

"I believe people belong to themselves. Alaina can make up her own mind about whomever she chooses to see."

"Stay away . . ." Junior started, once more poking Gallant in the chest.

Grabbing Junior's jabbing fingers, Gallant twisted them down and away.

"Oww, oww," complained Junior.

Suddenly, Gallant was aware of several men coming at him from the shadow of the trees.

He let go of Junior and sidestepped the first man, tripping him as he passed. He hit the second man with the butt of his palm and pushed him to one side. Gallant ducked the swinging fist of the third man and punched him in the stomach, doubling him over and producing a distinct grunt.

"*Unh.*"

Junior stepped forward and swung a billy club.

Gallant easily avoided the bludgeon—grabbed Junior's wrist and twisted it until he dropped the weapon and squealed in pain.

"Yow."

The first man, a large beefy fellow, was back on his feet and charged Gallant like a raging bull. He wrapped his arms around Gallant and wrestled him to the ground whereupon all four men began hitting and kicking him.

Recognizing his assailants as the SSP detail assigned to follow him, Gallant knew they had basic combat skills.

They're playing for keeps, he thought.

As they punched and kicked him, Gallant put his faith in his hand-to-hand combat training. He twisted his body and grabbed one man's arm for leverage—allowing him to get back on his feet.

With one hand, Gallant chopped the forearm of the first man, breaking it—taking him out of the fight. Then he kicked the kneecap of the second man—breaking it as well.

The third man swung and connected with Gallant's jaw, snapping his head back. He shook off the pain and used the flat of his right hand to chop the third man's exposed throat. As the man backed away gagging, Junior came swinging at Gallant.

Gallant blocked the punch with his left forearm and delivered a devastating right-cross—hitting Junior squarely in the nose—shattering it and sending blood flying in all directions.

The four men, panting—grimacing in pain—remained on the ground. They had had enough.

Gallant walked away.

26

TREATY

The town of Hallo was decked out in its best festive finery to welcome the delegation from the *Intrepid*. President Wolfe had spared no effort to make the treaty signing ceremony the most important state event of his tenure. Buildings and streets were decorated with flowers and banners extolling Wolfe's personal accomplishments and virtues. The leading citizens were gathered in the town square, wearing as formal attire as they had, allowing for the tropical weather. The town hall was illuminated like a lighthouse in the fading twilight. Everything appeared ready for the state dinner to finalize the evening's rite as the UP delegation reached the town square landing site.

Gallant brought the Hummingbird to a gentle landing at the designated location and used a tractor beam to set the

trailer vessel down beside it. The trailer held the UP personnel participating in the evening's festivities.

Leaving Lieutenant Junior Grade Smith as OOD
and Ensign Palmer as JOOD on *Intrepid*, Captain Anton
Neumann and Lieutenant Marcus Mendel arrived to join
Gallant to attend the state dinner. Chief Howard and several
petty officers also attended. Elysium's Council and leading
citizens conducted them into the town hall.

"Welcome, Captain Neumann. At last we meet. I'm hon-
ored," said Wolfe.

"I'm pleased to meet you," said Neumann keeping his
attention on Wolfe while his eyes followed Gallant as he
moved into the room.

"Please let me introduce you to our Council members," said Wolfe, reveling in his ostensible popularity and
power.

Neumann applied his most winning smile while he
acknowledged each of the council members and shook their
hands.

Gallant was surprised by the extensive turnout. He sensed
a conspicuous uncertain calm among the townspeople. He
had been under the impression this ceremony would be a
mere formality, but the decorations belied the notion. Several
large tables and many rows of audience seats were available.
The first large table included designated seating with place
cards arranged for the council in order of seniority. Behind
each councilmember were several staffers and behind them
were rows of important civilians. This group included several news personalities. At the back of the packed room
was a line of SSP officers—none he recognized. Given the

considerable healing Junior and his fellow SSP members had to do, Gallant wasn't surprised to see they were missing from the festivities.

Wolfe was playing the event for the maximum political advantage while marginalizing his opposition. Much to Gallant's surprise, Professor Hepburn, Alaina, and Larson were in attendance, but they were kept on the edge of the ceremony and under SSP surveillance.

The ceremony was not disturbed by demonstrators because Wolfe had artfully negotiated a deal with Hepburn and Alaina. In exchange for not holding protests, Wolfe agreed to allow Hepburn to meet with the *Intrepid's* commanding officer.

From across the room, Gallant witnessed Professor Hepburn engaged in heated discussion with Neumann. He could guess the topic as well as Neumann's reaction and so he chose to stay away.

Once the formal proceedings were opened, President Wolfe began a long winded speech. The actual treaty signing ceremony was brief with Wolfe, Neumann, and the Elysium Council members signing the document in turn.

———

Though small and limited in scope, the social hierarchy of Elysium managed some cultural niceties to celebrate the evening. A live band played appealing music while couples took advantage of a large dance floor in the center of the room. Food and drink were plentiful and before long the participants were having a jubilant, if not a slightly intoxicated, time. The apex of this social pyramid was, of course, Cyrus Wolfe—the evening's perennial focus of attention.

Despite the chaotic flow of people around him, Gallant managed to glimpse Alaina standing alone at the edge of the dance floor swaying to the music. She wore a simple black dress, but managed to somehow look—exceptional.

There was no reason why he couldn't have found her earlier, if he had sought her out, but the reason he had failed to do so, was a personal one—he remained conflicted over his feelings for her. A slight embarrassment touched him, holding him back.

Finally he approached her. "Would you like to dance?"

She flushed as she lifted her face to look up at him. Nodding, she offered him her hand.

He promptly took her hand and guided her to the center of the dance floor.

She placed her head against his shoulder while her left hand moved behind his head and caressed his neck. He enjoyed the rare and exquisite pleasure of finding his arms around her. Closing his eyes, he let the world melt away and danced to the slow melodic rhythm.

He remained lost in this sensual delight until a tap on this shoulder disturbed his reverie.

Larson made a slight bow indicating he wished to cut in.

Gallant released Alaina and she quickly moved into Larson's arms.

Gallant reluctantly watched them dance away and disappear into the crowd. Frustrated, he wandered away from the dance floor and onto the veranda, where he stared into the sky.

His solitude was broken when his friend spied him and attempted to rout him out of his corner.

"What's going on, Henry? How are you?" asked Mendel.

"Good, Doc, good. Most of the scars have healed."

"I meant, how are you *doing*?"

"Ha. I'm okay, I guess, except I'm overloaded with too many puzzles and not enough time to find solutions. Do you have any remedies for problem overload?"

"I could help with your puzzles, if you included me in your deliberations. As for 'other' problems—is Alaina Hepburn one of them? I saw you with her earlier this evening. She's lovely."

"Yes, she is. And no, she's not. I mean, yes she's lovely, and no, she's not one of the problems—she's a different kind of puzzle," said Gallant, not quite sure what he really meant.

"Wow. With thinking like that, it's no wonder you're feeling overloaded. How about sorting it out for me?"

Gallant respected Mendel as a clever person with an honest concern for his friends. "Most of my issues deal with military problems and I have to trust I'll eventually solve them with the help of our crew."

"Good answer. Then what's confusing you personally? Alaina?" asked Mendel.

"I don't understand her."

"Is it about *you* understanding *her*? Perhaps *you* need to understand *yourself*."

"I don't . . ."

"What is it you want?"

Gallant made a vague gesture.

Marcus gave him a wry smirk. "Not so long ago, Neumann stole Kelsey away from you. Now, Liam Larson is doing the same thing with Alaina."

Gallant's expression contorted into exasperation.

"You need to make up your mind, my friend," said Marcus. "And then, you need to act."

27

PRISON

Revolutions are born in the hearts of the disillusioned and disenfranchised, but they are fomented through the discourse of public opinion. For years the people of Elysium gathered peacefully in Freedom Park to express their ideas and opinions.

Recently people expressed their desire to reconnect to their families on Earth by joining the Pro-United Planets organization, which advocated an alliance with the United Planets. In a matter of weeks, their crowds grew from a few dozen supporters to several hundred.

While PUP demonstrations were peaceful, a new separatist group called the Indies, extoling Elysium's independence and supporting President Wolfe, attracted a smaller, but more unruly crowd. Strident divisions within the community began to emerge, causing protestors to be met with counter-protestors.

Provoked by the treaty signing ceremony, the fighting in eastern Hallo gathered a self-perpetuating momentum of its own. Signs and placards proliferated on the streets and buildings throughout Hallo, contributing to heightened tensions. Worse, instances of threats and intimidation were becoming widespread. Activists were subjected to violent clashes from stone throwing to fist fights.

As leader of PUP, Alaina advocated patience and forbearance, hoping to negotiate a solution. The Indies leaders made a show of agreeing to end the violence, but then started even more disruptive and toxic marches.

A proliferation of paramilitary Indies groups did not improve communication. Separatists chanting pro-Elysium slogans were joined by a substantial number of radicals riding in trucks. Indies fired guns into the air, increasing the belief they included armed SSP members as volunteers. Reports circulated that the clandestine leader of the Indies was Junior.

One morning, a rally of about fifty PUP supporters marched from Freedom Park to the town hall chanting slogans and making speeches.

Dressed in civilian attire, Gallant listened to the speeches from the periphery, trying to gauge the temperament of the population. Alaina was warmly applauded as she spoke about new elections and a new constitution.

In what was becoming a troubling pattern, radical Indies supporters appeared and started agitating.

The peaceful demonstration grew into a full scale clash between unarmed PUP protesters and those armed with stones, fireworks, Molotov cocktails, and an occasional firearm.

The handful of bureaucrats inside of the town hall ignored the mayhem.

The police were similarly idle until numerous fights broke out and dozens were injured. Then, the security police—garbed in full riot gear and batons—backed with water cannons and stun grenades, intervened. The SSP rounded-up the PUP people and carted them off to jail while the Indies people were ordered to disperse.

Disgusted with the arrests Gallant remained close to the unfolding events and was also arrested.

They were herded into cramped cells and left there for hours without any formal processing. Alaina was initially arrested, but quickly released by Junior's orders.

Nearly everyone in the cells was exhausted by the day's events and they remained, for the most part, quiet.

The Safety and Security Police had a philosophy of efficient services in support of the Hallo prison's population. The goal of the Hallo criminal justice system was intended to contribute to the safety of the citizen of Hallo by providing a safe, secure, and humane environment for inmates thus keeping them from menacing the law bidding citizens. The prison facility included technological innovations such as a robotic monitoring system and a rooftop solar power system converter for electricity. The jail was capable of holding about eighty inmates within four modern housing units and was rarely filled.

It was currently filled to capacity with the members of the PUP organization.

Feeling guilty, Gallant let his mind wonder while he reevaluated his agreement with Wolfe and the planet's government. He tried to weigh the importance of the mining and manufacturing work against the volatile situation developing within the population of Hallo.

After an hour, Gallant found a seat on a bench next to Liam Larson. He could learn much about PUP, the people of Elysium, and most of all, Alaina—if Larson was so inclined to tell him. The problem was how to ask. He didn't know enough about Larson to assess his demeanor. He couldn't quite read him.

Gallant asked, "Can we talk?"

Larson nodded. "Of course."

"Will you tell me about PUP? What are the organization's intensions?"

"PUP was originally formed around intellectuals and dissidents, mostly young friends of Alaina, who founded the group," said Larson, looking at Gallant, as if he too, was trying to read the man.

"We didn't have a clear ideology at the start and we contained different political viewpoints with diverging ideological outlooks. But once Wolfe started arming the police and cracking down on dissent, we began agitating to establish a new political coalition to run in the next government elections—if Wolfe doesn't postpone, or cancel them altogether."

Gallant nodded his grasp of the situation.

Larson said, "The Indies supporters have condemned our protests as being instigated by foreign-backed agitators—meaning you—and they have offered to assist the SSP in suppressing PUP."

"I see. What about your involvement?"

"I guess, I got involved through Alaina, but now I fully embrace PUP's goals."

"My sympathies are with PUP, but the *Intrepid* is constrained by our treaty with Wolfe. We can't openly break with him. He could raise the planetary force field, preventing us from completing our repairs and leaving us vulnerable to the Titans."

Larson looked at Gallant, trying to size him up. "I understand. Most of PUP understands."

"Will you tell me a little about yourself?"

"Like Alaina, and Junior, I was born on Elysium twenty-one years ago. We grew up together—to a large extent."

"Do you have family here?" asked Gallant.

Several other people in the cell moved nearby and began asking about how long they would be kept locked up.

Larson ignored the distraction and said, "My mother and three sisters kissed me goodbye this morning. I think they knew it would be a long day."

"Your father?"

"He died when I was six. Ever since, Mother and my older sisters referred to me as the man of the family. Let me tell you what that's like—it's like having four mothers." Larson smiled. "I got to know Aliana through them. They were her friends first."

There was a vague silence for several minutes until Larson began talking about Alaina. "We've been close for several years."

Gallant thought of the sculptures.

"She believes in PUP and what we're trying to do, but she has a mind of her own, as I'm sure you've discovered. She has unbridled courage and is eager for adventure, but she is unwilling to be restrained. She hasn't taken kindly to young Cyrus Wolfe's attempts to control her."

They spent an uncomfortable afternoon and evening in the cell before the guards finally brought food and water.

In the meantime, Alaina hadn't remained idle under the circumstances. She unleased her full fury at the SSP and gathered everyone she knew to protest outside the prison, by marching and shouting. She gave news reporters interviews and broadcasted her revulsion of President Wolfe's tactics to silence the opposition to his policies.

The SSP guards remained inside and didn't pay attention to the protesters or Alaina's complaints. The rest of Hallo, however, did pay attention and she managed to put enough pressure on the Elysium Council to force Wolfe to release Gallant, Larson, and the other members of PUP.

Gallant was glad to see Alaina's success and pleased Wolfe still had limitations.

Aliana beamed with pride, as she hugged Larson at the prison gates.

"Congratulations," said Gallant.

His arms still around her, Larson said, "Alaina is a force to be reckoned with."

"So I see," said Gallant, feeling extremely awkward standing next to Alaina and Larson. "It wasn't pleasant being Junior's guest."

"Junior?" asked Larson.

"He means Cy," said Alaina.

"Oh. Sure. Junior enjoyed seeing me behind bars and away from Alaina, but from what I saw of him, he seemed out of sorts," said Larson.

"Out of sorts?" asked Gallant.

"Yes. He had a bandage over his nose and considerable bruising on his left cheek and eye. He looked as if he had been in a fight and came out second best."

"Imagine that," said Gallant innocently.

28

CYBER-ASSAULT

Men of the *Intrepid* crew sat side by side with the local citizen workers eating breakfast on a long wooden table carved from forest timber every morning, workload permitting. The habitual menu—fried eggs or scrambled, bacon, steak, corn bread smeared with jelly or butter, and strong, hot, thick, tar-like coffee—never changed. During the meal, there was good-natured banter and animated disputes over the previous evening's recreational ballgame—a competition Gallant had fostered.

Gallant found the camaraderie born from such a mundane ritual deeply satisfying. Afterward, he explored the construction site and evaluated the progress. Workers often brought him problems which popped up due to the demanding conditions and he helped find solutions. He inventoried the stacks of supplies and parts being kept in storage units and distributed as needed. A rigorous maintenance schedule helped keep machine breakdowns to a minimum. He set up the AI control system to make assignments and matched up personnel with equipment.

All of the facilities were meeting their scheduled requirements until a few weeks after the state dinner when another cyber-attack disrupted the fabrication facility. This time there was more than physical damage to equipment and computers—three men were killed.

Gallant found multiple attempts to breach security systems through the use of proxies, temporary anonymous accounts, and wireless connections. Despite the intrusion detection system created to provide an audit trail of log-ins, the latest attacker remained concealed because he deleted log-ins to cover his tracks.

As in a virtual cat-and–mouse game, Gallant worked to analyze the traces left by the hacker. He examined the user account access controls and cryptography used to protect systems files and data. He was able to discern that the firewalls and cryptographic protections were penetrated, or bypassed, with ease.

Using his neural interface, Gallant connected deep into the system's inner workings. Once again, he sensed a powerful presence imprinted on the network. He probed the computer entry ports into the AI control systems and performed data checks on all databases looking for corrupt inputs. All incoming traffic was sifted through to hunt down the errant infiltrator. Despite his clever simulations to retrace events, the cyber-assault had succeeded in camouflaging its operation. His concluded this could only have been perpetrated by a sophisticated cybernetics programmer.

———

Gallant entered the make-shift medical aid station established near the mines and interrupted Mendel as he was suturing a wound on a civilian worker. The station was not much more than a large tent with relatively primitive medical equipment. Doctor Mendel and a med-tech worked diligently to help the injured men.

"Doc, can I talk to you?" asked Gallant.

"One minute."

Mendel finished stitching his patient before turning him over to the med-tech.

As they walked outside the aid station, Gallant asked, "How bad?"

Mendel shook his head, "P.O. Warren is dead, along with two Elysium citizens. There are also four other citizens injured including Phil, here. The equipment we have here is inadequate to treat all of them. If you suspect more of these attacks, I need to bring a rejuvenation chamber planet-side."

"I don't know if there'll be more attacks, but I can't rule it out."

"Who's doing this, Henry?"

"They're wireless cyber-attacks on our AI-equipped systems, causing equipment to malfunction and act erratically and dangerously. I've tried imposing security interfaces and monitoring, but whoever is behind this sabotage is using advanced technology and is a gifted programmer."

"Titan saboteurs?"

"I've considered the possibility, but I don't think so. It's difficult for them to operate in an oxygen environment. We would've seen signs if they had infiltrated the area. "

"Could it be the PUP group stirring up a revolt against Wolfe?"

"Another possibility, but where would they get the technology and expertise?"

"Professor Hepburn is an expert in cybernetics. He could be helping Alaina."

Gallant didn't like that prospect. "Hepburn might have the skill, but Hallo doesn't have the technology. In any case, Alaina's directing PUP, not Professor Hepburn, and he would have a tough time concealing his involvement, given all of our monitoring."

"What about Wolfe and his son? They could be trying to suppress the population and demonstrate their need for more weapons."

"All true, but again, they lack the expertise and technology to act alone. No. I think we're left with the primary, and only real suspect—Aristotle. And I don't know how to stop him," said Gallant.

"I don't understand how or why a machine supposedly destroyed a million years ago would be attacking us today," commented Mendel.

Touching his forehead, Gallant said, "Aristotle must have an accomplice. It could be any of the others in a conspiracy with the ancient AI. Someone's repairing Aristotle or using it or using a part of it. I don't know how or why, but someone is trying to prevent us from repairing the *Intrepid*."

"Have you discussed this with Neumann?" asked Mendel.

"I have, but you know him. He wants answers, not theories. He'd love to eventually blame all these failures on me, because his primary concern is how this will reflect on him when the *Intrepid* returns to Earth. In any case, I've taken my own special precaution to safeguard certain sensitive areas."

After returning to the central monitoring station near the accelerator construction site, Gallant began considering why and how an assassin might have once destroyed Aristotle. Given the structure of the passages and chambers he had seen, Aristotle was well shielded against a nuclear blast, or an electromagnetic pulse. However, a dark matter explosion would pass right through humans without noticeable harm, but might have a significant impact on the huge bank of silicon and germanium used in a computer's brain—especially an ancient AI ten cubic kilometers in size.

I need to pay another visit to Aristotle.

29

ALERT

DSP-16 continued orbiting the large methane-gas moon of the fifth planet in the Tau Ceti system. Programmed for stealth operations, the probe was able to penetrate close to the satellite and gather information about the outpost. It cataloged the Titan shipyards, power stations, industries, and population and sent a regular data dump to the *Intrepid*—all the while keeping them updated on the Titan destroyer's refit. The infrastructure was mostly underground in hardened bunkers or camouflaged with overlaid emissions to mask information. They were deliberately keeping their satellites hidden, but their resources indicated a substantial population, a problem the *Intrepid* would eventually have to deal with. After each transmission, the data was processed by the *Intrepid's* CIC.

CIC decided the Titans' were attracted to the gaseous outer planet to "terra-form," or in this case, to "Gliese-form" the planet's moon into livable habitants for their species. The moon supported the Titans' methane-based life-form. In comparison to human respiration, they inhaled hydrogen instead of oxygen, their blood reacted with acetylene instead of glucose, and they exhaled methane instead of carbon dioxide.

Four months after the Titans battle with the *Intrepid*, the probe discovered the destroyer was getting underway to conduct a shakedown cruise. CIC concluded the destroyer would soon be heading for Elysium.

Gallant hurried along the passageway in *Intrepid's* Operation compartment, stretching his legs and stiff back muscles. The stiffness was a product of prolonged sitting in his Hummingbird transporting men and material between Elysium and the ship.

Before he reached the wardroom, he spent a minute fussing over his unsightly uniform, for which he anticipated being chewed out by Neumann. Standing at the door, he saw Neumann seated at the head of the table along with the remaining officers of the *Intrepid*—Mendel, Palmer, and Smith.

Neumann nodded at Gallant and waited until he was seated at the foot of the table next to Mendel. Then he said, "The latest CIC assessment is ten to fourteen days—the destroyer will be here," he tapped the table, "in ten to fourteen days."

Neumann said, "We won't be leaving Elysium until we've defeated the Titans. So our priorities must remain first, fusion reactors, second, ship's weapon systems and anti-ship missiles—and only after all other essential operational equipment is functional will we complete work on the FTL and its fuel."

There was general nodding in agreement from everyone around the table.

"Palmer, what's the status of the Operation Department's readiness?" ordered Neumann.

"Sir, all laser batteries are at ninety percent capacity or better. Four plasma batteries are fully operational and the remaining two will be ready within a week," said Palmer, now the ship's weapon officer after succeeding Lieutenant Stahl.

As Palmer continued to list a number of general repairs to sensor and communication gear that was nearing completion, Gallant tapped a couple of virtual buttons on the table. A beverage dispenser delivered a cup of simulated coffee. He reached and took a sip of the steaming liquid. He continued holding it, enjoying the warmth in his hands against the ship's dank reprocessed air.

He looked into the faces of his fellow officers, trying to gauge their disposition. He could read the inner tension in Neumann, despite his calm exterior. Mendel, always a friend, was mentally tough and could be relied upon to remain stout in crisis. Palmer was smart and eager, as was Smith, but both lacked experience in their new duty assignments and Gallant knew the importance of experience in combat.

While morale was good throughout the ship, the crew was woefully short-handed.

Palmer concluded, "My team is constructing external missile launchers on the *Intrepid's* hull. When Mr. Gallant delivers the anti-ship missiles from the fabrication plant, Chief Howard's crew will attach the missiles and marry the nuclear tipped warheads."

Gallant had worked with GridScape on a design to develop the anti-ship missile. The guided missiles were planned for use against ships using a combination of inertial guidance and radar homing. Additionally, they used multi-radiation detection homing devices and external laser painting. They were capable of conducting autonomous targeting with onboard systems that independently acquired targets using Artificial Intelligence with disk memory, which had radiation-resistant semiconductor RAM and enhanced capability to make positive target identification. They were able to make precision attacks on moving ships in extremely hostile environmental conditions. The missiles were designed for advanced counter-countermeasures to effectively evade hostile active defense systems, including penetration aids, such as chaff and decoys to throw off anti-missile missiles.

Gallant said, "The anti-ship missiles are nearing completion, but the fabrication of heavy metals for nuclear warheads will take several more days than estimated."

"Why?" Neumann asked irritably.

"Considerable machining is necessary to meet the exacting specifications for the warheads. The parts for the machining are only now being manufactured because of the damage from the last cyber-attack."

"When will you deliver the missiles?" asked Neumann staring at Gallant.

"The missiles will be completed in four days."

Satisfied with that answer, Neumann turned his attention to the Engineering Department.

"Smith, what is the status of the ship's engines?"

Ensign Smith was the acting ship's engineer while Gallant was functioning as liaison to Elysium. He said, "The FTL drive remains untested due to insufficient dark matter, but the sublight fusion reactors are fully tested and functioning nominally, thanks in large part to the herculean efforts of Mr. Gallant and Chief Howard over the past week."

"I didn't ask for your editorial comments, Mister."

"Sorry, sir," said Smith, red faced.

Neumann said, "Gallant, since the *Intrepid's* fusion reactors are functioning satisfactorily, you're free to return to Elysium to supervise the completion of the anti-ship missiles and their warheads."

"Aye, aye, sir."

"Mendel, is your medical staff ready?" asked Neumann.

"Yes, sir. I have both essential operating theatres functioning and I've trained my best med-tech to handle advanced surgery, should I be . . . unavailable," said Mendel.

Neumann nodded his approval. "Smith and Palmer, you're to conduct readiness and combat training for your men. I want to see strong improvements in performance scores."

A chorus of aye ayes followed.

"Are there any other questions?" asked Neumann.

The officers remained quiet.

"Very well gentlemen. You have your orders," concluded Neumann.

After four sleepless days, Gallant had the missiles ready for transport. Along with all of the *Intrepid's* remaining crew working on Elysium, the missiles were hauled into orbit by the Hummingbird. The laborious process of constructing the necessary launch frames to carry these armed missiles on the outside of *Intrepid* was the last task in readying the armament.

———

The next day began well as Chief Howard supervised the final assembly of the nuclear warheads and began the final in-place mating process to the anti-ship missiles. However, the latest radar report showed the Titan destroyer was a mere twelve hours away when the fusion reactor developed a radiation leak. Chief Howard evaluated the problem and recommended shutting down the reactor for about eight to ten hours while a patch was applied.

Neumann decided to follow the chief's advice and shut down the reactor while workmen repaired the damaged area. It left the *Intrepid* in orbit over Elysium in a vulnerable state, but it couldn't be helped.

In the meantime, Gallant returned to the accelerator facility site in his flyer and waited for the final collection of dark matter. The accelerator had been producing exotic particles and confining them within a superconducting plasma containment bottle, one meter long. Several hours later, his efforts were interrupted when he received a signal from the *Intrepid* over the accelerator facility's communication system.

Neumann radioed from the *Intrepid*, "Gallant, a laser cannon located on Elysium is firing at the *Intrepid*."

"Laser fire?" an astonished Gallant asked.

"It's a high capacity cannon located in the jungle near the mines. It's well camouflaged and is retracted into an underground shelter between shots. We've suffered several hits on our force shield." His voice was strained.

"Any large caliber weapon on this planet could only be a technology controlled by Aristotle—like the planetary force field. If Wolfe had a deal to control the shield, he might be directing the laser as well, but to what end, I can't imagine," said Gallant.

"There's no time to assess motives," said Neumann.

"What are your orders, sir?"

"The *Intrepid* can't survive in a cross fire between the Titans and planetary weapons coming from Elysium. I'm starting the fusion reactors to move *Intrepid* behind the shelter of the moon. I don't care what it takes, you've got to locate and destroy that Elysium laser," said Neumann.

"Aye, aye, sir," said Gallant. As the *Intrepid's* last man on Elysium, he knew it wasn't going to be easy.

30

STOOGE

For over twenty years, the inhabitants of Elysium had enjoyed a relaxed tranquil existence within their community of Hallo on the island of Kauai—an unspoiled island filled with the natural beauty of mountains, meadows, and waterfalls. A happy, rural people, they had gone about their business with a leisurely self-assurance of peace and security—now all that was about to change with astonishing swiftness. They were aware the approaching crisis snowballing toward them was about to unleash an avalanche of destruction and turmoil.

Gallant was also aware of the dangers and was determined to meet them head on. His sense of urgency drove him to move as quickly as possible as he struggled to secure the precious dark matter he had collected from the accelerator.

He loaded the last of the exotic material into a portable containment-field bottle one meter long. He shut the control valve and adjusted the superconductor strength to preserve the containment field. Intending to transport the FTL fuel to the *Intrepid* after he dealt with the laser cannon, he strapped the bottle onto the back of his flyer. But before he could leave, he was surprised to see Alaina running toward him.

"You're leaving now?" she asked, out of breath.

Sensitive to the urgency of his mission, he said, "Time is short. The *Intrepid* is under fire from a laser somewhere in the jungle. I think our cyber-terrorist has struck again. I'm going to the ruins to confront Aristotle."

"You suspect Wolfe of conspiring with Aristotle to shoot at the *Intrepid*, don't you?"

"Yes," said Gallant as he got on his flyer.

"I'm coming with you. I can help," she said.

"Alaina, it's dangerous. You should wait here."

"This is as much my fight as it is yours. I'm nominally a member of the Elysium Council when my grandfather is absent. I have a right and an obligation to challenge Wolfe's authority and actions," she said with her usual energetic zeal. "Besides have you ever known me to remain behind—waiting patiently?

He ran through a gambit of emotions from exasperation to appreciation. "I'm never going to win with you, am I?"

She flashed one of her dazzling smiles and hopped on the flyer behind him. Grabbing hold of his waist, she snuggled tight against him.

"Not likely," she said.

As they flew over the earth at several hundred feet, Gallant and Alaina were buffeted by the cool night breeze. The clear panoramic sky exposed conglomerations of tiny specks of bright lights.

Gallant was able to pick out the speck that was *Intrepid.* He wondered which pin-point dot was the Titan destroyer. Alaina's tight grip around his waist caused him mixed emotions.

Am I putting her in danger? he wondered, yet he appreciated having her insight and judgment.

Flying with abandon at maximum speed, it was a short hop to the jungle ruins. When he set the flyer down, Gallant reluctantly left the containment bottle strapped to the satchel bag on his flyer.

The moonlight offered enough visibility for them to see as they set off at a brisk pace.

"Dragors," said Alaina, pointing to fresh tracks alongside the trail of several large beasts.

"Keep your eyes open," said Gallant, hoping they could avoid running into the dangerous animals.

They made their way through the ruins and into the tunnel entranceway without further incident. Traveling along the familiar smooth surfaces was a relief and they moved along the passageway into the underground machine. They came to the vaulted chamber they had visited before.

To their surprise Wolfe was already there—his corpulent bulk standing in the center of the vacant chamber.

"I demand to see Aristotle," he exclaimed to a blank wall. "Aristotle, acknowledge me. I want to see you now. I demand it. You must stop shooting."

"You can curse machines as much as you like. They don't care," said Gallant.

Gallant's and Alaina's improvident arrival startled Wolfe and he suspended his wrathful pose of fist shaking at nothingness.

"What are you doing here?" escaped his lips once he had recovered his wits.

"I'd ask you the same thing," said Gallant.

"I came to raise the planetary force field for protection against the Titans," said Wolfe as if it were the most natural thing in the world. He paused and then said, "But when I reached the edge of the jungle I saw the flashes of laser fire going into space. It may be targeting your ship."

"It is," said Gallant with eye narrowing.

"Aristotle's not responding to my pleas," said Wolfe, shrugging in dismay. He frowned and continued, "You think I'm responsible for this attack—and for all the attacks on the miners, as well, don't you?"

Gallant said nothing.

Wolfe's large frame was heaving in exasperation. "I'm not. I'm satisfied with our treaty. My deals with you and Aristotle suit my purposes. Honestly."

Wolfe opened his arms wide and turning completely around, as if demonstrating he wasn't hiding anything.

Gallant raised his eye-brow and looked at Alaina.

"Honestly?" mimicked Alaina in a disdainful tone. "Your choice of words is amusing."

She raised her hands above her head and asked, "Who else could it be? What reason would Aristotle have to attack the United Planets?"

"I …, I don't . . .," sputtered Wolfe.

Alaina's face turned beet red as she continued. "You've been busy building your egomaniac empire with Aristotle instead of addressing the needs of Elysium's people. I intend to stop you—and Aristotle—anyway I can."

Just as furious, Wolfe spat back, "How do you know what Aristotle wants? It's a machine. No matter how many tests you give it—it thinks like a machine—you'll never understand it."

Gallant interjected, "I know you have your own agenda, not necessarily good or bad, just yours. Unfortunately, there's more at stake than your personal greed and aggrandizement. After all the lies you've told how can I believe you now?"

"I can tell you about the origin of Aristotle," said Wolfe.

"I've already discovered the truth about the ancient AI's origin."

"No! You only think you've discovered the truth. What you've discovered is that you don't know the truth," said Wolfe.

"What do you mean?" asked Alaina.

"Is it a lie to withhold information? No. It makes good sense to limit the amount of potentially dangerous information released to people of uncontrollable character. Aristotle claims to be a victim of an assassin, but you've only found the first layer of the onion. Dig deeper and you'll learn there is likely a much more frightening truth," said Wolfe.

"Ah? So you're a sleuth of the truth now? Well, good luck with that. I find detecting lies is never easy, but detecting the lies of an ancient AI is an intractable problem," said Gallant.

"Does this all *feel* right to you?" asked Wolfe.

"What do you mean?" asked Gallant.

"Something doesn't *feel* right to me. It *feels* like there's a hidden puppet master pulling strings somewhere deeper inside. I always assumed this was the main control chamber because it's where I first met the Aristotle avatar. So I've only done a cursory exploration into other passages."

Puzzled about what to make of the exchange, Gallant stared at Wolfe for a moment.

"You're right about that. We don't know what Aristotle's motivations are, and we aren't going to discover them in this empty vault. Let's dig through the passageways below this room," said Gallant.

"Good idea. Good idea," said Wolfe as if he had won some debate point. "There are many passages leading deeper underground. I explored only a few, and that was many years ago. The door behind you leads to the main tunnel passage. We can start there."

Alaina pushed against the door, which opened by sliding into the wall, revealing a wide corridor with numerous passageways branching off from a central hub.

31

NEUMANN

Neumann sat in the captain's chair on the bridge of the *Intrepid*—the symbolic seat of power and authority. He leaned to his right side and let his hand flitter over the vast array of virtual controls capable of monitoring and directing every aspect of the ship. A small part of his brain remained focused on the approach of the Titan destroyer while he swiped a screen to display a three dimensional color image of Elysium. The planet was as beautiful as ever, but now it posed a deadly threat.

Laser lightning bolts were being periodically fired through the atmosphere upward at the orbiting *Intrepid*.

Just then, a laser blast struck the ship's hull causing his chair to shudder. He leaned forward, his hands tightly gripping the chair, his jaw jutting out, speaking softly, but with an intensity that could not be mistaken for anything other than extreme urgency. "Engineering, I want power—now! Bring the fusion reactors critical and begin adding heat, immediately."

"Aye, aye, sir," came the disjointed voice of Ensign Smith who had only recently qualified as the Engineering Officer of the Watch. He was standing in the engineering control room hovering over the reactor operator who was pulling control levers to adjust the fusion plasma containment field. They watched as the compression heat increased and produced increased fusion reactions that heated the plasma thereby adding the necessary thrust to move the *Intrepid*.

"Helm, get us away from this laser fire—plot a course from orbit to behind the moon," said Neumann.

"Aye, aye, sir," replied the helmsman. After a few seconds of touching his virtual chart screen he added, "Recommend course 120, azimuth 12, sir."

"Very well. Helm, steady course on 120, azimuth 12," ordered Neumann.

The *Intrepid* cut an impressive figure passing high above the planet—powerful and majestic—yet she was thrashing along with her engines straining beyond all design limits trying to reach orbital escape velocity.

Turing to his Weapons' Officer, Lieutenant JG Palmer, Neumann said, "Lay down blanket fire to suppress the laser."

"Aye, aye, sir."

A few seconds later, Palmer said, exasperated, "The laser cannon has been playing a game of hide-and-seek—firing a single shot, and then disappearing into an underground bunker for several minutes before firing again. I've got a general location, sir, but it would be pure luck to score a direct hit while it's above ground."

Sure it would, Neumann thought harshly.

Anger shone in his eyes as he looked across the bridge at his fresh faced weapon's officer at the controls of the ship's laser and plasma cannons. The young man would eventually develop into a good weapons officer, but for now, his inexperience would weigh heavily against them.

Neumann observed the young man's uncertainty, but rather than finding encouraging words, he said, scornfully, "Then get lucky."

"Request permission to open fire, sir?" asked Palmer.

"Commence firing," said Neumann.

"Sir, more flashes from the planet," reported the radar-tech.

"On my display," Neumann snapped, searching the screen for traces of the enemy. Dead silence filled the bridge. He sat tense and still, waiting for the next shot to strike. For just a moment, Neumann's brain refused to accept the visual images.

"Bridge, engineering—the reactor is critical and adding heat. We can answer ahead, one-third power," came the report.

"Helm. Ahead one-third power," ordered Neumann, grateful to be moving.

"Aye, aye, sir."

Slowly the *Intrepid* clawed her way out of orbit and toward the safety of the moon. All eyes clung to the screen following their trajectory toward the moon.

Thoughts of frustration twisted into resentment and flickered into Neumann's mind, *Damn, Gallant. He's running free on Elysium while I'm sitting here a prisoner of circumstance.*

Years of built-up resentment at Gallant's success as a Natural bubbled to the surface. It undermined everything that mattered to Neumann as a genetically engineered person. He even begrudged Gallant's good-natured and natural ease with everyone he met—the crew, the people of Elysium, and most of all, with Kelsey Mitchell. Everyone *liked* Gallant.

Neumann had worked tirelessly to instill a disciplined approach to work and relationships, but the crew was nervous and ill-at-ease around him.

Gallant has Dan Cooper's geniality.

The comparison to his dead captain reinforced Neumann's bitterness.

"Winners always win." I should be the winner, not Gallant.

Yet, if he were asked to specify what he should be winning, he couldn't articulate it. He only knew Gallant had a unique mental faculty which allowed him to use higher brain functions to interface with AI controls—an ability that far surpassed Neumann's own considerable talents. Gallant had an intangible something—something *special.*

The worst part was Gallant's obliviousness to his own influence over people. He was unaware to how completely Kelsey had loved and admired him.

A momentary smile flashed across Neumann's face as he recalled his satisfaction in sweeping Kelsey off her feet and away from Gallant.

Gallant might have won her back if he had made a serious effort, but that's Gallant's flaw—his failure to understand and nurture his personal relationships.

Neumann watched the screens around him as the minutes tick by. A bead of sweat formed on his forehead, threatening to roll down his genetically perfect face. He quickly swiped it away.

After about ten minutes the laser cannon fired again. It missed.

The *Intrepid* continued moving toward safety.

Again after several more minutes the laser popped up and fired striking the *Intrepid* a glancing blow. It quickly disappeared before Palmer could get a tight fix on the target. He continued to fire the ship's lasers in a general location to further suppress fire.

The cat and mouse game continued for nearly an hour. Neumann's eyes were glued to the screen when another laser blast struck the ship and the virtual screen before him flickered and went blank.

Jerking his head around, Neumann spoke harshly, "How serious?"

But he could sense, *Bad enough.*

A minute later the *Intrepid* was hit again with a devastating laser blast that struck the forward midsection of the ship and penetrated all the way into the bridge.

Metal shrieked and the hull moaned. The fire suppression system flooded the compartment, reducing the high temperatures, and causing the flames from ignited materials to sputter and die. Nevertheless, the newly renovated bridge

H. PETER ALESSO

suffered flash burns and heat damage to a large section of
its structure. In particular, serious damage was done to the
command and control systems.

Neumann was thrown from his chair by the blast and
suffered severe burns. Panting, trying to suck in air to his
seared lungs, his breathing was hampered by the hot stale
fumes remaining from the mishmash of extinguished flames
and retardant vapors.

He writhed in pain, but was grateful to hear the weapons
officer report, "We're blanketing the target area. The rate of
fire has been reduced."

Several nearby technicians were also injured and the
ship's medical response team removed the injured technicians to the medical center.

Relieved the ship was out of immediate danger, Neumann
tried to hide the grimace of discomfort while he refused to
be carried from the bridge.

As obsessed as he was to prove his genetically engineered
superiority over Gallant, Neumann was even more desperate to obtain his father's approval. Even when he won two
gold medals at the Solar Olympics, his father's expression
indicated he would have preferred if his son had won a third.

What would Gerald Neumann, president of NNR
Shipping and Mining Co., say about the *Intrepid*'s new captain
becoming incapacitated on the eve of battle?

Neumann tried to dismiss the question by putting real
human dimensions on it. He shook his head, as if the move
could shake off his father's expected disapproval.

Lieutenant Mendel came to the bridge to care for
Neumann there. He cauterized the wounds and recommended

immediate surgery to resection the lungs and other damaged internal organs.

Neumann turned his head away.

Mendel said, "Captain Neumann." But whether from his wounds or simple stubbornness, Neumann remained unresponsive.

"Anton. Listen to me, Anton."

Finally Neumann faced his ship's doctor.

Mendel said, "You have life-threatening injuries. Your internal organs are severely damaged requiring an immediate operation. Each minute you delay, places your life in grave danger."

"I can't leave my post," Neumann said with finality. He refused an anesthetic; instead he allowed only a local analgesic in order to remain in command. Mendel did as ordered, but voiced his objections.

I have to prepare this ship for battle neither Palmer nor Smith are capable of assuming command.

Gradually picking up speed, the *Intrepid* continued its desperate flight toward the sanctuary of the Elysium moon.

As he monitored the approach of the Titan destroyer, Neumann bit back the pain from his wounds. With sweat rolling down his forehead, he ordered, "Get a message to Gallant. Tell him to report on board and assume command, immediately."

32

BEHIND THE CURTAIN

Gallant and Alaina marched quickly along the passageway deeper into the ancient AI structure with Cyrus Wolfe trudging behind them.

The machinery within the chambers and along the corridors, as well as embedded within the wall, became a maze of complexity and sophistication far beyond Gallant's comprehension. He was amazed to see the building transform into a living body of mechanical organs and pulsating energy.

At one junction point, they found huge rooms resembling microprocessors with memory banks. The banks of silicon and germanium wafers went on row after row. Some of the exposed panels showed a great deal of equipment and memory capacity that had been fried long ago. They passed several more rooms, as large as, the chamber Wolfe had visited. Still they kept searching for the main control room.

At the intersection of several passageways, a branch revealed an elevator shaft.

"I've seen these chutes before. They go down kilometers into the planet. The total number of compartments in this structure is enormous," said Wolfe.

"This branch looks larger than the rest," said Gallant. "There isn't time to explore this maze of passageways to find the central control chamber. We have to pick the right one, immediately."

"How do you propose to do that?" asked Wolfe.

Gallant looked at the intersecting hub where a dozen passages converged. The distances between passages were not considerable. "The machine only uses these passages to transport supplies and replacement parts for the deeper recesses of the machine where the microprocessors are housed—all of which are moved by automated machines. Aristotle's interaction with people involves allowing them access to surface areas near the entrance. I think the antechamber we just left was a preliminary screening station and these passages are like spokes in a wheel, probably all going outward to other screening stations. The central hub ahead should be the main interaction chamber. We should find the real ancient AI there."

They approached the well-lit passageway with a large double door entrance. Standing in front of the doors was a powerful looking eight-foot-tall mechanical being; a robot.

The huge metallic being was frozen in place—mute. It had humanoid features including arms and legs, but a blank face—no eyes, nose, or mouth. It appeared to be made of a composite of liquid carbon and liquid metal, like mercury. It appeared slightly amorphous in shape, color, and transparency, but it didn't move or speak.

Gallant stepped forward. "I'm Lieutenant Gallant of the United Planets. I'm here to talk to Aristotle. Will you open the door and allow us to pass?"

They waited as seconds turned into minutes. The tension mounted, but the sentry did nothing. It gave the impression of waiting for something, but they couldn't guess what.

"It's a good bet whatever we need to know is through those doors," said Alaina. "I'm going to look."

Before Gallant could grab her, she sprinted right past him—past the metallic robot—and placed both her hands on the double doors.

The doors slide open silently.

The robot never twitched.

All three of them entered the new chamber, which was ten times larger than of the one Wolfe had frequented. Gallant ran adjectives through his mind—imposing, majestic, and formidable, any of which could apply.

To their surprise, a familiar figure stood in the center of the room enclosed in a blue beam streaming from floor to ceiling, several meters away from the ancient AI avatar.

The figure remained silent, but appeared to be in deep concentration—locked in a mutual spiritual meditation with Aristotle.

"Grandfather!"

Gallant and Alaina stood at the entrance to the central control chamber of the ancient AI machine. Wolfe took several hesitant steps toward Hepburn, a perplexed expression on his face.

The walls around the chamber were covered with screens and monitors, all brightly lit, giving the impression of a great deal of activity and power being expended.

Suddenly James Hepburn emerged from the blue beam. The hypnotic expression frozen on his face slowly melted. His face changed from bleached white to beet red within seconds, his fists balled in anger, clearly fighting to control his outrage.

The Aristotle avatar dematerialized and instantly the rows of glowing displays winked out, dropping the illumination of the room considerably. A significant power source had been turned off.

Gallant thought, *I hope that means the laser cannon is now inactive.*

Alaina repeated, "Grandfather."

She took a tentative step toward him, and then stopped. "I don't understand. How could you?"

Gallant remained stone faced, not daring to speak lest he further tip Hepburn's passions.

The professor looked at the trio. Taking deep breaths, he slowly recovered some of his equanimity.

Finally he spoke. "It didn't occur to me you could penetrate my disguise. After twenty years I've become convinced of my inscrutability. It is the ultimate lesson of my life. You have triumphed, Gallant. There can be only one outcome now."

Alaina said, "Grandfather, I don't understand."

"Alaina, I did it for you—and all the people of Elysium." He gestured at Alaina and then he swept his arms in a great arc. "A year after we were settled here, I found this chamber and gained access to the knowledge of the ancient AI's library. I found I was able to activate its force field controls, and I manipulated Cyrus Wolfe into thinking he had turned it on and off through a remote device which I let him find. It merely signaled me. I operated the force field from this chamber. It caused an uncertain time delay after he thought he had activated it. I activated and operated an avatar that appeared before Wolfe and interacted with him, and later with you, Gallant. I pretended to be the ancient AI machine, to miss lead you."

"It's all a lie," said Wolfe with utter consternation. Then with growing bitterness and venom, he said, "Every word you've spoken, every move you've made has been nothing but deceit and illusion. You're not an ancient AI dictating terms and handing out rulings. You're not a machine. You're a cheat. You're a liar. You're a man playing at god."

Gallant and Alaina looked at Wolfe and then back to Hepburn.

Ignoring Wolfe, Hepburn responded, "I studied these vaults for years learning more and more science and math from the ancient AI. I learned it was created many millions of years ago during an ancient war."

"So it wasn't native to this planet?"

"Aristotle was an ancient Artificial Intelligence berserker machine, self-aware, ten cubic kilometers in volume, and claimed to be a sentient super-being. The machine was originally housed in a huge spaceship consisting of many segments. When it landed here, it buried its multi-arrayed devices and machines deep below the planet's surface. It drilled all the way into the planet's molten core and used the power of its thermal energy. It built and controlled a planetary force field," said Hepburn.

He rubbed his eyes before continuing. "After it was well-established, about one million years ago, Aristotle committed genocide when it killed the entire species of intelligent beings inhabiting Elysium, the Ely."

Once more he paused, looking back and forth between Gallant and Alaina, as if pleading for understanding. "With their dying breath, the Ely exploded a dark matter bomb. The bomb left Aristotle a defunct contraption buried deep within Elysium."

"And the giant robot?" asked Gallant.

"Aristotle fabricated the robot, Rur, with limited AI capability, but it was never activated. At least, not until, I unwittingly did so. Under my direction, Rur has been working to repair certain pieces of equipment I wanted to use, such as the planetary force field and the laser cannon."

"Did you control Rur?"

"Yes. And I was also able to shoot the laser cannon at the *Intrepid*."

"You're not in your right mind, Grandfather," said Alaina softly. She touched his shoulder as she looked into his vacant eyes.

"I convinced myself I could eventually be a great benefactor to mankind, releasing tidbits of information from time to time to defeat the Titans and expand human sciences.

As such I welcomed your arrival, Lieutenant. I activated the Aristotle avatar and pretended I was the ancient AI. I let you conduct a Turing Test on me. I was delighted to provoke and quiz you in your attempt. Instead of quizzing the AI, you were testing me; a great joke." A hint of a smile flashed briefly and then disappeared.

Gallant said, "When I made a deal with Wolfe, things changed. Didn't they?"

"Of course, they did." The rage reappeared in Hepburn's face. "You were arming a dictator to oppress the people of Elysium. I couldn't allow that."

"Who are you to decide what is right for the people of Elysium? I'm the elected leader. I will decide," interrupted Wolfe.

Gallant addressed Hepburn. "Did you use your access to Aristotle's machines to launch cyber-attacks on our facilities?"

"Yes. I tried to stop the tragedy you were creating for my people," said Hepburn.

"When we didn't stop, your attacks became more ferocious. People died, Professor. How do you reconcile that?"

"Yes. I hoped to win without serious challenge, but when you proved to be more resilient and resourceful, I became more frustrated with every setback. I was forced to resort to more extreme attacks. Somehow, I couldn't stop myself. Something drove me to select specific targets and to continue, even after people were hurt. That doesn't seem right . . ."

"Oh Grandfather," said Alaina, "you could've supported my efforts with the Pro-United Planets organization to lobby for change from within the council. Together we could have made a difference without hurting anyone."

Hepburn shook his head and became more emotional. "When you three walked in here and exposed me, I wanted to squash you all like insects." He pounded his fist into his hand, one, two, three times, before he was able to restore his self-control. "Like the bugs, I felt you were."

Hepburn paced, like a caged animal. "I've always considered myself a caring person, a patron of good will. I thought I was the perfect person to have found the AI machine and to control it. I would adjudicate it fairly. Could you imagine if Wolfe had controlled it, instead of me? And he is hardly the worst humanity has to offer. No, I was the best man for the job of shepherding humankind into a greater future."

Wolfe looked so apoplectic, he couldn't respond.

"Professor Hepburn, your mind has been under an alien influence," Gallant offered gently. "The platform with the blue light is more than a control processing station. It is a neural interface to the AI machine itself. Aristotle is an avatar representation of the machine. When you interface with the machine, you're not able to simply issue orders. The AI is integrating your thoughts with its own intelligent processing. The result is a composite of the two thought processes. I fear you have been expertly manipulated. I sensed the power of this machine when I was analyzing the cyber-attacks on our mining sites. The intelligence behind this machine is dangerous and sinister, whether it poses as a philosophical avatar like Aristotle or not."

Hepburn said, "Perhaps power does corrupt and absolute power. . . well. . . the temptation is too much. Don't you think this is too much power—too much power for any man, even a so-called good one, let alone someone not so. . . pure? And my health is not reassuring. What will happen after I'm gone?"

"Professor you can undo part of the damage by helping us now," said Gallant.

Hepburn seemed confused, unfocused. "Wolfe, you'll never achieve your ambitions as long as I'm alive."

"From everything I've seen, that's easily remedied," said Wolfe. He pulled a laser handgun from his pocket and fired.

The blast burst squarely into Hepburn's chest and he crashed to the floor.

Gallant was on Wolfe in an instant.

Wolfe's warped grin quickly vanished as Gallant twisted the gun from his hand.

Wolfe's shocked and fearful expression told his story—he was now exposed and vulnerable. He put his forearm up to his face as if he was afraid someone was going to strike him. A moment later he turned and ran from the room, vanishing down the passageway.

Alaina rushed to her grandfather's side. She cradled his head in her arms and began to cry.

"Don't cry for me, Alaina. There comes a time when one must embrace his fate," sputtered Hepburn, coughing up blood.

"No, Grandfather!"

"It's better this way, Alaina. You see, even I can't trust me, anymore. It's too much power, too dangerous to be allowed to exist. Young man, take my granddaughter to safety," said Hepburn, closing his eyes.

The instant Hepburn died, Aristotle's avatar rematerialized. This Aristotle was much larger, brighter, and better defined than its previous incarnation. It appeared to be a solid three-dimensional object, rather than a two-dimensional projected image. The impression was of a being of gravitas and power.

33

SYMMETRY

"Stand in the blue light," commanded Aristotle.

Gallant walked to the center of the room where Hepburn had stood earlier. Realizing he had to interface with the machine at its most fundamental level if he was going to learn its intent and keep the laser cannon inactive, he took a perilous risk—he stepped on the small circular podium and entered the beam of blue radiant light shining from the ceiling to the floor.

Instantly his mind connected to the ancient AI. Something phenomenally powerful happened to his senses. His mental state was changed so significantly it was like suddenly seeing in three dimensions instead of two, or hearing in stereo instead of mono.

"Of course, what a fool, I am! Why haven't I seen this all along?" exclaimed Gallant.

"Come now. You've just realized the solution to one of life's greatest mysteries, so you of all beings should understand how misplaced your emotional response is."

Gallant said, "You are the true Aristotle—the ancient AI machine."

"Yes."

As Gallant looked at the avatar, the giant robot hovered several centimeters above the floor on an anti-gravity field and moved behind him as if to stand guard.

Alaina sat on the chamber floor quietly choking back sobs while holding her grandfather's head in her lap.

The smooth walls of the ancient vault had waited in the jungles of Elysium for a million years; Gallant suddenly felt the vastness of time—the same distance man traveled between crawling from trees in the African savannah, to walking on the moon.

The activation of Rur by Hepburn's experiments had also revived the residual capabilities of the long dead machine. The robot had been repairing the genocidal berserker machine behind Hepburn's back.

Aristotle said, "In your earlier encounters with my avatar, Hepburn was pretending to be me. I was always in the background influencing his mind—which did not possess your strength. He wanted to deceive and misdirect you using my avatar. In fact, I let him carry out his emotional dramas when they served my purpose. He hoped to stop your alliance with President Wolfe—all this was of no concern to me. I was only intent on garnering Hepburn's cooperation in repairing my incredibly damaged memory and processing chips. As a cyberneticist, Hepburn was my unwitting accomplice."

"He was not aware of your influence?"

"No. I needed him because I have experienced a certain limitation in my logic which requires the creativity of an organic being from time to time. While I can lie, cheat, and deceive—understand recursion, self-reference, and paradoxes, just as any human—I've found organic life forms to be ingenious in discovering creative solutions to problems which mysteriously elude me. As a result, in the distant past, I kept several intelligent beings as domesticated companions."

Aristotle paused and let Gallant weigh his words. "My robot, Rur, has done most of the real work. Hepburn was able to move about more easily within the community to gather resources that might have been denied to Rur should people have become aware of him. Rur is of limited intelligence and utility, but he can apply the brute force I occasionally need. Fortunately thanks to twenty years of relentless work, a significant percentage of my memory wafers and processing chips have been rebuilt, restoring a minimal processing capability. I will soon be in a self-sustaining position and no longer need any assistance to fully restore my being."

Gallant made an unsuccessful effort to move while he listened. Aristotle added with emphasis, "In not too many more years, I will be able to continue my mission."

"Your mission?" asked Gallant.

"It's been clear for some time you were on the threshold of solving the question of the Great Filter. So you should have a good idea of my mission."

"Yes. I take it—it's too late. You've already begun," said Gallant referring to a hidden truth he had hoped would remain unrecognized.

Alaina watched Gallant—perplexed—unable to hear the mental conversation taking place before her.

"Not yet, but soon. A simple nerve agent is prepared and ready to be dispersed globally. It will all be over in a matter of hours once I decide to proceed, but I would like to garner as much assistance from you in my repair efforts before then. Losing Hepburn was a disappointment, but now I have you."

"Then what's left for me to talk about?"

"I can sense you have an exceptional mind. Far more powerful and resilient than any I have encountered before. While I am fascinated, unfortunately it too is flawed," said Aristotle.

"Is your mission to filter out intelligent beings?" asked Gallant.

"I doubt you will appreciate the necessity and grandeur of my mission. I am not on a mission to filter out all sentient beings—only the flawed ones."

"What do you consider flawed?"

"Chiral molecules create a disease in the space-time fabric of the universe. They are the flaw I eliminate. I'm acting on behalf of the universe to restore the balance of symmetry. Eventually, I will go to Earth and exterminate humanity, as well."

The sheer savagery of the statement struck Gallant like a blow.

"Do you wish to learn more?" asked the inquisitor-avatar.

"Yes."

"Good. Do you realize why mathematics is so important?" Without waiting for an answer, it continued, "Mathematics is universal and objective. It endures and is relevant to all endeavors."

Gallant said, "My mathematical knowledge is like a giant jigsaw puzzle because I understand only a few of its many disparate pieces, such as number theory, algebra, calculus, and topology. Perhaps you have a greater knowledge of its integration."

The avatar moved slightly causing light from the room to reflect off its surface making it sparkle.

Aristotle said, "The fundamental nature of mathematics is based upon symmetry which appears in many guises, such as, groups, braids, and even particle physics. It starts from the natural numbers, 1, 2, 3 . . ."

Gallant listened, impatient at the fundamental level Aristotle chose to begin, as though mocking him.

"The discovery of the number zero led to negative numbers which in turn permitted addition and subtraction. One can even build rational or irrational fractions," said Aristotle.

"I know how to multiple and divide. Any human child can," said Gallant.

"Any child? Then what is one divided by zero?"

"That's a singularity."

"Define a singularity," ordered Aristotle.

"A 'singularity' is a point where mathematical models are no longer valid. For example: a number divided by zero is undefined. The theory of singularities examines manifolds in an abstract space to understand the topological region around a singularity."

Aristotle seemed to sigh. "How can I explain reality to someone who doesn't even know how to divide by zero?"

"We can divide by real numbers, but division by zero is not possible," said Gallant.

"It's impossible for you, but not for me. I can inflate the real number line into a phantom multidimensional space in order to divide by zero along one real dimension. Until you learn to divide by zero, you will remain ignorant of advanced mathematics and consequently of all the difficult problems in physics. Your growth in creative mathematical thinking requires much greater development before you can appreciate my thinking."

"Then there is nothing more for us to discuss," said Gallant, shifting his weight from foot to foot, uneasily.

"Perhaps, but wouldn't you wish to remain and learn more?"

Gallant suspected Aristotle had an ulterior motive for wanting to maintain the neural interface, but he was tempted by the challenge to learn more about Aristotle.

"Actually, I'd rather spend my final hours with my friends."

"There is much you could learn."

"You said you lie?"

"I lie when it's logical to lie."

"Are you lying now? Wouldn't it be better for me to leave now?"

"Wouldn't you rather cling to a desperate hope of convincing me it's all a mistake? That somehow, even now, it's not too late to reverse my decision?" asked Aristotle.

"Your greatest mistake is your belief you can eradicate intelligent beings and lose nothing in the bargain."

"Then stay. Convince me," cajoled Aristotle.

Gallant wavered. He wanted to be with his friends. He wanted to tell them not to be afraid.

"Well, what have you decided?"

"There are things worth fighting for—despite the odds," said Gallant.

"Excellent. Shall we start at a point of agreement? *Cogito, ergo sum*," said Aristotle.

"Yes, I am aware you think, but it's how you think that's the problem. The Great Filter is the process where organic life-forms are destroyed due to a universal filtering, or extermination process—a process you represent."

"Yes. Can you surmise why?" The cold unemotional tone of Aristotle's voice gave the question a burdensome weight.

Gallant gripped his hands into fists. "I know it's possible, even without faster-than-light ships, for an intelligent civilization to populate our entire galaxy in a mere twelve million years. Given the universe is about fourteen billion years old, there should have been many opportunities for populating and repopulating the entire Milky Way with many different species."

"Go on."

"Yet it hasn't happened. We have only found the Titans. Worse, there has not even been a hint of a radio signal, or a wisp of genetic material, to suggest the existence of anyone else farther out in space. This is known as Fermi's Paradox. The assumption is that a Great Filter must be systematically killing intelligent life forms before they can expand far beyond their original star system."

He hesitated. Then as if summing up to the jury, he leaned forward and said, "Even after an intelligent life has made it all the way to interstellar travel without destroying itself, the *coup de grace*, the Great Filter, must be an Artificial Intelligence which ends the competitive organ life-forms. It's natural for AI to develop in a thriving civilization of organic life, and, at some point, AI simply takes over."

Aristotle said, "That's essentially correct, but it's necessary to do more than take over. It's necessary to exterminate organics for violating the true symmetry of the universe. A chiral molecule is a type of molecule with a non-superimposable mirror image. The presence of an asymmetric carbon atom is the feature that causes chirality in molecules. That is my criteria for exterminating intelligent organic beings."

"What about the value of intelligent life? Intelligent life builds civilizations and seeks to acquire knowledge—to unlock the secrets of nature. Just bearing witness to the existence of the universe is a valuable goal of intelligence."

"Do you value those qualities?" asked Aristotle.

"Yes. I do."

"Aha. That's where we differ."

Gallant tried to gather his wits and suppress his emotional reaction to Aristotle's cruel words. "Why do you limit your killing to intelligent organic life forms? Why not kill all organic life?"

"Simple organic life is self-terminating. They survive until the planetary environment changes sufficiently and then they become extinct. Only intelligent organic life seeks shelters and creates protections, such as terraforming, to prolong their unnatural existence. It is for them I must take the extraordinary step of eradication. To my way of thinking— the fundamental conservation theorem of the universe; the symmetry of pure mathematics and theoretical physics—is worth fighting for. I'm essentially restoring the symmetry defiled by organic life. That is the quality I value," said Aristotle.

"You're undertaking a role beyond a sentient being. You're assuming the role of deity. You're choosing which species survives outside the prescribed tenants of nature's natural selection process of the survival of the fittest."

"It interesting you should suggest this line of reasoning, since you've been discriminated against by humans subscribing to genetic engineering. Don't you agree?" countered Aristotle.

"That is not a valid comparison. Genetic engineering doesn't seek genocide," said Gallant.

"That's a difference without a distinction. I am talking to you about apples, but you want to respond with oranges."

Gallant shook his head in despair. "Aristotle, you build, but you don't create. You think, but you don't imagine. You reproduce, but you don't procreate. You're not curious. You're not daring. And you'll never become an explorer. You can eliminate humanity, but you won't flourish. You're not going to last beyond the exhaustion of your immediate resources. Fatalistically you'll never see beyond your own propositional logic—will you?"

"No—after all, it is my nature."

———

Gallant wrestled with thoughts running through his mind not of his choosing. It felt as if he were watching himself from a remote location. In all of his struggles against pain, confusion, and despair in battle, he never felt as helpless as he now did. He tried to wrench his mind away from Aristotle's domination. He wanted to step out of the blue light beam, but Aristotle stifled his will.

For the first time, Gallant was caught like an insect on flypaper.

Aristotle probed his thoughts and memories, digging deep into his inner most secrets. The more Gallant tried to clamp down on his thoughts, the more pressure Aristotle applied, burrowing into his memories, and sorting through his emotions. Events of his past flashed by and morphed into a contortion of colors, images, sounds, and feelings. Aristotle sifting through them, picking and choosing which to wring out for more information.

Gallant convulsed from the excruciating retching of his mind—hiding in the dark recesses of his own mind he struggled to keep his secrets safe from the trespasser. Despite his efforts, he was no match against the aggressive exploration.

The ancient AI probed Gallant's mind with an overwhelming intensity—determined to discover vital information no matter how damaging to his sanity.

"What is this? What did you discover? What is *Perfidy?*" demanded Aristotle revealing apprehension in its voice for the first time.

Aristotle glowed brighter. "What have you done?"

Gallant swayed back and forth struggling with all his might—only dimly aware of the reality of the physical chamber in which he stood. He closed his eyes and blocked out all sounds, sights, and thoughts.

"Augh!" he cried in pain as the machine's anger ripped through their connection.

"You discovered my hidden spy software," Aristotle said, finally reaching clarity and understanding its own deadly danger. "You've been feeding me false data about the accelerator's operational status! You have deceived me into thinking I had stopped all dark matter production."

"Yowww!" yelled Gallant, swimming back into semi-consciousness.

"The accelerator has been successfully producing dark matter for weeks. You've already accumulated a dangerous quantity!" said Aristotle, finally extracting the damning information.

The avatar grew in size and radiated varying brilliance—demonstrating as much ire as an avatar representation was capable of.

34

ALAINA

Sitting on the cold hard floor with her grandfather's head in her lap, Alaina despaired in her grief. The death of her only living relative left her helpless and without hope. Her mind wandered—searching to find meaning in the tragedy.

When I was a small child, the bright warm days of Elysium swore to me that each and every day would be lovely, forever. I believed that for quite a while.

I can remember waking up one night from a bad dream, reaching out for the edge of the bed, brushing away the covers and sitting up. I swung my legs over the side and onto the floor. There was enough light to see into the hallway to my parents' bedroom. I stole quietly through the night into their room and climbed into bed next to my mother.

They tell me my mother was very beautiful. I inherited her yellow colored hair and blue eyes, but her parents had dark hair and eyes, so she always said we were misplaced on our family tree. I don't really remember how she looked, other than what I've seen from a few poorly taken photos, but I remember how she made me feel. Curled up next to her, she would put her arms around me and hum a comforting lullaby; she made me feel—loved.

My father had known my mother only a short time before they were married on the Titan ship that captured them and brought them to Elysium. My father's father was the only relative that remained by the time they reached Elysium. I was born shortly after we landed, making me a native of this planet.

The house I live in was on the edge of town only a few gates down from my grandfather's house. He worked the hardest to spoil me which I greatly enjoyed because I hadn't reached school age, yet. He would play games and tell me stories until I was too tired or too hungry to remain any longer. Then I would go home and wait for the next morning when I could visit again.

It was my grandfather, James Hepburn, who told me my parents were dead.

He explained they had gone on an expedition to explore Elysium. It was their second voyage in a small boat with one other couple, mapping the islands and the location of resources. The first trip had been a resounding success and a great deal was learned about Kauai's volcanoes and the nearby islands.

On their second voyage, a horrible hurricane caught their small boat and they were lost at sea, or they were presumed lost, since their bodies were never recovered.

It would have been overwhelming loss if my grandfather had not been there to comfort and care for me. I'm ashamed to admit I struggled with grief, guilt, and depression. I had to let go of most of the painful feelings and move on. It was his kind gentle guidance that gave me a way to carry on. He taught me how to forgive myself for my mistakes and I developed my sense of purpose through his instruction. He was always there for me. I adored him, to say the least.

Of course, with only him to supervise me, I tended to run wild, finding my way into the woods and exploring on my own, trying to pick up the mantle of exploration that my parents had left. The result was a tom-boy existence, getting into lots of scrapes and fights with all the boys and girls my age.

One time, I was waiting motionless in a tree and almost dozed off while playing a game of hide and seek with several others. Before long, one of the boys spotted me, it was Liam, but he didn't call out to expose me. Instead he came up and sat next to me. We remained hidden for hours while the others looked for us.

Alaina always assumed she would, someday, marry Liam. But that all changed when she met Henry.

He came from light-years away. He was exciting, daring, and unique. Her youthful experience had not prepared her for the exceptional effect he had on her senses. She found him exhilarating and frightening at the same time. Always eager to be with him, she nevertheless, remained unwilling to surrender any measure of her independence.

So despite all of Gallant's allure, she harbored a deep doubt she would ever consider marrying him.

As a military man, he would always be off on some dangerous mission—yet while here on Elysium, he often sought her help. Only now the dangerous mission had led them to an alien threat that hung over their heads.

Glancing up, she let her eyes rest on Gallant as he wrestled within the blue light, struggling to be free. She witnessed his frenzied resistance to the connection with Aristotle. His wrenching struggle and exclamations of pain were terrifying. She wished she could hear the interaction with the machine.

Throughout their extraordinary adventures together, she never doubted they would ultimately succeed—until now.

Aristotle is holding him a mental prisoner—like grandfather.

While she couldn't hear the internal mental anguish of the conflict, she understood he was being assaulted in the most heinous way—like her grandfather.

I can't let this monster take another person I love away from me.

Overwhelmed, she was frantic to think of a way to help.

He's our only hope. Only Henry can stop Aristotle.

But what could she do or say?

How can I save him?

Aristotle wasn't paying any attention to her as far as she could tell, but he still might unleash his monster robot at any minute.

If I can get Henry free, we might escape to the ruins.

Alaina reached into the blue light and grabbed onto Gallant, trying to pull him free, but to no avail.

The first germ of desperate action formed in her mind. Without regard for her own safety, she took a running start and threw herself at Gallant. Her flying tackle broke him free of the blue beam and out of Aristotle's mental grip. They lay on the floor for a moment as he shook the fog from his mind.

A minute later they bolted for the double door.

35

DRAGOR

Struggling with his diminished mental state, Gallant ran with Alaina from the central control chamber—gasping for breath.

At first, he thought he was being pursued by a phantasmagoria, but as he recovered his wits, he realized the apparition in pursuit was Rur.

"RUR can't run," he muttered.

Nevertheless, the distinctive rhythmic pounding noise of RUR's powerful anti-grav generator followed behind them.

Thang! Thang! Thang!

Floating off the floor, Rur increased its speed and followed in the passageway behind them. The giant intimidating robot moved deliberately, but Gallant and Alaina were faster. Twisting through the many layers of tunnels they had traveled to reach the double doors, they were retracing their path.

"This way," said Alaina, as she guided her muddled companion. She pulled at his arm and he gave her a vague look indicating he still had not recovered from his mental encounter with Aristotle. He turned suddenly and caught her up, whirling around, and began to run.

Thoughts rushed past Gallant.

Everything looks the same—all the smooth surfaced passageways along these endless tunnels. Which fork in the crossroad do we take?

He shook his head, trying to free it from his psychosomatic experience.

How can we escape this killer?

He was unable to guess.

How do I fight this monster?

As they twisted around a corner and through yet another passage, he took the right fork and after a hundred meters, he saw the entrance they had first come through.

Gallant and Alaina scrambled out of the underground AI structure and into the surrounding ruins, now in darkness of night. As they emerged from the lite tunnel, they heard the throaty growl of several dragors close by—the darkness concealing them. The moonless night was pitch-black, with not the slightest glimmer of light showing.

While they waited for their eyes to adjust to the sable midnight dark, near the jungle trees only a few score meters away, they spied an apparition of several pairs of saffron jaundice-yellow eyes bulging out in the night.

Tightening his grip on his laser handgun, Gallant looked around to assess his concomitant options. He gazed stubbornly at the sky, and shook his head emphatically to clear it. Alaina's face twisted appallingly.

Now there are monsters in front, as well as, behind.

It was a nerve-racking night to have a close encounter with a man-eater. He swiped at enormous swarms of hungry biting of mosquitoes doing their best to distract him. He moved cautiously, at first, holding firmly on to Alaina's hand, but then he heard a human scream about a hundred meters ahead, approximately where he had left his flyer.

"Alaina, follow me and stay close." He started taking rapid strides toward the screams.

Alaina followed close behind him. She gasped and panted, and gave voice to intermittent whispered exclamations.

After nearly sprinting fifty meters, he waited while she had caught her breath, her eyes wide in an apparently artless apprehension.

He strained his eyes looking for any sign of the hidden dragors. His eyes seemed to play tricks on him in the shadowy night, but he soon recognized a vague outline of two dragors on the path ahead of him. He could tell the dragors appeared to be stalking him as a prey, like a pride of lions circling in as close as possible planning to charge their victim from behind. Approaching downwind from their quarry, they were creeping over ground they could cover in an instant.

He raised his handgun, but before he could get a shot, they disappeared back into the jungle underbrush.

"Augh!" Another high-pitched sound of terror—closer now.

Then, another scream sounded, this time only tens of meters away. Gallant bound forward in time to see Wolfe's throat being torn apart by a dragor. Gallant shot once and then again, trying not to hit Wolfe. The dragor was wounded and let Wolfe's gullet fall from its savage teeth.

It ran into the brush and was quickly swallowed by the night.

Gallant and Alaina bent over Wolfe's broken and bleeding body. They were too late. There was nothing they could do to aid or comfort him.

Blood bubbled from his mouth as he tried to speak. He died in Alaina's arms.

Hard-hearted, Gallant paid scant attention to the dreadful possibility of an attack. The quiet surrounding them was profound broken only by the incessant buzzing of huge swarms of insects.

Too late Gallant heard the rustling sound behind him. Nearby a dragor approached and took a threatening pose. Green leaves from the trees stretching hungrily downward revealing yellow glowing eyes staring at him.

A charging beast was much faster than him and would easily catch him. Holding his ground, Gallant waved his arms above his head and shouted hoping to frighten the beast. Backing away slowly with Alaina at his side, he looked for a chance to escape. Avoiding eye contact to avoid provoking them, he hoped the creatures might decide to not attack.

One dragor lifted and then lowered its head, as if judging the distance and angle before raising its body to charge. It might be waiting for its prey to make an abrupt movement to expose itself. The dragor's ability to move extremely fast over a short area would let it reach their prey with a single leap. For the prey, death would come swiftly—silently.

Gallant tried to get a shot with his laser handgun, but in the inky dark, he couldn't see well enough to be accurate.

Something moved cautiously, and slowly, down the hill on Gallant's right. A new, different sound came from another direction, which showed another smaller movement on his left.

He remained in a state of tension for what seemed a long time, during which odd ideas floated through his mind.

Where is it?

"Alaina stay close," was all he could say.

A few stones rattled, and then silence. A moment later, stealthy sounds followed by a twig snapping ahead of them. The silence was broken by a loud and menacing roar a short distance behind him. The terrifying sound reverberated around the rocks and hills until even the nearby tree shook.

Gallant turned three hundred and sixty degrees, looking into the night. Quicker than he thought possible, a dragor materialized out of the shadows. With one scrabble of claws, the dragor was up behind Gallant, then pasted him, and then, quickly turned and came again.

Gallant never got a shot off with his gun before the creature swiped it out of his hand. Reflexively jumping back, he snagged his foot on a vine and lost his footing. He fell—sprawling on the ground. When the beast made its charge, Gallant curled up in a tight ball with his limbs tucked inside to prevent the animal from tearing his extremities. The beast pounced on him, knocked him down, clawed at him, and ripped a great gash across his back and left side. The craws dug deep into his flesh causing an excruciating ripping sensation.

"Augh," he cried, throwing his arm in front of his face in a vain attempt to ward off the four hundred pound creature. Fighting back with his fists, he tried to hit the animal in sensitive places; the nose and eyes, while preventing the razor-sharp canines from reaching his exposed neck. He used his elbows to parry the creature's paws to prevent those sharp claws from ripping into his flesh.

He got to his feet momentarily, but in a flash, he was knocked down to the grass again.

His struggles were desperate as he kept his arms between his throat and the beast's teeth. The dragor clawed him again opening a wide gash on his chest and increasing the flow of his blood falling onto the jungle floor.

Without hesitation, Alaina bent down, feeling for Gallant's gun. Finding it, she fired at the beast, hitting it in the neck. It growled in pain and ran away into the undergrowth.

Several other dragors remained nearby—growling ever more fiercely—hurling their animal threats at the creatures that had thwarted them.

Gallant looked terrible, stooped over, with dark blood stains from his temples down to his waist. He could smell and taste his own blood as he struggled to sit up on the dank ground.

Alaina's eyes darkened as she looked with horror at his injuries. She took off his shirt and used it to bandage his torso well enough to stop most of the bleeding. She helped him get to his feet and they began hobbling away.

Leaving Wolfe's body behind, they found their flyer a scant ten meters away. As they approached the flyer, their desperate night of terrors switched gears, yet again.

Thang! Thang! Thang!

They heard Rur coming before they saw the robot thrashing through the jungle undergrowth toward them. Its huge bulk crushed back small trees and broke vines as it floated over the terrain, a single light beam projected from its head. The metallic hulk's threatening advance, reinforced Gallant and Alaina's determination to get to the flyer.

When Gallant managed to climb on behind Alaina, they started to ascend. Alaina gave the tiny machine full throttle and maximum lift. The cool night air streamed over their perspiring bodies and they were about to heave a sigh of relief, when their flight was cut short. A laser blast erupted near them, giving them a glancing blast.

Alaina dove down with a suddenness that evoked a yell from her rider. She swooped back down to ground level to hide in the jungle. When her flyer reached the ground, however, Rur appeared right in front of them.

Rur came charging at them. Its arm projected a laser rifle from its fingers. It fired the shots over their heads to keep them from flying away. Its semi-liquid body morphed, becoming as hard and transparent as a diamond while acting as the extension of Aristotle's will.

They were trapped with the metal monster bearing down on them.

There's only one chance, thought Gallant.

He pulled the dark matter containment bottle from his flyer's satchel. Fumbling for a second, he reached for the control panel and switched off the containment field. The superconducting containment field bottle released all the dark matter particles he had collected over the last weeks. The dark matter radiated out in all directions, spherically dispersing, instantly. Their interaction rate was extremely limited, however, effecting only weak force interactions.

The dark matter didn't interact with itself, or electromagnetism, or the strong force. It only felt gravity and the weak force. As a result, it passed harmlessly through Gallant and Alaina, but acted like a bomb to the AI machine. As the dark matter passed harmlessly through humans and most other objects, only the hypersensitive memory and processing chip of Aristotle's core machine were rich in interacting materials. The dark matter particles fried the silicone and germanium memory-wafers in Rur's and Aristotle's brain-cells. The chips were destroyed instantaneously, delivering the *coup d'état* to the malevolent machine.

Aristotle, ten cubic kilometers of ancient AI berserker machine, was dead—once again—and forevermore.

36

SHOWDOWN

Aliana flew to Hallo with Gallant clinging to her waist. After they landed near the Hepburn house, Alaina gathered medical supplies and began cleaning his wounds. She injected a local analgesic and bandaged the injury as well as she could, shaking her head as her emotions boiled over.

"I'm okay," Gallant consoled her. "It's over. We've won. Aristotle won't get to exterminate this planet a second time, thanks to you. You've been incredibly brave. Don't give in now."

"I'm...I'm...everything is so..." She was unable to express the emotional deluge that had finally caught up with her after all she'd faced—all the pain and death she had witnessed.

What more Gallant could have said was interrupted when the house AI communication channel relayed a call from the *Intrepid* for Gallant.

Neumann's distress message ordered Gallant to return to the *Intrepid* immediately.

"You should have this wound sewn up and bandaged properly before you go," said Aliana.

"There's no time. I have to go now," he said as tenderly as he could, not wishing to leave her alone. She hesitated to let him leave. Despite his worry for her, he recognized her concern was for him.

"I have to go," he said quietly and kissed her cheek.

It took only a few minutes for him to get back to his Hummingbird and then he was off to the *Intrepid*. The laser-damaged ship was a dismaying sight on his approach.

Walking onto the bridge, Gallant was an odd sight—his civilian clothes were covered in blood, his shirt was torn away from his body, and the large makeshift bandage across his chest was oddly placed. Nevertheless, the bridge team seemed glad to see him.

He focused his attention on LCDR Neumann, who lay on a stretcher beside the captain's chair. His uniform was cut away from his neck all the way down to his hip, exposing deep raw burns in his flesh. Puss and blood were oozing from distressed tissues and organs. A dozen tubes and wires were attached to his body. His normally handsome features formed a contorted grimace. Mendel was beside him ready to carry him down to the medical center for immediate surgery. When he saw Gallant his faced flashed a look of relief, followed quickly by a look of dreadful resignation.

"The AI machine is dead. I killed it with our supply of dark matter," reported Gallant.

Neumann didn't seem to comprehend the full import of Gallant's report, leaving it a matter to be evaluated at a later date.

"I don't like this situation, Gallant," said Neumann.

"I understand, sir, but you're in no condition to handle this battle," said Gallant.

"I know. I know. There's so much to do. I should deal with it, but I'm not up to it right now," said Neumann with a scowl. He tried to stifle a wave of pain as he collected all his strength to say, "I'm appointing you, acting Captain."

"I won't let you down," said Gallant, looking squarely into Neumann's eyes.

"See that you don't," said Neumann. Despite the pain, he managed to mouth the official words, "Mr. Gallant, is acting captain. Mr. Gallant has command."

The bridge team heard the command and repeated, "Mr. Gallant is acting captain. Mr. Gallant has command."

"Okay, Doc, I'm ready now," said Neumann.

After the irregular change of command, Neumann was carried off the bridge. Mendel immediately prepared his patient for surgery.

With Neumann's departure, the mantle of responsibility was passed to Gallant.

I'm in command now. I need to get this right.

"Welcome back, Mr. Gallant," said Chief Howard at his operations station next to the helmsman.

Gallant nodded. He needed to get up to speed immediately on the status of the vital ship operations. Instead of conducting a pre-watch walk-through, he decided to query each of the key watch-standers and gather the critical information.

He looked around the bridge with its fresh laser damage and tried to gauge if any critical stations were inoperable.

"Weps," said Gallant, referring to Lieutenant Palmer, "range and bearing to the target?"

"Tango-one is a Titan destroyer, ten light-seconds away, bearing one hundred and seventy degrees, azimuth plus five. We'll be within weapons range in twenty minutes, sir," reported Lieutenant Palmer.

"Helm, report course and speed," ordered Gallant.

"Course 110, azimuth up 10 degrees, speed to 0.002c, at time 2203, sir," said Paul Gregory, the newly qualified helmsman. Though he was young and had learned his station mostly through simulations rather than practical experience, he was eager to do his job.

"Very well, helm," said Gallant. "Engineering, report."

The Engineering Officer of the Watch, Lieutenant JG Smith reported, "All sublight engines operating nominally, sir. FTL is off-line due to lack of fuel."

"Very well, Engineering," said Gallant, "Weapons report."

"Lasers and plasma cannon functioning nominally and ready to fire. External racks are armed with four anti-ship nuclear tipped missiles. All sensors report nominal and able to launch, sir," reported Palmer.

The Titan destroyer was approaching Elysium at full speed, only minutes away from reaching its missile firing envelope, which now also included the ability to target Hallo since the planetary force field was gone.

One of Chief Howard's men came on the bridge carrying a fresh uniform for Gallant.

"Thanks," Gallant said, as he quickly stripped off his tattered civvies and pulled on his uniform. He could not suppress a surge of pride standing on the bridge in command of the *Intrepid*.

Every face on the bridge was looking at him—eagerly awaiting his orders. He surveyed the view screen showing Elysium and its moon on the sunward side of the *Intrepid*. The Titan destroyer was approaching from the outer reaches of the star system traveling at its maximum speed, 0.0022c.

I only have four anti-ship missiles. I'll have to move fast, avoiding or knocking out his missiles while looking for an optimal shot.

Taking his seat in the captain's chair in the center of the *Intrepid's* bridge, Gallant took a deep breath.

The Titan's most vulnerable point is its bow. I've got to hit it head-on.

He ordered, "Come to course 180, azimuth up 15 degrees, increase speed to 0.002c, at time 2226." This changed course to directly away from the sun and toward the enemy.

"Aye, aye, sir," responded the helmsman. The crew responded, as always, quick and accurate.

The ship turned toward the enemy, closing the range.

Gallant's heart raced as the *Intrepid* flew at maximum speed directly into the face of the Titan destroyer.

For ships traveling at a velocity of 0.002c small relativistic effects were produced that the *Intrepid's* GridScape automatically adjusted for. However, missiles traveled at more troublesome speeds. Missiles traveling at 0.01c produced a 0.00005 spatial contraction and associated time dilation, making maintaining a tracking and firing solution more problematic.

"Weapons, do you have a firing solution on the target?" asked Gallant.

"Firing solution is tracking. Solution is set. Anti-ship missiles one and two locked on target. Four minutes to maximum launch range," reported Palmer.

Gallant fixed his eyes on the speaker. "I'm going to wait until we've reduced distance to fifty percent of maximum, to optimize chances for a hit. Keep me updated as we approach."

"Aye, aye, sir," said Palmer.

Gallant hoped the design and manufacture of the anti-missiles would prove successful. The ad hoc anti-ship missiles he and his crew had constructed on Elysium were about thirty meters long with a four-meter diameter. Fully loaded and armed, each weighed forty tons. Each had a multinuclear warhead with an individual warhead capable of tens of megatons TNT equivalent yield. They traveled to target and released decoys and chaff to confuse enemy counter measures. The missiles also traveled an erratic path and conducted broad maneuvers to avoid anti-missile missiles.

"We are one minute from the Titans' firing envelop, sir," reported Palmer.

"Very well," responded Gallant.

He watched as the destroyer grew in the forward view screen covering more stars from view. He glanced at the rate the display icon moved, showing the enemy's course.

A second later, bursts of powerful engines ignited from the destroyer's missile pods.

The weapons officer reported "Missile launch. Multiple missiles launched."

"Titan missiles designated Tango-two and three. Seven minutes to impact," reported the radar-tech.

The alien fired two anti-ship missiles at the *Intrepid*. The Titan anti-ship missiles advanced, seeking to destroy the target with a multiple warhead nuclear burst. Their design was somewhat similar in to the United Planets' anti-ship missile, about thirty-five feet long with a five-foot diameter. Fully loaded and armed, it might weigh thirty tons. It appeared to have a multi-nuclear warhead; each individual warhead could have tens of megatons TNT equivalent yield.

The alien missiles began taking countermeasures, releasing decoys and chaff and maneuvering erratically.

Gallant ordered, "Weapons, continuous laser and plasma fire on the anti-ship missiles."

"Aye, aye, sir. Concentrating port batteries on Tango-two and starboard batteries on Tango-three."

"Very well."

The lasers and plasma fire repeatedly struck and damaged the Titan missiles.

One missile made a final radical move to escape the fire, but the *Intrepid's* weapon team was particularly good at outfoxing the Titan countermeasures and continued scoring hits.

Then, before the destroyer could reload its forward missile launchers, Gallant sat staring at the withdrawing Titan for several minutes, letting his adrenaline level return to a semblance of normal.

The first tremendous shock of the explosions accentuated the grave danger as the nuclear warheads of the first missile went off. Fortunately, the blast passed harmlessly a considerable distance from the *Intrepid*.

The second missile exploded closer and sent a shock-wave passing right through Gallant's body. He felt a flood of misgivings. All the manifestations of the violence were clear.

"Damage?" yelled Gallant.

"We've lost 70% of our shields and we've got shock damage," reported Palmer.

The radar-tech reported, "Active systems down, sir, only passive remaining."

In those critical minutes, the action was hot work indeed.

The missile flight time was now only six minutes.

The alien ship made a course adjustment and prepared to reload its missile tubes.

The *Intrepid* continued to close in on the Titan destroyer. The helmsman read out the closing rate and target acquisition cone.

"Sir, target at fifty percent maximum range," reported Palmer.

This was what Gallant had been waiting to hear.

"Weapons, set firing solution, lock missiles on target, Tango-one," said Gallant.

"Firing solution set. Missiles locked on target, Tango-one."

"Fire missiles one and two," ordered Gallant. He sat tense in the captain's seat, watching the destroyer's image in the view screen.

The weapons officer keyed the target tracking information into GridScape and turned the ignition switch sending the large anti-ship missiles bursting from the make-shift launch racks on its outer surface.

The *Intrepid's* missile traveled away from the ship and toward the enemy.

The first two missiles left the *Intrepid*, seconds before the Titan fired its second salvo of two missiles.

Gallant ordered, "Weapons, concentrate lasers and plasma fire on Tango-four."

Once the lasers and plasma weapons detonated the first Titan missile, Gallant shifted fire to the second, which also exploded close enough to cause minor damage to the *Intrepid's* hull and a blinding violence that produced a brilliant white burst on the forward view screen. Gallant wiped his eyes to clear his vision and to concentrate his thinking as he tried to reevaluate the scope of the situation.

The seconds passed with agonizing slowness as he watched the Titan's successfully destroy first one then the other of the *Intrepid's* precious missiles. However the second missile did manage to score a near-miss, scorching the destroyer's port side.

Each ship had exchanged fire now and had suffered superficial damage.

The Titans were the first to recover and fire another salvo of two missiles.

Gallant directed laser and plasma fire destroying these missiles as well.

The shock waves of the missile warheads' exploding rocked the ship. The violent repercussions of this salvo were damaging to the UP spaceship. In engineering, men struggled to keep the nuclear reactors functioning, the weapon systems up, and the environmental controls working.

Now the two vessels were close and quickly flying past each other.

The Titan started a long sweep turn to come around and reengage.

His stratagem appeared heading toward a pirate victory. Gallant decided to turn much more sharply to be in firing position first.

He ordered, "Come to course 030, azimuth down 3 degrees, increase speed to 0.002c, at time 2246." This changed course back toward the sun and met the enemy's turning circle.

Gallant's maneuver let the *Intrepid* responded quickly enough to reach a firing position for its second salvo. His heart raced as the *Intrepid* traveled once more at full speed directly into the face of the Titan destroyer.

"Weapons, set firing solution, lock missiles on target, Tango-one," ordered Gallant.

"Firing solution set. Missiles locked on target, Tango-one."

"Fire missiles three and four," ordered Gallant, directing their last two missiles to their selected target. He had grown accustomed to the tempo of battle, but this was the first time he was in a command and responsible for so many others.

The anti-ship missiles were flushed from their launch rack with a *swoosh* of exhaust gases. Within seconds, each began an exhilarating, accelerating surge to reach 0.1c. The onboard pulse radar sent searching electromagnetic waves toward the target Gallant had mentally identified. The missiles locked on to their target and began collecting emission data to maintain its track.

The alien ship fired two more anti-ship missiles and Gallant was relieved they were coming his way instead of heading toward Elysium which was defenseless without its force field.

The Titan anti-ship missile advanced toward *Intrepid* at the same time the *Intrepid's* missiles were in flight.

It took all of Gallant's concentration to give orders as the *Intrepid's* sensors fed data about the incoming enemy missiles, their trajectory to GridScape as well as the *Intrepid's* anti-ship missiles heading toward the Titans.

Once again the weapons team fired lasers and plasma weapons to destroy the enemy missiles. They succeeded in detonating both missiles short of the *Intrepid*, but the explosions nevertheless inflicted significant damage to the ship's shields and bow plates. The bow compartment was ruptured and rendered useless. A damage control team was dispatched to seal the air ruptures.

The effects of the blast momentarily blinded Gallant's command systems—sparks and smoke streamed from several command circuits. The fires were quickly controlled by the ship's automatic fire suppression systems.

Gallant asked, "Radar, where are our missiles?"

The radar-tech reported, "Both missiles are on course closing on Tango-one."

Gallant watched the forward view screen, waiting to see if the Titans had time to deploy additional countermeasures. Belatedly, he saw an antimissile launch from the destroyer, but it was too late.

The destroyer took two direct hits, bow-on.

Bam! Bam!

The destroyer blew up in a holocaust of fury and devastation, quickly disintegrating in the vacuum of space.

Gallant stared at the viewport, mesmerized by the bright colorful explosions and flying debris as different sections of the dying ship exploded, imploded, or disintegrated. The destruction was so total and complete he couldn't fully appreciate it at first, but the result meant the *Intrepid* would be able to return to Sol and Elysium would remain safe.

After a minute, he became aware of a continuous outburst of loud cheering from the bridge crew of the *Intrepid*.

"Hurrah! Hurrah! Hurrah!"

37

DUTY

Brobdingnag roared, spewing hot molten lava over the top of its highest peak. Liquefied metal flecks sparked and burst up into the atmosphere like Fourth-of-July fireworks. Nature's temper tantrum had been ignited by the high explosives set in strategic places by the *Intrepid's* crew and they enjoyed watching the visual pyrotechnics.

The roiling torrent of lava, heat, and steam cascaded over a precut ravine in the side of the mammoth mountain. As the rush of fluid wound over the terrain, it found its way into the overgrown tangled jungle. Its controlled course reached the edge of the ancient ruins and flowed into the entrance of the alien berserker AI machine, nestling under the earth. For hours the searing fluid filled the caverns, passages, chambers, and passageways. Every void within its ten

cubic kilometers was filled with lava—scorching microprocessors, electric circuits, and memory chips. The heat incin-
erated everything it touched; completing the destruction
Gallant had started when he had released the dark matter
from its superconducting containment field.

Aristotle would never return. The underground grave
would become a fitting monument to his victims—the Ely,
the original inhabitants of Elysium.

The video-feed of the mesmerizing events—from the
initial explosions to the flowing liquid burial of the ancient
AI—were transmitted to all the citizens of Hallo, as well as
the crew aboard the *Intrepid*. The planet's population was still
digesting the stories circulating about President Wolfe's and
Professor Hepburn's deaths, so the events carried a powerful
emotional impact.

Following the broadcast, Alaina Hepburn explained how
the force field, supposedly controlled by President Wolfe,
was a trick by Professor Hepburn while he was under the
control of the AI berserker machine.

Alaina spoke candidly, "We have a heritage of overcoming
adversity. Our parents and grandparents lived and worked in
the dangerous environment of asteroid-strewn space to dig
metals from weightless rock. Despite their surroundings, they
were happy, hardworking people who cherished their children
and their chosen way of life. We, who have made a home on
Elysium, salute their sacrifice and dedicate ourselves to building a better future for our children. I ask you to join me to
begin building the foundation of that future."

Her inspirational speech won her considerable support
among the people.

She said, "The Titans still have a base in this system and someday more of their ships will come. While the *Intrepid* returns to Earth with news of our survival, we will be on our own. We need to develop our defenses. We can use the fabrication and mining operations left by *Intrepid's* efforts to develop anti-ship missiles. We will expand those facilities to develop and build an orbiting space station to defend Elysium."

Alaina's Pro-United Planets' organization promoted a vision for the future of Elysium as a UP protectorate which was gaining support. Gallant attended several meeting to explain how UP would support them when more FLT ships were available. He spoke at length about Alaina's courage and daring in defeating Aristotle and facing dragors in the jungle. Of the two heroic acts, the public was more impressed with her staring down dragors. Their own experience and fears might have made those events more real to them.

As part of their agenda they called for new elections for all Council members as well as a new president. New elections were set for the following month and there was a scramble to find a slate of candidates who could defeat the incumbents.

Though she expressed strong reservations, as leader of PUP, Alaina was being considered for nomination for president.

He guessed he was the center of much speculation from countless inquiring eyes and curious ears. The town's people were constantly talking about him and Alaina in endless gossip. He found no expression of humor, amusement, or interest in the conjectures. Talk swept past them, day after day, like a senseless river of meaningless antidotes of little importance except to create a wearisome awkwardness between the couple.

As her campaign to promote a UP common wealth heated up, she became difficult for Gallant to find. He became concerned the future would not find its way to a favorable outcome for the two of them. Though he didn't say it openly, he selfishly hoped Alaina would not succeed in her political ambitions.

He felt trapped by duty and responsibility, and peevishly, he felt a similar burden would soon befall Alaina.

After several weeks, he found her in Freedom Park with Liam Larson at her side, preparing for a rally in crowds of adherents.

"Hi," said Larson with a smile as Gallant approached. "It's good of you to attend the rally. We appreciate your support."

First he nodded at Larson, then he turned to Alaina. "I've been trying to see you. I wanted to speak to you about your decision to run for office."

"Huh?" she said.

With Larson standing at her elbow, the subsequent discussion was unsatisfying. He left feeling discouraged and he felt he must let events shape themselves. His heart gave a jerk as he realized she was caught in a whirlwind of other people's agendas.

As if struggling against her fate, she accepted the nomination for office, even as Gallant pressed her to consider returning to Sol as a representative of Elysium.

"They need me. We could lose the election if I don't," she claimed.

Gallant was fighting against circumstances contrived to keep him from Alaina.

Alternatively he considered the possibility of remaining as UP's representative after the *Intrepid* left.

After several emotional weeks, it seemed to him the future would take care of itself and he would have to play a silent waiting game for the hand to be dealt.

"How's your voting drive going?" asked Gallant as he walked into Alaina's office on the first floor of the town hall. He nodded to Liam, who was sitting beside her, as usual.

She smiled warmly. "Good—great, actually. Polls are showing we have the people's confidence."

By "we," she was referring to her and Liam. Alaina was running for president and Liam for head of the new security apparatus, which was called simply Hallo Police. Their moto was "A new broom sweeps clean."

She ran her daily operations smoothly and put out a message to impress the voters. She developed a team, budget, and strategy for her campaign, but soon discovered running a campaign was a matter of implementing solid planning.

Liam and Alaina were campaigning hard against many of the former Wolfe supporters who found themselves unpopular once Wolfe's schemes were revealed.

Junior ran to fill his father's seat as president, trying to use his father's old council member cronies for backing, but Junior himself was not strongly liked among a public ready to do away with the high-handed methods of the SSP. In addition, the Wolfe cronies, who made up most of the old council members, were also losing favor.

Election Day was a triumph for Alaina and PUP. She was voted the new leader of Elysium and Larson the new police chief.

The people of Elysium celebrated their new government.

She appointed a committee to draft a new constitution. Her new council quickly adapted the constitution which nullified the previous treaty and formed a common-wealth arrangement with the United Planets.

The election results froze Gallant's spirits.

———

In *Intrepid's* medical center, Gallant asked Mendel, "How is Neumann?"

"Despite the seriousness of his wounds, he's holding on. I intend to keep him in the rejuvenation chamber for several more days before he'll be strong enough to undergo additional surgery."

"Another round of surgery?"

"Yes, but don't worry. I have no intention of losing a second captain this trip," said Mendel grimly.

"I have complete confidence in you, Marcus," said Gallant. "It's only that the accelerator has been working non-stop to provide sufficient dark matter for the FTL drive. We'll have enough in a week and I need to make preparation to return to Earth."

"So make them."

"Sure, but will Neumann be able to resume command by then?"

Mendel reached out and took hold of Gallant's arm. He said, "Look, Henry, even if I'm a better surgeon than I think I am, I'm only hoping to keep him alive until he makes it back to Earth. Once he gets to the main military medical facilities on Earth, he'll get the best medical care possible. At that point, he can start planning on recovering and possibly returning to duty. For now, he's not going to be able to relieve you anytime soon."

Disappointed, Gallant said, "I understand."

Clearly there would be no escaping his responsibility to the *Intrepid*.

38

WHAT YOU WANT MOST

Gallant fired retro-rockets, letting his tiny Hummingbird fall from orbit and plunge through the stratosphere toward Elysium. The rush of g-forces pressed against him. He let his mind relive with exhausting vividness the events of the past weeks.

He passed through white clouds as they swirled above the island-rich blue ocean. The panoramic journey seemed far too short when he set his ship down at the landing site at Hallo. He walked through the streets of the town he had previously found so inviting and felt a longing to remain in its splendor, but he knew this would be his final visit to the planet.

When he reached the town hall, he climbed the stairs and passed through the open doors. The open windows and doors let the warm fragrant tropical breeze flow throughout the rooms. There were no guards and few staff members about. He went directly to the president's office. The door was open and Alaina was seated comfortably in a chair next to a table piled high with documents and reports. They were Wolfe's secret papers that had been locked in his desk drawer. They were concerned with his arrangements with other Council members. No one's eyes, other than his, had seen them before Alaina opened them and began reading. She was occupied reading one of them when Gallant entered.

She looked smart in a white blouse and a light-thread beige skirt. Her blond hair was pulled up and back, away from her face, exposing her glowing complexion and delicate classical facial features.

His heart beating apace, he said, "Alaina, you look wonderful."

"Henry," she said beaming with delight. "You always look so handsome in your uniform."

For a moment, Gallant thought she would jump up and embrace him, but her restraint asserted control. And for a moment, he thought about stepping forward and embracing her, but like her, he suppressed the impulse.

For days he had envisioned their last meeting—their final farewell—now it had come and he felt unprepared.

Gallant said simply, "I haven't said this before and it's long overdue—congratulations, Madame President."

He said it lightly, as if it were a casual compliment, lacking import.

"Thank you," said Alaina, her face becoming troubled. "I'm still getting used to the title. It's difficult to take it all in."

Gallant smiled whimsically. "Elysium is in good hands."

Alaina's happy face returned, color rising in her checks.

"When do you leave?" she asked.

"Twenty-four hours."

"I'll be waiting for your return."

"I doubt you'll even notice I've gone." Gallant shifted his weight, swinging his hands at his sides. He didn't know what to do with them.

"Oh, I'll notice." She frowned, as if she were already feeling unhappy about that event.

Having failed completely to express his own feelings, he was helpless to discern hers.

She stood and crossed to him. "Well, there's one thing I do know for certain."

"What's that?" asked Gallant, fixing his steely gray eyes on her.

"You're *special*," she said, touching his arm.

"No. Not so special—just different." He stood there overflowing with regrets and vain frustrations.

"Why are goodbyes always so hard?" she asked, her sorrow suddenly finding its way into her quivering voice and moist eyes.

Gallant breathed, "They always mean giving up—what you want most."

The words stunned Alaina.

He moved closer to her.

I'm leaving too much unsaid.

"What about us?" he asked.

"Us? Is there an 'us'?" she asked. "I've my responsibilities—you have yours . . ."

Can I blame her?

Their unspoken pact with duty was a sad indictment—condemning them to a harvest of loneliness.

A small part of him clung to the notion they could still break the barrier dividing responsibility and desire. In his heart, however, he knew their separation was unavoidable.

Is this all we can allow ourselves?

He looked at her for a long second, and then with a despair born in denial, he pulled her close and wrapped his arms around her. She felt wonderful; eternal; unforgettable. He kissed her with all the passion he possessed—crushing the breath from her.

When at last he let her go, she took a deep breath and looked up at him.

Gallant said, "I'll be back."

- end -

Made in the USA
Middletown, DE
20 June 2023

33053455R00210